SIREN'S SONG

AN ASPECT SOCIETY NOVEL

MICHELLE MANUS

For Drew.
We've been through a lot of shit together.
Somehow you still like me.
Thanks for always having my back.

CHAPTER

ONE

S iren had long ago learned to listen to the itch that sometimes started beneath her skin. The itch that whispered awake the flames of power inside her, telling her to move on to a new town, and soon, before *he* showed up and the nightmare things came for her.

Before she got someone killed.

Again.

She gathered her power, steadied her breath until she calmed enough to send it back to sleep. Relief hit her as it settled. Her control was uncertain at best, and it was safer when her power slumbered. Still, she couldn't shake the longing that rode twin to the relief, the hollow feeling that some integral part of her faded along with the power.

Too soon, she thought. *It's too soon to have to leave again.*

When she'd first started running, she could stay in a new town for six months. Over the last couple years, she'd been lucky to get three or four. One and a half, though, *that* was setting a new record. One she didn't care for.

Siren started the coffeemaker and pretended the day was as close to normal as her days ever got, and *not* the day she would have to pack everything up and leave. The hissing and spitting

1

as the machine gurgled to life comforted her. It also sent a twinge through her chest as it reminded her of her favorite coffee shop in town, and a certain blond-haired, entirely-too-handsome man who could reliably be found there on Tuesday afternoons.

She'd enjoyed flirting with Jace Winters over the last few weeks. She thought he'd enjoyed flirting with *her*, too, despite the fact that they'd been introduced when she tripped and her latte nearly destroyed his laptop. She'd known it couldn't last— long-term attachments weren't really a thing for her, given the necessity of her on-the-go lifestyle—but she'd thought she at least had more time.

Get over it, she told herself. *It's your own fault if you got attached.*

She'd crafted a set of rules over the years to keep her emotionally sane, and the foremost of those rules was that she never spent time with a man she actually liked. She'd broken it when she'd let Jace buy her a coffee to replace the one she'd spilled on him. She'd broken it again when she'd sat down and talked to him.

The first time he'd made her smile she'd realized she'd made a terrible mistake, and shouldn't see him again. But she had. Every Tuesday, she told herself she wouldn't go, and every Tuesday, she wound up right back in that damn cafe, lying and telling herself it was the last time. She left the coffeemaker to its work and promptly tripped over a pile of discarded clothing on her way to the bathroom. She wasn't usually so messy, since tidiness lent itself to the ability to run quickly when necessary, and she recognized the disorder as a sign that she'd gotten too comfortable tossing things any which way when she got home.

Home. When had she started thinking of this crappy seventies-era studio apartment as *home*?

This development was far, far worse than any silly fantasies she'd had about dating Jace. She hadn't thought of any place as home since she was sixteen, and she hadn't been in this town long enough to warrant feeling so comfortable. Still, she rebelled against the knowledge that she had to leave. It was as if when she'd stepped off the bus into the little town of Seclusion, some missing part of her had clicked into place.

Now that she looked, signs of undesirable entrenchment were everywhere. The pile of books stacked by the bedside. The dirty coffee mug in the sink that meant she now owned two and could leave one dirty for a day. The small print of Munch's *The Scream* she'd picked up for a couple bucks at Goodwill.

She hadn't been stupid enough to buy anything decorative since Phoenix. It was a waste of money she didn't have on just another thing she'd need to leave behind. She showered and then dressed, ignoring her reflection in the mirror that showed just how prominent the dark circles beneath her eyes had grown. Clearly, her recurring nightmares weren't doing her any favors.

She put her coffee in a travel mug and left the apartment. Once the itching started, she had a couple days to skip town, and since today was payday, she needed to go to her job at Hand Me Down Sound, the used music and movies store over on Main Street. After, she'd come home and pack, then buy a ticket on the first bus out of town.

Simple. Easy. Nothing she hadn't done dozens of times before.

Usually, she felt a sense of relief when it came time to move on. Too many months in one place built up pressure inside her, and leaving released it. She didn't feel relieved now. She felt tense. Unsettled. She searched every innocent shadow for hidden threats and jumped at the skittering of dry leaves on the sidewalk.

She was so keyed up that when an awful, ravenous hunger slicked over her, she convinced herself it was in her head.

It's just the nightmares, she told herself. The gray-eyed man wasn't here. The itching had just started this morning. She had time.

A harsh buzz filled Siren's ears, grew louder as a wet lick of foul power teased up her neck. The stench of stagnation and rotting meat hit her nostrils, and she knew it wasn't just her nerves. She threw one look over her shoulder, unable to believe it was happening so soon, in broad daylight, on a public street.

The swarm of flies loomed a block away, six feet tall and roughly in the shape of a man. They closed in on her, streams of the black insects branching off from the main unit toward her, and she stood frozen as they neared.

A tired voice in the back of her mind whispered that she could just…stop. If she sat down in the street and let him take her, she could finally be done. No more running. No more being afraid.

The power of habit saved her. Her muscles responded to the adrenaline that hit the back of her throat with a copper tang, and she turned and ran. Her hesitation had cost her, and flies crashed into the exposed flesh on her nape, the pain from their bites unnaturally sharp. The need to brush them off burned in her throat, but doing so would make her lose speed she couldn't afford. If the thousands of flies in the main swarm enveloped her…

She pushed her body to its limit, turned the street corner and closed the thirty remaining feet between her and Hand Me Down Sound. She barreled inside and slammed the door shut behind her with enough force to rattle the pane. Flies crashed against the glass, a driving rain of black wings.

"Somethin' interesting going on out there?" Old Hank's voice rumbled across the store.

Though her throat burned, she managed to send a smile his way.

"No. Nothing going on." Siren turned her gaze back to the door and realized her words were even true. The swarm had disappeared.

She took a deep breath and told herself she was safe. The nightmare things, the swarms, they never followed her into buildings if other people were in them. Of course, given that she'd just been chased in broad daylight for the first time, she wondered how long occupied buildings would continue to prove safe.

She pushed the thought away. Acting like everything was normal would serve her better than spending the day tied up in worried knots.

"Good morning, Hank." She infused brightness into her voice to hide her trembling speech, and also because she knew the chipper tone would make Hank grumble with an irritation that was all show.

"Ain't seen nothin' particularly good about it yet," Hank replied. He presided over his store with a kingly air, his throne a battered old barstool, the seat of which had been torn and duct-taped back together so often that the original material likely existed only in Hank's memory.

She had never asked his age, but judged him at a mean seventy-five. He was bald on the top of his head, with flanks of white hair on the sides. Every day, without fail, he wore pressed khakis and a long-sleeved button-up shirt, completely at odds with his battered pair of sturdy work boots.

Siren grinned. "That's what you always say, but I bet Betty Lou came in this morning."

Betty Lou, an energetic woman in her late sixties who came in every Monday at seven-twenty on the dot, was, near as Siren could tell, the only reason Hand Me Down Sound opened at seven in the morning.

"Don't see what that has to do with anything," Hank muttered.

When Siren had applied here and gotten around to the paper-work phase, Hank had taken one look at her ID, snorted, and said, "Hope you didn't pay much for this."

He'd hired her on the spot and proceeded to treat her like a wayward grandchild upon whom to unload his pent-up years of advice and wisdom. He'd made it clear he thought she was running from the law and, as he wasn't particularly fond of the law, he found this supposed fact endearing.

"When are you going to stop torturing yourself and ask her on a date?"

"I'm an old man. I don't go on dates."

"Of course not. How silly of me. When are you going to ask her to go steady?"

He turned a calculating eye on her and said, in a low drawl, "Oh, I reckon about when you give the time of day to that well-dressed feller's always coming in here."

Heat flushed Siren's cheeks. If she had a habit of wandering into a certain coffee shop every Tuesday, it might also be the case that Jace had a habit of wandering into Hand Me Down Sound every Friday.

"He's not my type," she lied.

Hank snorted. "What? Young, good lookin', charming?"

"Well, if you like him so much, maybe *you* should date him."

Hank grunted, pretending to take the suggestion seriously before concluding, "Nah, too young for me."

They passed the remaining five minutes until ten o'clock in companionable silence, Siren checking the till for the change Hank never seemed to restock, and Hank staring out at the shelves of CD cases and presumably pondering the vastness of the universe.

Or, Siren thought, *daydreaming about Betty Lou.*

The clock ticked over to ten, and Hank nodded goodbye. He'd be back later to take over the closing shift.

Siren spent the first hour dusting the displays and cleaning the area around the cash register. Hank had a fondness for sunflower seeds, and despite his always keeping a cup around for the hulls, she still found them everywhere. Next, she found a few CDs in the returns box and walked them to their homes. Only once she was satisfied that there really wasn't anything else to do did she settle into her chair behind the counter.

Truth told, Hank wouldn't have cared if she sat around all day as long as a customer wasn't in the store, but she had to do *something* to earn her keep. She'd only been here two days before making a few signs and displays and rearranging the music section; she wasn't sure what Hank's organization method had been, but she hadn't been able to make heads or tails of it.

When he'd seemed pleased with her changes, instead of annoyed as she'd feared, she'd made a few tentative suggestions when he put the weekly order in. The store dealt predominantly in used trade for CDs, movies, and books, but Hank ordered new as well to, "Keep things alive," as he put it. She'd just about worked up the nerve to ask if she could take over some of the ordering directly.

Not that she ever would, now, the prickling underneath her skin reminded her.

The first few hours of her shift, the store saw enough customers to keep Siren's mind off of nightmare creatures, but when the traffic died out and her brain wouldn't stop spinning, she pulled a paperback from beneath the cash register and settled in. She'd been saving this one, the latest by her favorite author, JC Morden, for a rainy day. It was the one series that, no matter what was going on in her life or in her head, could pull her completely out of herself and get her lost in the pages and the characters so she didn't have to think.

She was a hundred pages in and considerably more relaxed when the shop door opened. The old-fashioned Open/Closed sign clattered as the door settled shut. Siren looked to see who had come in, and her heart tripped over itself. She had forgotten, in the chaos of the morning, that today was Friday.

He wore black jeans today, hugged low on his hips and contrasting nicely with the plain white t-shirt stretching across the muscles of his chest. The blond hair that had been a near buzz cut when she'd first met him was now long enough to fall across his forehead, and the summer sun had bronzed his skin. Clear blue eyes looked out above high cheekbones and a strong, angular jaw, and his lips curved into a smile when he saw her.

He was headed straight for her when the door clanged open

behind him, and Lena Simmons walked in. She barreled past Jace to the cash register, a determined look on her face.

Siren groaned internally. Lena had a chronic inability to understand that the fact that she hadn't *liked* a movie or CD she purchased did not mean she was entitled to a refund on it. Jace, who had witnessed the woman's tirades before, mouthed "Sorry" at her and retreated to the relative safety of the DVD section.

Siren dealt with Lena on autopilot, an experience made vastly pleasanter by the view of Jace directly behind the woman. Lena was in such rare form that Siren eventually caved and gave her a fifty percent refund in store credit, just to get her to leave.

As soon as Lena was gone, Jace walked up to the register, handing over a DVD of Jet Li's *Hero*.

"Straying from documentaries?" she asked, tsking in mock disapproval.

"It's for my sister. I'm trying to do normal family things. Movie night is a family thing, right?"

"Right." Siren thought movie night could be a family thing. Surely that was a thing normal people did. "This would be the sister that has three black belts?" she asked, remembering an offhand comment he'd made once.

He grinned. "The one and only."

"In that case, I'd advise you not to forget popcorn, as she could literally kill you in a hunger-fueled rage, after which my Tuesdays and Fridays would be exceptionally boring."

The itch beneath her skin flared up, as if to remind her that she didn't have any Tuesdays or Fridays left in Seclusion.

"I'll do my best to stay alive for your sake, then. However, if you want me to survive tonight..." He pulled a gold envelope from his pocket and placed it on the counter.

At her confused look, he said, "I promised you an official invitation for the party tonight."

Shit.

"You forgot."

Prior to today, getting invited to his family's annual party had been the highlight of Siren's week. She wouldn't ordinarily go to something like that, as it screamed commitment, but Jace was...safe, in that regard. Over their first cup of coffee she'd learned he didn't live in Seclusion, and had only come home to help with some unspecified family matter.

If he didn't live here, then he wouldn't want anything serious with a woman who did, so attending a party with him, hosted by his family or no, wasn't a big deal. At least, it hadn't been, until her timetable on leaving Seclusion had been bumped up to *tonight*.

"I..." She trailed off.

His face fell. "You're not coming. Is it because I said the party would be boring and stuffy, or because I used the word 'drudgery' in reference to it? Because I can take those things back. Allow me to lie. It will be fun. There will be lots of nice people there. We won't want to get drunk ten minutes in."

Siren laughed in spite of herself. He *had* invited her under the pretense of needing to be rescued from the party in question.

"It's not that."

"Then what is it?"

She blurted out the first excuse that came to mind. "I don't have anything to wear." He'd said it was formal attire.

"Ah."

"But I'll find something," she added.

What? No, she would *not* find something. She was not going.

"Okay." He sounded understandably confused. "Should I pick you up?"

"No," she said quickly. The last thing she needed was him seeing where she lived. *How* she lived.

"But you'll be there?"

"I'll be there." If there was a hell, she was going to it, because she most definitely would *not* be there. It was just that she couldn't stand to see him look disappointed in person. Imagining him looking disappointed later, when she never showed up, was bad enough.

Maybe she could send him a note.

Yeah, Siren, a note. That'll fix everything. Dear Jace, I'm sorry I couldn't come to your party, but I'm being hunted by a madman with creepy nightmare creatures at his command. Oh yeah, and magic is real, and I have it, along with an unfortunate tendency to kill things. Again, so sorry about the party, but I had to leave town. Sincerely, Siren.

She snorted internally and waited until he was gone to open the envelope.

**You are cordially invited to the Gathering Ball
at the home of Elijah Winters and his children, Jace and
Valkyrie
21 Aspect Lane, Seclusion, AR
Please arrive promptly at 8 p.m.**

A ball? Seriously? Yes, Jace had said formal attire, but he didn't really look like he ran in the correct circles to be attending an actual ball. For one thing, his truck looked like the eighties desperately wanted it back.

Siren slipped the invitation back inside the envelope and tucked the flap closed. She wanted to go. She wanted to buy a dress she couldn't afford and spend the entire evening with Jace, dancing and getting drunk and pretending she was a normal twenty-two year old. She wanted to finally find out what he tasted like, if he kissed half as good as she'd imagined.

She wanted all of those things a little too much, so she tossed the invitation in the trash. If her mind hadn't been made up before, it was now. She was leaving Seclusion. Tonight.

CHAPTER

TWO

Hank arrived three hours early to relieve Siren of her shift, settling onto the barstool next to her without a word. She finished ringing up a high school student going through a distinct Goth phase and waited for the door to close behind the kid before turning a suspicious glare on Hank.

"You've never been early for shift relief before."

Hank crunched a sunflower seed and spit the hull into the little Styrofoam cup in his left hand. "Thought you might want to take off a little early."

Siren narrowed her eyes. "Why would you think that?"

He crunched another sunflower seed. "Heard you might have a party to go to. Thought you might want time to get ready. Do all that stuff women do before parties."

"Where did you hear I was going to a party?"

"Small town. Word gets around."

Siren crossed her arms and Hank relented.

"Bailey 'cross the street saw the Winters kid comin' in here with a gold envelope. Everybody in Seclusion knows what's in those." He frowned, looking at the wire mesh trashcan. "Why's your invitation in the trash?"

"Because I'm not going."

Hank sighed, adjusted a pair of plastic-rimmed glasses Siren was pretty sure he didn't actually need, and took on *that air*, the one that said his seventy-odd years of wisdom were about to be imparted to her and she had better listen.

"Siren, you been livin' here a couple months now. You don't have any friends and I've never seen you go anywhere or do anything 'sides read books. Now, there's a lot to be said for choosing your associates wisely and expandin' on literature and whatnot, but it don't mean nothin' if you ain't happy. You happy?"

Siren didn't know what to say, so she didn't say anything.

"That's what I thought. Now, I don't know what kinda trouble you're in, but I can't imagine it's too bad, you bein' a nice girl and all, and 'sides there ain't much trouble Jace Winters couldn't get you out of, if he put his mind to it. He seems to like you and you always get that flustered look whenever he comes in, so why don't you go and have a good time?"

"Jace Winters, huh? Why do you always refer to him as 'that well-dressed feller' if you know who he is?"

Hank spit another sunflower hull into his cup. "We-e-ll," he said, stretching the word into two syllables, "the Winters are the oldest family in Seclusion. Everybody 'round here pretty much knows who they are. You seemin' the skittish type, I didn't wanna scare you off. But seeing as how you're goin' to his party tonight and all, I figured you'd figure it out anyway."

"I am *not* going."

He gave her an old, worn-out hound dog look and she crumpled. She was leaving. What would it hurt to give him the happiness of thinking she was going to the stupid party? She fished the gold envelope out of the trashcan and waved it at him. "Fine. I will go. On the condition that you ask Betty Lou to coffee."

"I thought you might come up with somethin' like that, so you'll be pleased to know I already did."

"Really?" How did he know her so well in a handful of weeks? "And?"

"And we're going Sunday morning." He pulled a white envelope out of his back pocket and handed it to her. "That's the week's pay, plus a little bonus for doin' all the displays and stuff. Get yourself somethin' pretty and go have fun."

Siren took the envelope, embarrassed to discover her eyes had welled up. She didn't want to leave. She liked Hank, and Jace, and this store, and this entire stupid town.

"Thank you," she said. So he wouldn't see that she was about to cry, she threw her arms around him and hugged him. He smelled of leather and spice, just what she had always imagined grandfathers *should* smell like.

"Now, now, no need to go and get all sensitive on me." His words were as gruff as usual, but she could feel the smile beneath them.

She turned away from him, so he wouldn't see the water that spilled over her cheeks, and headed for the door.

"Go ahead and take tomorrow off, too," Hank called after her. "Just in case things go well."

The words made her laugh, even as they made the ache in her chest intensify.

JACE PULLED into the drive and parked outside the front doors of his father's house. He'd thought the mixed cocktail of anger and rejection that hit every time he saw his childhood home would fade with repeated exposure, but it hadn't. Some irrational part of him still expected Elijah Winters to walk out those doors, to coldly reiterate that Jace wasn't his son anymore, and that he had no business being on the property.

Never mind that his father had been missing for five months, now.

Jace went inside and found his sister in the upstairs gym,

sitting cross-legged in the middle of an alarming array of throwing knives and other paraphernalia, an oilcloth in hand.

Not a good sign. Some people meditated when they were upset. Some people did yoga or went running. Valkyrie cleaned weaponry.

She sat with a longsword in her lap, a thick braid of raven-black hair trailing over her shoulder. Strong curves of defined muscle etched her biceps, and Jace thought again that she was pushing herself too hard. She'd always been tough—she'd had to be, to survive their father and still remain in his good graces—but ever since Elijah Winters had disappeared, training had become Valkyrie's only god.

She turned at the sound of his footsteps, dark blue eyes winged gracefully by thick, arched eyebrows, her full lips pursed in concentration.

"I got a movie," he said by way of greeting, holding up the DVD as proof. "I thought we could have a movie night tomorrow. You know, a little post-Gathering brother-sister bonding time?"

Valkyrie returned her attention to the blade in her hands, wiping along its length with steady, careful precision. "Sure," she said, her voice passionless. "Did you learn anything from the Somersets?"

"No." He hadn't expected to, either, since Valkyrie had already talked to them. After their father's disappearance, she'd talked to every one of his acquaintances and connections. Only once she'd exhausted every avenue of investigation had she called Jace two months ago, told him Elijah was missing, and asked him to come home.

"He's been gone for months, Val, and chasing down every lead you've already followed isn't helping. I'm not sure why you even wanted me to come out here."

She didn't look up from the sword in her lap, but her hands stilled.

"Maybe I just needed my brother."

"You didn't seem to need me for the last six years." The words were out of his mouth before he could stop them. When his father had disowned him at eighteen, he'd expected it. Relished it, even. What he hadn't expected was that Valkyrie would turn her back on him, too.

And she hadn't, not exactly. But she'd ignored every one of his calls. When she *had* spoken to him, she had initiated, and she had never called on her own phone. Or from the same number twice. All of which told him their father had forbidden her to speak to him, and she'd wanted his approval more than she'd wanted to keep her relationship with her brother.

"You don't understand," she said, softly.

"Understand what? That our father's a controlling asshole? I'm well aware of the fact. What I don't understand is why you put up with it." She was five years older than him, and for a long time he'd thought the only reason she'd tried so hard to please their father, the only reason she'd stayed in this house into adulthood, was because she hadn't want to leave Jace here alone.

When his father had effectively banished him, Jace had honestly expected her to leave with him. Especially since Elijah wasn't even her biological father. He and Valkyrie shared a mother, but Jace was the only one who'd inherited DNA from the bastard that raised them both. But Valkyrie hadn't left with him. She had stayed, and she'd molded herself so far into what their father wanted her to be that when Jace had finally laid eyes on her again after over half a decade he'd been afraid there wasn't anything of *her* left.

"I didn't—" she started, then cut off with a short growl. Her Aspect roared to the surface in response to her frustration, and she funneled it into the blade in her hands. It swirled, etching a strengthening rune into the hilt that would render the weapon all the more powerful for the emotion given to the rune's creation.

"I understand why you're upset," she said. "And I know it must seem like I didn't care what happened to you, but I did. I do. My choices may not make sense to you but they were the ones I had to make. So please don't ask me to explain them."

He wanted to push her. But there was an undercurrent of *something* beneath her words that made him back off.

"Okay. I won't ask. But, Val? He might not even be missing. There was no indication of a struggle anywhere in the house. And, yeah, his truck's still here but it's not like he doesn't have the money to buy a new one or ten. Have you considered that maybe he just left?"

It wasn't an unreasonable possibility. After their mother had died, when Jace was seven, his father would sometimes disappear for weeks on end.

"I've considered it," she said, softly. "But it doesn't change anything. I need to find him."

"And when you do? What then? I leave and we go back to talking to each other once every six months?"

Valkyrie's fingers clenched around the sword, and not the dull part, either.

"It will be different this time."

Jace snorted.

She looked up and met his gaze. "It will. I'll *make* it different this time. I promise. But I have to find him."

He let out a long breath. There was no point in fighting with her. It wouldn't change anything. "Okay, Val. Okay. We'll keep looking."

"Thank you."

He started to walk out when she said, "Movie night sounds fun." Her voice held as much conviction as a person saying that walking over a bed of hot coals sounded fun. Then again, Valkyrie would probably enjoy the challenge of the latter. "It's not one of those boring documentaries, is it?"

"Uh, no. Action."

"Oh." She brightened visibly. "Good. Don't forget popcorn."

"I didn't." *Thank the goddess for Siren. Speaking of which...* "Is now a bad time to tell you I invited a guest tonight?"

"A guest?"

"A date," he clarified. "I invited a date."

Her eyebrows drew together, a frown line appearing between them. "The redhead from the movie store?"

"Her name is Siren, and yes."

"She's a Null, isn't she?"

"Far as I know." He didn't particularly like the word that was used to describe people without Aspect.

"You want to bring a *Null* to the Gathering Ball? Is that even allowed?"

"I checked the Council by-laws and, technically, it is."

"But no one will be able to talk about Aspect around you and —" she cut off with a glare. "Did you really invite her just to avoid having to talk to anyone tonight?"

"No. I invited her because I like her. The fact that no one will be able to talk to me about arcane magical societies and whether or not I intend to rejoin them now that I'm back in town is simply an added bonus. Please be nice to her."

"I'll consider it, if you get all of these things done before five." She picked up her phone and texted him an extraordinarily long list.

"You might have given me a little more advance warning."

She shrugged. "Do you want me to be nice to your date or not?"

"Fine, fine. I'm on it." One look at the list told him he was headed back into town. Trust Valkyrie to leave preparations for the last minute.

CHAPTER
THREE

Siren didn't know why she went down the street to Rise and Grind Coffee instead of going directly home to pack.

Okay, that was a lie. She knew exactly why. She'd wanted to sit at the table where she usually sat with Jace, and hold on to the way that talking to him there had made her feel like a normal person. It didn't work. It just reminded her that there wouldn't be a Jace in the next town, or the one after that, or the one after *that*.

She was so sick of running.

She pulled out the pay-as-you-go cell phone she'd bought just for Jace. She'd dodged the first two times he'd asked for her number, but the third time she'd known that if she didn't give in, he'd have thought she wasn't interested and moved on. She hadn't wanted him to move on, so she was now the proud possessor of an over-priced hunk of plastic and electronics, and his was the only phone number she had.

Maybe she should text him.

She should not text him.

She typed in "Hey" and hit the "Send" button, then spent the next thirty seconds waiting for his reply with an angst that more befitted a teenager than an adult.

Her phone dinged.

Hey, followed by a smiley face.

What are you doing?

Errands. What are you doing?

Drinking coffee alone.

Ten minutes ticked by and her last message elicited no response. Of course it didn't. The text practically screamed, *I'm lonely and pathetic.*

She drowned her idiocy in the inch of whipped cream on top of her latte, then nearly choked on it when she heard a low-level buzz. The sound was followed by a wave of hunger so strong it baffled her how no one else in the café felt it. They remained glued to laptops and coffee cups, and so Siren controlled her fear, sticking to her seat and pretending she didn't hear the buzzing. Until the window next to her fogged up from floor to ceiling and a long, thin finger traced out a name from the other side.

Siren.

She bolted out of her chair, the legs screeching across the concrete floor. Her back slammed against something warm and hard, and strong hands closed around her shoulders. Panic punched her. She shoved away and her hip barked hard against the table. She turned and expected to find the gray-eyed man, but instead—

"Jace." Her heart thudded erratically, even as she realized all sense of the gray-eyed man had vanished. Almost as if Jace's mere presence had driven him away.

Now *that* was wishful thinking.

Still, if it weren't for her name on the window, only half-legible now as condensation rolled down, she would have thought she'd imagined the entire episode.

"Is everything all right?" Jace asked.

"Fine. Everything's fine. What are you doing here?"

He held up his phone. "It seemed like you wanted company and I was in the area. Are you sure you're okay?"

"I'm fine," she repeated. But she wasn't. "I'm sorry, I just...I need to go."

She dodged around the café tables, burst out the exit and nearly knocked a woman over. She rattled off an apology and jogged to the end of the block, her head spinning. She sucked in air but felt like she couldn't breathe.

The gray-eyed man's presence returned, that low-level buzz and insatiable hunger just close enough for her to feel. She spun in circles, looking for the source, but she didn't *see* anything. No man, no hounds, not even any flies.

"Siren."

She startled, jumped, and knocked into Jace Winters for the second time that day. And, for the second time that day, the gray-eyed man's presence vanished.

"I'm sorry," she stammered.

"Siren, what's going on?"

"Nothing."

He leveled her with a single look. "You're shaking all over and you're white as death."

She looked down at her hands and discovered he was right.

"What happened?" he asked.

"It's nothing." But she was so tired of it all, so tired of never telling anyone anything, that a partial truth came out. "I thought someone was following me this morning, and I thought I saw them again at the coffee shop."

Jace's lips thinned. "Someone you know, or a stranger?"

"A stranger." Technically true. She'd never *met* the gray-eyed man. "Look it's not a big deal."

"Do you want me to call the police?"

"*No,*" she said, a little too forcefully if the look on his face was any indication. She tried for a more normal tone. "No. I'm probably wrong, and I can't describe them anyway. The police will think I'm wasting their time."

He hesitated, obviously not wanting to let it go.

"Please?" she added.

"Alright. But in the event you're *not* wrong, maybe you shouldn't be alone right now?"

Siren knew what she should say. But she couldn't deny that, twice, she had felt the gray-eyed man and, twice, Jace had showed up and her pursuer had withdrawn. So perhaps he'd gotten desperate enough to come after her in the day, but it was clear he had reservations about doing so in front of someone who knew her.

"What did you have in mind?"

He gave her a rueful smile. "I don't suppose you want to help me set up for a party?"

Jace's truck rumbled to a stop in front of a wrought iron gate over seven feet tall. The dark-gray stone wall connected to it ran farther than Siren's eyes could follow, so she could only guess at the total size of the estate that hid behind it. She was convinced he must have taken a wrong turn when he rolled down the window, punched a code into the sleek control box, and the gates swung inward.

She felt a flicker of something as they passed through the gate, as if the air pressure had abruptly changed without giving her time to adjust. Then Jace pulled the truck up the long drive and the feeling vanished, and she was too busy staring to remember it.

The grounds had been landscaped to within an inch of their life. Dogwood trees lined either side of the road, all the way up to the house, and the road itself culminated in a fountain of a rearing horse that was set dead center of the home's circular driveway.

Siren tried and failed not to stare at the house as Jace parked. It would have been perfectly at home splashed on the glossy pages of some country estates magazine, all gorgeous gray stone and rounded archways, three stories with balconies dotted here and there on the upper levels.

"Umm, Jace? Did you maybe forget to mention something?" She was now acutely aware of the dime-sized hole in her jeans, and how battered her secondhand Converses were.

Jace followed her gaze to the house. "Oh. Right. That."

"You're not supposed to be rich."

"Then I guess it's fortunate for me that I'm not?" he offered.

"I'm not joking."

"Neither am I."

"But you live here?"

"Ah, no. I got myself disowned, so I'm a temporary guest." He pointed at his old truck. "What you see is what you get."

She opened her mouth, closed it.

"Go ahead and ask."

"Why did he disown you? And why are you *here* if he did?"

"It's a long story. Suffice to say we had a difference of opinion on pretty much everything. As for the other, he isn't around right now and I wanted to spend some time with my sister."

Right. Okay. "Just one question. Am I allowed to go inside wearing this?"

Jace laughed. "There isn't a dress code for existing."

Siren wasn't so sure about that, but she got out of the truck and followed him up to the imposing entryway doors. Jace reached for the handle, but one of the massive black doors swung inward before he touched it, and Siren found herself in the presence of a goddess.

The woman stood at least six feet tall, barefoot in black yoga pants that showed off sculpted thighs, her arms lean with muscle. A thick rope of black hair hung in a braid over her shoulder, trailing down to her waist.

Siren couldn't see the family resemblance between Jace and this woman, but she *could* see her having three black belts.

"I thought you'd be back an hour ago, what—" she cut off when she noticed Siren.

"Valkyrie, this is Siren. Siren, my sister, Valkyrie."

"Nice to meet you," Siren managed.

Valkyrie's gaze swept over Siren, who couldn't help but feel the woman was searching for something very specific. Whether she found it or not, Siren didn't know.

"Indeed," Valkyrie answered. Jace gave his sister a pointed look and she added, "Please, come in."

Siren followed them into an enormous foyer with black and white tile, through a living area that sported a grand piano, and into a kitchen with gleaming granite countertops, dark mahogany cabinets, and shining black appliances. She was very careful not to touch anything as she moved and was more than half-surprised when no servants appeared to glower disapprovingly at her presence.

Jace had barely set down the many shopping bags he'd been juggling when Valkyrie subjected Siren to yet another piercing gaze and then said, "Jace, can I talk to you for a minute? Alone?"

Siren told herself it didn't sting. She didn't need his sister's approval. If she were a different person, one who could have an actual relationship with Jace, *then* it would sting. But she wasn't, and she couldn't, so it didn't.

"Val—"

"It will only take a moment."

The two siblings stared at each other long enough that the silence grew uncomfortable, and Siren decided to break it before the room spontaneously combusted.

"I'll just, ah, take myself to see the horses, then?" She pointed out the wide kitchen window, where two paddocks were bisected by a large, modern barn. The left enclosure held four towering black animals, and Siren would bet every minute of her equine-obsessed childhood that their flowing manes and feathered fetlocks marked them as Friesians. The other enclosure held a motley trio comprised of a bay, a palomino, and a fat dapple-gray pony.

Jace's jaw did not unclench at her announcement, but he did walk to the fridge, pull out three carrots, and hand them to her.

"Don't feed the Friesians," Valkyrie said, "they're—"

"The black ones," Siren finished. "Got it."

Siren slipped out the kitchen door and told herself, once again, that she didn't care about whatever Valkyrie said to Jace. She told herself this the entire walk down to the paddock. Once she was there, the great thing about horses was that they took her mind entirely off everything else. The rotund, dapple-gray pony was the first to approach. He shoved his head eagerly through the fence rails and reached for the carrots.

"Someone clearly spoiled you," she murmured, but she broke off a piece of carrot and held it out for him. Despite his eagerness, he wasn't nippy, and politely took the chunk from her hand. His success encouraged the other two to come trotting over.

The bay mare was five feet away when she froze and her head went straight up in the air, her muscles quivering. The palomino went stiff a second later and their tension bled through to the pony in front of her, who whirled and trotted back to the safety of his herd.

Siren turned and searched for whatever had set them off, but try as she might, she didn't see anything. Then again, sometimes a plastic bag blowing in the wind was all it took to set a horse on high alert. She'd just convinced herself it was something that banal when the bay mare reared up and uttered a whinny like a war cry. Her front hooves landed and all three horses split, galloping for the far side of the paddock.

Siren felt the harsh buffeting of wind a second before she thought to look *up*. Then the talons of a leathery, winged creature the size of a grizzly bear tore into her shoulders and lifted her off the ground.

CHAPTER

FOUR

Jace watched the door shut behind Siren and struggled to find a calm voice. "Do you want to explain to me why you're being unbearably rude?"

"Something about her isn't right."

"Please tell me you are not about to try and convince me she's a gold digger? Because she already knows I don't have this kind of money." He indicated the house. "It hasn't driven her off yet, though the behavior of my relatives well might."

"The wards noticed her, Jace."

He shook his head. "The wards don't recognize Nulls."

"I'm aware of that."

He didn't like what she implied. "Siren doesn't have Aspect. You just met her. I felt you search her—which is also rude, by the way—did you notice any power in her?"

"No. But the wards don't make mistakes. That's why I'm saying there's something not right about her."

"Look, she's had a really bad day, and—" he cut off as a flurry of motion jerked his attention to the kitchen window. He tore out the back door with Valkyrie on his heels, a short sword already in his sister's hand.

Siren screamed as a spectral harpy descended from the sky and its talons sank into her shoulders. She struggled against it, her weight and constant movement the only thing that kept it from getting her airborne more than five feet as it dragged her toward the thick of woods on the west side of the property.

A second harpy swooped down to join the first, and together they dragged her up, eight feet, then ten.

Aspect poured out of Jace. His instinct was to harden the air in the harpies' flight path, but if they slammed into it and fell, he could easily kill Siren along with them. Since air wasn't his primary affinity, he didn't have the precision to do much more than that. He called to the moisture in the air instead, thanking the goddess for Arkansas humidity, and spun chains of water he looped around the harpies' legs.

He tugged on that chain and brought the harpies down one foot, then two. They flailed and the chains broke, and Jace burned through Aspect too fast as he constantly reformed them. Water wasn't *meant* to hold in this fashion, no matter how solid he could make it, and it was only the strength of his connection to the element that made it possible at all.

A third harpy swooped down, and Valkyrie ran for it.

"Jace," she barked. "Jump point."

They hadn't done "jump point" since he was twelve. He split his focus long enough to harden a single square foot of air six feet off the ground. Valkyrie jumped. Her Aspect flared, enhancing her physical strength, and she cleared the distance. One foot touched down on the patch of hardened air and she leapt off it. Another pulse of Aspect carried her higher, and she brought the short sword down in a whistling arc that severed the third harpy's head.

She fell the twelve feet back to the ground and landed with bent knees as her Aspect absorbed the impact.

He turned his focus entirely back to the two harpies that held Siren as he struggled to bring them down. The first dug its claws deeper into her shoulders and a scream of pure, primal terror left Siren's throat. Power tore from her in a dizzying burst that dropped Jace to his knees. The harpies exploded. Whole one second, mere chunks of meat and leathery skin raining down from the sky the next.

Impossible. Aspect didn't work that way. It didn't just *obliterate*, but he didn't have time to contemplate it because she was falling, falling fast and from too high up. He called to the air first, drove every ounce of power and will he had into his plea for it to catch her.

He reached the ground beneath her just as the recalcitrant air acquiesced, wrapping tendrils around Siren like an invisible net. It couldn't slow her *too* much, or the abruptness would break her as easily as the ground, but it slowed her enough. Enough that when Jace caught her and called to the earth, it allowed them to sink into its depths like landing on a net, so that Siren hit with no more force than if she'd fallen off a bed.

Her eyes and nose ran with blood, and her shoulders were ragged strips of flesh where the talons had almost torn clean through her. Her eyes roved from side to side behind half-closed lids.

"Siren? Can you hear me?"

She shuddered, her skin hot and flush. Harpy talons secreted a substance that, when introduced into the bloodstream, induced fevers and vomiting and, in rare cases, death.

"Val!"

"I'm on it, I'll get Charles." His sister turned and ran for the house.

Siren opened her eyes, her pupils dilating.

"Jace?" She struggled to sit, but he held her back.

"Hey, easy, you're okay. Try not to move, all right?"

"Sure." She settled back, and her lids slid closed before fluttering wide open again. "You talked to the wind." She said it with a sense of mixed wonder and terror.

Then her eyelids shuttered closed, and she slumped. Only the feel of her pulse against his fingertips told him it was okay, would *be* okay, if he could get her inside. If Valkyrie could get Charles here in time.

CHAPTER

FIVE

Siren surfaced as if from the bottom of a deep well, all panic and furious motion. She scrambled to get away as her eyes opened and she realized she was not, in fact, in the grip of a monster. Her shoulders ached, but it was nothing compared to the pain of the winged creature's talons, nothing compared to the pain she *should* feel.

She looked down and found her shoulders covered in a thin white film, iridescent like spider silk. She rolled one shoulder experimentally. The film stretched and moved with her like a second skin. No blood seeped through the strange bandage, and when she tentatively pressed her fingers to the places she knew had been pierced by talons, she didn't find the holes she knew should be there.

She sat on a couch in the Winters' living room, no sign of either of the siblings, the door behind her open to the back porch. She walked to it and looked down to the paddock where she could just make out the remnants of the creatures.

She closed her eyes and leaned her forehead against the doorframe. She'd done it again. That chasm of power inside of her had opened, and rained death on everything around her.

But that wasn't the real problem. She was used to that. No, the thing that wouldn't stop bouncing around in her skull was that Jace—nice, ordinary Jace, who was supposed to be her nice, ordinary flirtation—had *spoken* to the wind, and it had answered. She had felt the exchange, like a conversation carried on without words, had felt the moment the wind had agreed to catch her.

Relief and fear warred within her. Relief, because she wasn't alone, because her long-held suspicion that if *she* had power, surely others did too, had just proved correct. Fear, because the only other person she'd known with power was the gray-eyed man. Fear, too, because she couldn't help but wonder if the only reason Jace had been interested in her was because of that power.

"You're awake."

She didn't have the energy to startle. She turned and found him in the opposite doorway, his hands in his pockets, and an unreadable expression on his face.

"Are you okay?"

She laughed, and it was mirthless. "Sure." She tapped the film covering her shoulders. "Looks like I'm good as new. Care to explain?"

"Charles patched you up. That will purge any venom from the harpy talons. It also feeds off your Aspect to expedite your healing."

"My what?"

"Aspect." At her blank look, he said, "Your power. What do your people call it?"

"My *people*?"

He frowned. "I didn't mean to be offensive. But you're obviously not Aspect Society or Wild born, or you'd recognize the term."

"Back up ten steps to the part where I have no idea what you're talking about. You're telling me this kind of power is prevalent?"

Every time she spoke, all she seemed to do was make him

more confused, which was rich, because he obviously had some idea of what was going on here while she didn't have a clue.

"You didn't know anyone with power outside of your parents?"

"Before today, I didn't know *anyone* else with power." *Aside,* she thought, *from the psychopath trying to kill me for the last six years.*

"So you didn't recognize what I was?" He looked relieved, of all things, and an absurd part of her wondered if he'd had the same fear she'd had about him with regards to her interest.

"I could ask you the same question. I don't know what you are. I don't even know what *I* am. All I know is I was just attacked by another nightmare creature at the end of a very long list of nightmare creatures, and I'm really hoping that you aren't involved in any of it."

"If you mean did I have anything to do with the attack, the answer is no. I should think that would be obvious."

Logically, it was. He and Valkyrie had stopped those things—harpies, he'd called them—from taking her. Illogically, she'd needed to hear him say it.

"As for what I am, what *you* are…you really don't know anything?"

She shook her head.

"The short version? This kind of power is hereditary. In the U.S., you either fall under the governance of the Aspect Society Council or the Wild Magic Alliance. Basically the same fundamental rules, just a very different attitude. Seclusion is Council territory. The heart of it, in fact. The spectral harpies that attacked you outside would fall under the category of forbidden uses. We call that Dark Aspect."

Siren barely heard most of his words. She was too hung up on one in particular. "Hereditary? So my parents were like me?"

Jace nodded. "They didn't tell you about any of this? What did they do when you manifested?"

"They died right after I was born." At least, that was what

she'd been told. Given the source, she didn't know if she could trust the information or not. "I was adopted out of the system."

Jace frowned. "It's rare that an Aspect bloodline doesn't make provisions for their children to be raised by another Aspect family in the event of their death. It does happen on occasion, but the Council tends to find those children very quickly when their adoptive parents start making claims about their kids making strange things happen. What did yours do when you manifested?"

"When I what?"

"When you first showed signs of Aspect? Typically, it happens between three and five. Valkyrie, being a force of nature, managed enhanced strength at eighteen months, but I didn't create a whirlpool in the lake until I was three."

"I thought I was normal until I was sixteen."

The look on his face said he didn't just think that was abnormal, he thought it was impossible, but he didn't say it.

"And what happened then?"

She swallowed. *I saw the gray-eyed man for the first time, and I watched someone I loved die.* Aloud, she just said, "The nightmare creatures came after me. I panicked. It felt like something inside me broke and power came out. After that, I ran. They followed." She attempted a wry smile. "Rinse and repeat."

His frown deepened. "Outside the café, you said you thought someone was following you. Who?"

"I can't tell you, Jace."

He looked away from her, and when he finally looked back she had the sense he'd chosen his words very carefully.

"I know you don't have any reason to trust me. I can't even imagine what your life has been like, having no idea what you are. But I can help you, if you let me. I *want* to help you."

"It's not that I don't want to tell you." A very large part of her wanted nothing more than to dump this problem at his feet and have him explain, in that intellectual manner she was so fond of hearing him talk in, how this could all be fixed. "I mean that I literally can't tell you."

"I'm not following."

"Ask me what the person stalking me looks like."

"Okay, what do they look like?"

Silver glasses. Gray eyes. Mid-forties. Light-brown hair. Siren opened her mouth and tried to force the description out. She couldn't speak. She tried harder, focusing on the first two words.

"Sil—" Her voice cut off. Her *breath* cut off and pressure built behind her temples until she broke into a coughing fit. It was worse than the last time she'd tried to talk about it, maybe because Jace would actually believe her, while the police she'd tried to tell back then wouldn't have.

She fell to her knees. Her entire body shook as moisture rattled in her lungs and she coughed blood into her mouth.

Jace's arms wrapped around her, a steadying force. She closed her eyes and stopped thinking of the gray-eyed man, thought instead of how nice it was to be held. How very much she liked *Jace* holding her. She'd imagined it any number of times, though admittedly she hadn't been choking in any of them. And her clothes weren't covered in harpy gore.

In retrospect, maybe this wasn't a good thing. She probably smelled awful.

Her lungs finally quit trying to kill her. Jace did not let go of her, so maybe she didn't smell too bad, after all. He brushed a lock of sweat-damp hair out of her eyes, his mouth set in a hard line.

"Told you so?" she offered.

"You knew that was going to happen?"

She nodded.

"Then why the hell would you make me ask you a question you know you can't answer?"

"It seemed expedient."

"It seemed *expedient?*" he echoed. "Do me a favor. Next time, save me the expedience if it ends with you coughing up blood."

"Okay. You don't need to get all bent out of shape about it."

"You nearly hacked up a lung and *I'm* the one getting bent out of shape?"

Siren nodded. "It's cute."

Those words made her recognize the onset of what she had long ago termed the *I-almost-just-died* high. She felt a little light-headed, a little drunk, and a lot more interested in doing anything with Jace Winters other than talking to him. He, however, looked entirely too serious, and there was also that unfortunate matter of her being covered in harpy remnants.

"Cute," Jace repeated. He closed his eyes and took a long, slow breath. She had a suspicion he was praying to whatever he believed in for patience. "You're cursed, but it's *cute* that I'm concerned?"

"Cursed?" She managed not to giggle. Practically everything was funny to her in the throes of an *I-almost-just-died* high. "Cursed as in, like, prick-your-finger-on-a-spinning-needle-and-fall-into-a-long-deep-sleep cursed?"

"Same basic principle."

She tried, very hard, to be serious. "Any way to break it?"

His eyebrows drew together, a line appearing on his forehead. He looked positively sexy if one was into that whole deep-in-thought, scholarly type. She was very, very into it.

"The problem is that curses are illegal and therefore there aren't any standard ones to study. They're highly specified to the Aspect user who created them. We *might* be able to break it, but it will take a lot of trial and error."

Siren decided she absolutely deserved a medal for not asking him if true love's kiss would do the trick. When a handsome, dark-eyed stranger appeared on the back porch and walked inside, she wondered if she had progressed to full-on hallucinations

Tall, with bronze skin that didn't come from the sun, his hair was as dark as Valkyrie's and just long enough to look properly rogue-ish. Chocolate eyes gone almost black blazed with mischief. He looked like he belonged on the cover of a romance novel, leaning against a motorcycle and staring moodily into the distance.

He glanced at Siren and frowned. "Jace, you have a bleeding woman on your floor." He produced, of all things, a handkerchief, and handed it to her with a flourish that would have done any street magician proud.

"I'm Random," he added as she took the handkerchief.

"I'm methodical," she answered, drawing a laugh from him as she moved to the couch to wipe the blood from her mouth.

"Oh, she's *funny*. Wherever did you find her?"

Jace rubbed his temples. "The music store. Siren, this is my best friend and hopeless idiot, Random. Random, this is Siren."

"Hope*ful*," Random corrected. "Hopeful idiot."

Siren played along. "Hopeful for?"

"For the opportunity to steal you away from this brooding moron." Random threw an arm over Jace's shoulder. "He's no fun. All intellectual and serious. Spends all his time on world peace and saving defenseless puppies. You don't want him."

Siren's *I-almost-just-died* high very much approved of having someone around with a sense of humor. "But I *love* puppies."

"Well, yes, everyone loves puppies, but—"

"Did you really come here to talk about puppies, Random?" Valkyrie, her voice a solid sheet of ice, stood in the doorway. She had thunderclouds in her eyes, and power crackled around her wrists and knuckles.

Random's eyes changed when he saw her, softening. "Hey, Kyrie. I didn't know you were here."

"Last time I checked it *was* my house. What are you doing here?"

"I asked him to check the perimeter wards," Jace said.

Valkyrie looked like she'd swallowed a frog. "You asked him to check *my* wards?"

"I wasn't sure how long it'd take you to get Charles home. I didn't want to leave Siren alone and I wanted to make sure nothing else could get in. It wasn't a criticism."

She turned back to Random. "Well, did you find anything?

"Whoever sent the harpies busted through the wards on the southeast perimeter, and they were careful. Didn't even leave a trace of power to Track."

Jace frowned. "You never felt the wards break, Val?"

She looked away. "They're keyed to Dad and they won't accept a transfer of authority. I put my own wards over the front gate but I didn't see the point in going over the entire estate when no one's ever broken in before." She strode to the porch door.

"Where are you going?"

"If the wards are broken, they need mending."

Random walked after her. "Kyrie, wait, I'll come with you."

"I don't need your help." The screen door slid shut behind her, neatly cutting Random off.

"I already patched the damn wards," he called after her.

She acted as if she hadn't heard him. She turned the corner of the house, leaving Random staring at the spot where she'd disappeared, and Jace staring at Random.

"What's going on with you two?" Jace asked.

Random sighed. "Nothing, man." He ran his hand through his hair in what looked like a habitual move that artfully tousled it. "You know how Kyrie is. Sometimes she'll bite your finger off for trying to feed her.

"Anyway, let's not talk about that." He turned to Siren. "Let's talk about you. You really killed two harpies?" Random asked.

"I guess so. What exactly are they?"

"Spectral harpies, technically," Jace told her. "They're Dark Aspect constructs born of blood and will. They're illegal to make and extremely difficult to kill."

"Right," Random jumped in. "So take out all the boring stuff he just said and go straight to 'extremely difficult to kill.' How'd you do it?"

Siren blinked. *How* had she done it? The same way she did almost everything with power. "I panicked and they sort of just exploded."

Random nodded sagely, as if she'd just given him a highly detailed response. "That is *so cool*. Jace, isn't that cool?"

"It's unexplainable in terms of magical theory, considering the power expenditure necessary to make two creatures of Dark Aspect actually explode should have killed her, but sure, Random, it's *cool*."

Random shot Siren a look of long-suffering. "You see what I mean? No fun. If you let him, he'll drone on all day about the fundamentals of magical law. He did his academy thesis on Aspect differentiation throughout the bloodlines, dating all the way back to colonial days, for goddess sake."

At that moment, a falcon landed on the back of one of the patio chairs, screeching loudly at Random through the screen door. Neither Jace nor Random appeared to find this at all unusual.

"You're right, Nelsen, I *am* late." Random turned to them, bowing with a flourish. "Lady, gentleman, I'm afraid I have important affairs to see to."

"Picking up Aunt Ella from town?" Jace guessed.

"Yes." Random gave him a withering stare. "A task I used to have help with, until *someone* ran off into the great wide world to find fame and fortune."

"We all have our crosses to bear. Tick-tock." Jace tapped his watch. "You know how she gets if she has to wait."

Random muttered something no doubt unpleasant under his breath and then he was out the back door, the falcon screeching at him and taking off into the air ahead of him.

"You have unusual friends," Siren said dryly. She didn't think her brain could handle asking about the bird right now, so she didn't.

"You have no idea. That was Random being well-behaved."

Siren lapsed into silence, her emotions a chaotic mess, relief and uncertainty and hope all tangled into one convoluted ball. She kept coming back to one question, one fragile hope.

"You said you could help. How?"

CHAPTER

SIX

"Aspect Society doesn't look on stalking any more kindly than Null society does."

Siren did not interrupt him to point out that Null society, or at least its justice system, did not give two figs about stalking. If it did, fewer women might die.

"Everything the person following you is doing is illegal under Council law, especially the use of Dark constructs. If you register with the Council for inclusion and it's approved, they will use their resources to find whoever's doing this."

That all sounded very good and well, but Jace had paced the entire time he spoke.

"I sense a catch."

He stopped pacing and met her gaze.

"You're very old to have had no standard training in the use of your Aspect. The Council will want to know that you have control over it. That you aren't a danger to anyone."

"And if I am?" she asked softly. She was more than a danger, more than a potential threat. She'd killed Dark constructs, yes, but other things, too. Some nightmares, she had learned all too well, wore human faces.

There was the man in Houston who'd dragged her into the

bathroom, his hands fumbling beneath her clothes until she'd screamed, power bursting out of her, and his heart had just stopped. The cop who came into the diner in Milwaukee every Sunday night with his wife, her makeup inadequate to cover her bruises. He'd mysteriously developed a cancer that killed him in the space of one week, and she had known, somehow, that that had been *her* doing, even though she hadn't consciously tried to cause it. She'd just wanted his wife's pretty blue eyes to not look sad, for once. For her not to flinch every time someone spoke to her.

She could keep the list running in her head, all of the incidents justified, in one way or another, and she'd never meant for any of them to happen, but they *had* still happened.

"I won't lie to you; your Aspect is unusual. Power calls to power, and people with it recognize others who have it on sight. But even seeing what you did out there" —he pointed at the backyard— "I can't *feel* anything from you. Add in that you only seem able to access your Aspect when you're panicked, and the Council will have legitimate concerns over whether you can manage it safely.

"But," he continued, "a good lawyer can argue that since none of this is your fault, all of these issues can be sorted out under the guidance of a trainer."

"I can't afford a lawyer."

"I know one that'll do it pro-bono. He has an annoying tendency to always get his way."

Okay... "And the trainer? Who will that be?" The idea of spending countless hours working with a stranger while they tried to figure out what made her tick filled her with an anxiety she couldn't tamp down. Jace's obvious reluctance to answer the question didn't help either.

"They'll want it to be someone with an extensive background in magical theory, who can help you learn to control it and also explain to them why you're like this."

Flashing back to some of the things he'd said about the

harpies, to what Random had said about Jace's school thesis, she thought she understood his hesitation.

"I'm qualified to do it, if you want."

Let's see, did she want a random stranger treating her like a magical abnormality, or did she want Jace?

"I don't want you to feel obligated."

"I don't."

She took a deep breath. "Okay, then. If I'm going to do this, I want it to be you."

Valkyrie chose that moment to storm back into the room. "The wards are fine."

"Did you find anything Random missed?"

Valkyrie shook her head. "He's a pain in the ass, but he knows what he's doing." Her voice held a distinctly bitter tone.

"*What* is going on with you two? You used to get along."

She shrugged. "You've been gone a long time, Jace. People change."

"But—"

"So what's going on here?" she interrupted, pointing at Siren.

Siren might have been offended at being pointed to like an object, if she hadn't figured out by now that that was just how Valkyrie was. Jace brought his sister up to speed far more succinctly than Siren could have managed.

"In that case, you both need to get dressed."

"Dressed?" Yes, her clothes were in a state of dishevelment, but the last time Siren had checked, she was still wearing them.

"For the ball."

Siren laughed. The Winters siblings did not. "Seriously? After everything that happened today I'm supposed to care about going to a party?"

"The Gathering Ball happens once every five years, and it brings together the most powerful families in Aspect Society. If someone using Dark Aspect is after you, the Gathering is the safest place you could possibly be for the evening," Valkyrie explained. "Jace should also send your petition in to the Council now, and we can circulate the news this evening."

Siren understood the benefit of being surrounded by powerful magic users, but try as she might, she couldn't grasp the benefit of spreading gossip. "Why?"

"Because it will make you interesting, and because you will be arriving on my brother's arm. He may be legally disowned, but the people in that room care more about the genetic bloodline than they do familial squabbles, and the Winters bloodline dates back to the founding of Aspect Society. Having public attachments to us will give the Council a reason to treat you more considerately at your hearing than they would if no one knows who you are."

Siren looked to Jace for confirmation.

"She's not wrong."

"And you're okay with me using you to make a public statement?"

"It's nothing I'm unaccustomed to."

"Don't be so dramatic," Valkyrie snapped. "You haven't had to deal with any of this in half a decade. So go get dressed, and remember to smile."

"Umm, there is one problem," Siren said. "I really don't have anything to wear."

CHAPTER
SEVEN

That was how Siren found herself on the third floor of the Winters' home in a walk-in closet the size of her apartment, an entire wall of which was comprised of nothing but evening dresses.

"Not that I'm ungrateful," Siren began, "but I don't think anything of yours will fit me." Siren was shorter than Valkyrie, narrower in the waist, and larger in the chest.

"These aren't *mine*."

Valkyrie looked horrified at the very idea, and in retrospect the lack of black in the closet should have clued Siren in.

"They were my mother's," she said softly.

"What happened to her?"

Valkyrie's expression hardened.

"I'm sorry. It's really none of my business."

"It's fine. She had health problems. Having Jace exacerbated them, and she died a few years later. It's part of why of our father's so hard on him. Anyway," she said brusquely, "you're welcome to anything that fits. You can use the guest bedroom across the hall to clean up."

Valkyrie left, and Siren went to shower off the grime and gore of obliterated harpies. The film on her shoulders had blended color to match her skin tone, and when she ran her fingers over it, she couldn't even feel the seam where her skin ended and the patch began. Only the fact that she couldn't feel the sensation of her fingers over the patched area told her it wasn't, in fact, her own skin. It was both cool and creepy. She wanted to know who the mysterious Charles was that had done it for her, but finding that out was at the bottom of her list of current priorities, number one of which was to survive the evening.

Once she was clean and dry, she returned to the enormous closet. Valkyrie's mother had been much closer to Siren's size, and she finally found a soft yellow gown that fit. Elegant in a classic, timeless style, and mock-corseted at the waist, the skirts flowed loose in long ripples that hid the bite scars on her ankles. The straps were a wide strip of the same material as the skirts, each side clasped with a series of gold rings that bunched the material together right above the bodice and let the rest of the material fan out as it went over her shoulders in a halter-style tie.

She'd just selected a pair of shoes that fit, if they were a little small and pinched her toes, when she heard a raised curse and the shatter of breaking glass. She ran out of the room, skirts bunched in her hands to keep from tripping. The sound had come from the end of the hall, and she rushed into a room bedecked with mahogany furniture and dark, drawn drapes. It looked, in short, exactly like Siren had imagined Valkyrie's bedroom *would* look.

She found Valkyrie in the bathroom, wearing a one-shouldered black gown that fit her like skintight body armor. A furious snarl lit her face. Her left fist brandished a hand mirror, its glass shattered on the floor around her, and her right fist held a curling iron in a death grip.

Her hair…Well, Siren wasn't quite sure what the woman had tried to do with it, but she obviously hadn't succeeded.

"Are you okay?"

"No," Valkyrie growled. "This thing is obviously defective."

She glared at the curling iron as if it had challenged her to combat.

"Right." Siren had the sneaking suspicion that Valkyrie's sudden decision to style her hair, something it appeared she'd never before had the impetus to do, had a direct correlation to her and Random's caustic interaction earlier.

Not that Siren was foolish enough to *ask*.

Valkyrie stared at her hair in the mirror. "This was the dumbest idea I've ever had."

"It's not."

A ripped-out page of a magazine lay on the counter. It showed a woman with long hair that fell in loose, shimmering curls. Siren pointed to it. "You want it to look like that?"

Valkyrie gave her a suspicious look, but she nodded.

"All right, then. I can fix this."

"You don't need to—"

"Please. It's the least I can do." Siren pulled over a wire-backed chair that matched the vanity—the bathroom was as absurdly large as everything else in this house—and ordered Valkyrie into it.

"Why do I need to sit?"

"Because you are tall, and I am not."

Valkyrie sat, but one would have thought it a valiant sacrifice by the way she moved into the chair. Siren grabbed a brush and combed the newly made tangles out of Valkyrie's thick mane, silently whispering her thanks that Valkyrie had not put any of the hair products—newly bought, if the Target bag beneath them was any indication—littering the vanity in it.

Turning to the array of products, she selected a shine spray, misted a small amount over Valkyrie's hair, and then combed it through. Then she pinned all but the bottom layer of hair on top of Valkyrie's head and began curling it in sections. She worked layer by layer, adding a small amount of hold spray here and there, though never very much. Valkyrie's hair was so thick Siren thought it could probably hold a curl for days.

When she got to the top layer, she drew back a portion of hair from the front middle, securing it on top of Valkyrie's head with a couple of bobby pins, and curled the trailing locks so they ran down and blended in with the rest of the curls. She set the curling iron down and gently finger-combed the curls, just enough to loosen them slightly, giving them a freer, more natural look.

"All done. You can open your eyes now."

Valkyrie had shut her eyes when Siren first started work, her face clenched in an expression of a woman proceeding to the gallows. When her lids flickered open, she just…stared. After a few seconds, she lifted her fingertips and hesitantly touched the loose tendrils tumbling down her shoulders.

"It will look like this all night?"

"The curls may loosen a little over the night, but more or less, yes." Siren grinned. "So whoever it is you want to impress or drive mad with longing, I'd say mission accomplished."

Siren immediately regretted the words when thunder clouded Valkyrie's eyes, but she gave no admission of noticing the woman's change in mood. "If you don't mind, I *would* like to borrow your makeup. I don't have anything with me."

"Help yourself." Valkyrie consulted the time on her phone. "I need to check on the arrangements. Can you find your way downstairs on your own?"

"I think I'll manage."

Valkyrie looked in the mirror again before leaving, as if she couldn't quite believe the transformation she saw.

"Thank you," she said softly, and then she was gone.

Siren stared after the spot where Valkyrie had disappeared. The woman had whispered her thank-you like no one had done her hair for her before. It occurred to Siren that maybe no one ever had. She didn't know how old Valkyrie had been when her mother died, and Siren strongly suspected that Valkyrie did not have many female friends.

She felt a pang of sadness for the isolation Valkyrie seemed to wrap herself in, then shook her head at the ridiculousness of *her* pitying *Valkyrie*. She doubted the woman wanted anyone's pity.

Still amused at herself, she turned her attention to Valkyrie's scant supply of cosmetics. The foundation was a shade too dark for her, but she could work with the loose powder. Her complexion might be pale, but at least it was smooth. She dusted it across her face, blending it carefully where skin met hair and where jawline blended into neck.

She might not be able to take out a two-hundred-pound linebacker with her bare hands, something she suspected Valkyrie could do with ease, but eyeliner and mascara were their own forms of battle armor, and as she applied both and surveyed the end result, she couldn't help but feel well-equipped, indeed.

Even if her battle was only a ball.

CHAPTER

EIGHT

As it turned out, Siren didn't have to find her way downstairs after all. She opened the bedroom door and stopped an inch shy of running smack into Jace's chest. After her eyes did a quick once-over, she regretted she *hadn't* run into him.

He wore dark gray dress pants with a wide belt that accented his lean, flat stomach. A light blue dress shirt fit him as if it had been tailored—then again, it probably *had* been tailored—emphasizing broad shoulders and hinting at the muscles beneath the silky fabric.

Had she thought men's dress clothes boring and businesslike? She had been wrong. They were devilish and sensual. He didn't wear a tie, and the top button of his shirt was undone, giving her a tantalizing glimpse of skin. The shirtsleeves were rolled up to just below his elbows, exposing well-muscled forearms that somehow looked more tempting partially covered than bared completely in a t-shirt.

She realized she was staring. Warmth flushed her cheeks as she raised her gaze to his face. The heat in his eyes made her certain not only that he'd noticed her inspection, but that she'd been subject to one of his own.

All thoughts of ballrooms and dancing fled her, replaced with thoughts of her mouth on his, of her body crushing against him, of finding the nearest room with a bed that was *not* Valkyrie's and distracting herself from everything that had happened today in the oldest of ways.

His gaze fastened on her mouth, and she felt his desire in the coiled tension of his body, in the slow, hard swallow that had her following the up-and-down slide of his Adam's apple. She felt brazen, possessed of the confidence conferred by good clothes and the certainty that she wore them well.

"How do I look?"

"Perfect," he said, his voice a low rumble.

Then he kissed her.

She met him eagerly, parted her lips as his tongue thrust between them. Liquid fire spilled through her and she pressed against him, acutely aware of his hand splayed across her lower back, of her hips pressed against his thighs. She ran her hands up the planes of his back and reveled in the hard, defined muscle. Unable to resist, she dug her nails in.

He groaned low in his throat and pushed her back against the door frame. One of his hands tangled in her hair and the other trailed up her side, coaxing every nerve ending in her body to glorious life. When his lips left hers, she nearly growled in protest.

"We're going to be late," he whispered. It was the kind of protest a person made when they thought they ought to be making a protest, the kind meant to give the other person involved the opportunity to elegantly exit the current scenario if they wished.

She had no desire to exit the scenario. She wanted *this*, the pure physical feeling of need that wiped away the necessity of thinking, of worrying. When she kissed him, when she touched him, she didn't have to think about what would happen next. She didn't have to *be* anything.

"And if I want to be very, very late?"

"Then we'll be very, very late."

He kissed her again, walking her back down the hallway. When she stumbled—because walking backwards in plush carpet while wearing three-inch heels was not her forte—his hands slipped down to grasp her thighs, lifting her up. She wrapped her legs around his waist, grateful for the accommodating slits on either side of the dress's skirts.

She was momentarily confused when she realized they were exiting the hallway back towards the staircase, until she caught sight of a second hallway and deduced his room must be there. They rounded that corner when Siren caught a silhouette in her peripheral vision, almost directly behind her but clearly in Jace's line of sight.

He froze.

Siren slipped down, heels landing gently on the ground. She turned toward the staircase, but Jace's arms around her waist prevented her from stepping away from him entirely.

A woman stood there, her expression unreadable. She wore a silver evening gown that Siren suspected cost more than most cars, and she was undeniably beautiful. Blonde hair fell in soft, natural waves to her waist, and the artful cut of the gown's skirts showed off one long, toned leg. Full, expressive lips were painted a deep red and set against pale skin, high cheekbones, and ice-blue eyes.

Siren was caught between mortal embarrassment at being walked in on when she'd been wrapped around Jace, and the desire to know why he was doing his best to imitate a statue.

"I'd heard you were back," the woman said. Her gaze swept over Siren. "Clearly, I should have called. We can talk later, when you aren't so...busy."

She turned on four-inch stilettos and walked back down the stairs, her hand trailing the banister like a queen descending the staircase in her own castle.

"Who was that?"

Jace ran a hand back through his hair with a sigh. "That was Meredith. My ex."

~

MEREDITH. The name sent a sinking feeling through her. If *that* was the previous girlfriend, what the hell was he doing with her?

"*There* you are." Valkyrie strode up the stairs, her gaze fastening on Jace. "The opening dance is in twenty minutes. I need you downstairs."

"Right."

Valkyrie's gaze flickered to Siren then back to Jace. "Can I talk to you alone for a moment?"

"If you wanted to tell him that Meredith is here, there's no need. She was *quite* comfortable letting him know that herself."

And *that* hadn't sounded insecure or clingy at all. Yes, she had just been about to engage in certain carnal acts with Jace, but it wasn't as if they were dating.

Were they dating? She'd never had to figure this sort of thing out before, because she'd never stayed in one place long enough for it to matter. If she was dying to know just how recent of an ex Meredith was, she would just have to suffer through the curiosity.

"When did you find out she was going to be here?" Jace asked, voice clipped.

Did he sound angry? And why did that make her very, very pleased?

"I found out a few minutes ago when she blew past the doorman. For some reason, he didn't think she would stay in the public areas of the house."

"Well, she damn well will now." Jace shoved the sleeves of his shirt back up to his elbows, and put his hands on the banister. A sheen of gold power rolled over his eyes, the only warning before a soundless shockwave buffeted the house. Siren stumbled at the unexpected shock, caught herself on the banister, and gasped as her hand brushed a current of power. She closed her eyes and slipped into that current, felt where it flowed and twisted through every wall and doorway in the house.

"There." Jace's eyes still crackled with power as he linked one arm in Siren's, the other in Valkyrie's and walked them down the stairs as if the entire matter was settled. Valkyrie and Siren exchanged a wordless glance as they wound their way out of the center of the house to the east wing. A steady stream of men and women in formal wear made their way toward a grand set of French doors that opened onto a stunning hardwood floor.

"Jace! Kyrie!" a familiar voice called.

Random walked toward them, his arm looped through that of a distinguished older woman with coiffed gray hair and a ramrod straight spine. Her skin was a shade darker than Random's, a beautiful deep bronze set off to perfection by the soft cream color of her gown and the evening gloves that went up past her elbows. Though she must be somewhere in her seventies, it only showed in the gathers at the corners of her lips and eyes.

"Aunt Ella, this is Siren, who I told you about." Random said, "Siren, my great-aunt, Ella Tremayne."

"It's nice to meet you."

Ella Tremayne did not return the greeting. She stared at Siren as if she'd seen a ghost, and then she rattled off a stream of Spanish that made Random's eyes widen.

"Could we all duck aside for a moment?" Random asked. "I think we might want to revise our entrance strategy."

Siren did not have a good feeling as Random ushered them into a side room. The door had barely closed behind them before Ella Tremayne's gaze pinned Siren in place.

"How old are you, child?" she demanded.

The intensity that rolled off the woman made Siren take an

inadvertent step back, right into Jace. He settled a comforting hand on her hip.

"Aunt Ella, it's been a very strange day," Jace said. "What's going on?"

When she spoke, it was directly to Siren. "You look just like Mara Savage. Which is why I'm wondering how old you are."

It took a moment for the implication to sink in, another for her to fight down the rush of excitement.

"Twenty two. You think," —she broke off, hardly able to get the words out. "You think you know who my mother is?"

She'd been *told* her parents were dead, yes, but after what had happened that night her power first woke, she'd questioned everything her foster parents had ever told her. It made a great deal more sense, in fact, that she'd been kidnapped.

"I'm fairly certain I know who she *was*," Aunt Ella said, gently.

Just like that, the hope that had blossomed in Siren's chest died.

"Savage," Jace said, "Isn't that the family that used to live next to us?" His thumb stroked across her hip bone, a silent offer of support.

"Yes," Valkyrie said. "John and Mara Savage. They were friends with Mom."

"They're both dead?" Siren asked. It shouldn't hurt. But a small part of her had always hoped that maybe they were still alive, and looking for her.

"I'm sorry, dear," Aunt Ella said.

"What happened to them?"

"It isn't pretty," Valkyrie said. "Maybe now isn't the best time."

"I don't care if it's the best time. I've waited twenty years, I deserve to *know*."

Valkyrie gave her a measured look and then nodded.

"They were killed inside their home on winter's solstice. Dark Aspect was involved but the Council never discovered who was behind it. Given that their wards were intact, it's likely it was someone they knew. Mara was eight months pregnant before she died." Valkyrie swallowed. "They…she wasn't pregnant when they found her body. Someone took the baby."

Took me, Siren thought. *Someone killed my parents and took* me.

CHAPTER

NINE

"How certain are you that you're right?" Siren asked Ella.

"You're practically a carbon copy of Mara. And Siren *was* the name they chose for you. But even without that, my Aspect has an…affinity for bloodlines. I'm certain."

"She's never been wrong," Jace murmured. "I'm sorry."

"It may seem insensitive," Random said, "but her best advantage is to announce her tonight under the Savage name."

Siren tensed.

"Random," Jace began.

"He is right," Aunt Ella interrupted, and she turned her full attention back to Siren. "Random informed me of your situation. The circumstances of your Aspect are unusual enough. Add in the mystery surrounding your parents' deaths, all of which point to the likelihood of you being raised by Dark Aspect users, and the Council is going to have concerns. I should know." She gave Siren a tight smile. "I'm a member.

"So you can let your emotions cause you to stumble, or you can do this the strategic way."

Frustration, along with the desire to run back upstairs and hide from all of this, warred with the knowledge that none of it was going to just go away. Not unless she ran again. Part of her whispered that that was exactly what she *should* do, but running wasn't a life. Running didn't have Jace. Running didn't have safety.

She wanted all three, and she wasn't going to let it go just because hearing her actual last name caused her pain. "Fine. Do it, then."

"I'll make the change with the announcer," Valkyrie said, and left.

"There is one other thing," Random said. "Aunt Ella's never wrong, but her results aren't official, so to speak, without a more invasive use of her Aspect. It *will* have to be done at some point. You're best off doing it publicly."

"When?" she asked. It made little difference to her at this point.

"It won't take long for the gossip mill to question your heritage tonight. Aunt Ella can contrive to put those questions to rest at an opportune moment."

Jace's hand tightened on her hip. "You don't have to do everything tonight."

"It's okay. I'd rather just get it over with."

"You'll do fine, dear," Aunt Ella said. "Jace, escort me into the ballroom? Random can take Siren."

When he protested she said, "You can have her for the opening dance and the rest of the ball, but it will do her good for everyone to know that she has the Winters *and* the Tremaynes behind her."

Jace glanced down at her. She nodded, because if she had to say some variation of "It's fine" one more time she'd feel too much like a broken record.

Jace shot Random a warning look. "Behave."

"Don't be ridiculous, you know I never do."

Jace and Aunt Ella left the room. Random bowed to Siren in a faintly ridiculous manner that made her laugh despite everything, and she took his proffered arm.

"So," he said, leading them from the room at a glacial pace, "what pissed Jace off?"

It was an obvious attempt to distract her, and she was grateful for it.

"You felt what he did?"

"Honey, everyone in this house felt what he did."

"And what, exactly, was that?"

Random eyed her speculatively. "If I answer your questions, are you ever going to answer mine?"

"Yes."

"He activated the interior wards of the house, blocking everything but the path from the front door to the ballroom to everyone but him and Valkyrie." He was silent for a couple steps, then added, "And you."

"Is something like that always noticeable?"

Random laughed. "No. It was noticeable because he wanted it noticed. Are you going to let me in on why?"

"Meredith decided to let herself in."

Random stopped walking. "She actually showed her face here?"

"Yes? Look, I get that he wasn't expecting her, but why everyone is so shocked? What happened between them?"

Random opened his mouth, then shook his head. "Normally, nothing would delight me more than to gossip about all of Jace's dirty secrets, but in this instance, the tale requires proper telling, and I'm afraid this isn't the place."

"That fills me with confidence."

"I aim to please." Random resumed walking. "I haven't seen Jace *that* gloriously pissed off in years. You say all she did was wander in on you two coming downstairs, then?"

"We weren't precisely heading downstairs."

"No?"

"We might have been heading more toward the bedrooms."

Random mock-gasped. "You little tramp. Consider me properly appalled," he replied in a stiff, cultured voice while a smile cracked at the corner of his lips. He held up his free hand for a high five.

Siren stared at it.

He waved the hand. "Come on, don't leave me hanging."

"You realize I'm not a dude with a conquest and also that nothing actually happened, right?"

"Hey, ladies have a right to conquest, too, and intention counts for something." He waved his hand again. "Come on."

Siren high-fived him. It seemed like the only expedient way to get him to put his hand down.

She hadn't realized she was nervous until they stepped through the ballroom door. The room was so eerily silent that Siren's heels clicked audibly on the polished hardwood. It wasn't hard to guess the cause of that silence. Jace, halfway across the ballroom and heading toward Valkyrie, had drawn every eye in the room.

There were a *lot* of eyes. Well over one hundred pairs of them. Guests lined the perimeter of the dance floor, collected together in little groups. They gathered around standing cocktail tables, holding fluted champagne glasses and tracking Jace's every move. He strolled across the dance floor, politely chatting with Aunt Ella and acting as if he didn't notice the attention.

Random leaned over and whispered something to the announcer by the door, who then spoke into his small microphone, "Random Tremayne and Siren Mara Savage."

Every eye that had previously been trained on Jace turned to the doorway in a concerted movement, like a pack of hyenas scenting a wounded animal. She only started walking when Random did because, since he held her arm, she'd cause a scene if she didn't.

"Easy does it," Random murmured. "Halfway there."

"How do I make them stop staring?" she asked, more because she wanted something to say than because she thought he had an actual answer.

"Well," Random considered, "I could always kiss you."

That brought a genuine smile to her lips. "And that would make them stop looking at me because…?"

"Because Jace would feel obligated to punch me, and then everyone would be looking at him again. You know, now that I think about it, a love triangle with two handsome, powerful men is just the thing your strategic entrance into Aspect Society is missing. The only decision to be made is if we're staying PG or going NC-17."

"You're ridiculous, you know that right?"

"So I'm frequently told. You have about ten seconds to make up your mind on that kiss. I promise, it's an experience you won't want to miss."

Siren laughed. "I'm sure. While I appreciate the generosity of your offer, I'm not sure I want anyone getting punched out of a sense of *obligation*."

"Who is getting punched?" Aunt Ella asked as they walked up to her, Jace, and Valkyrie. The old woman had a look of excited anticipation in her hawkish brown eyes. Apparently, Aunt Ella enjoyed a good brawl.

"I would be, Aunt Ella, if I were to kiss Siren."

"What part of 'behave' was unclear?" Jace asked. He *looked* calm enough, but underneath the cool exterior, Siren could tell that the crowd and Meredith had bothered him more than he let on.

Siren slipped her arm out of Random's and traded it for Jace's. "He was just being polite. He thought it might take the attention off me if everyone was busy watching you pummel him."

"Did he?" Jace glanced at Random. "I had no idea you'd turned so self-sacrificing."

"Yes, well. It's interesting what happens to you when a beautiful woman tells you that you don't have a single useful bone in your entire body."

Jace laughed, but Siren caught the trace of genuine anger in Random's voice, and she didn't miss how Aunt Ella's lips thinned, *or* the look the woman flashed at Valkyrie. An angry blush crept up Valkyrie's high cheekbones, and her jaw was clenched so tight Siren expected to hear teeth crack at any moment.

"Random, in all the years I've known you, you've had a different beautiful woman on your arm every other month and never made any of them *that* angry," Jace said, oblivious to his sister's reaction. "What did you do to this one?"

Random grabbed a champagne flute from a passing server and downed the contents in two swallows. "I told her I loved her, and I meant it." He flashed a grin. "Now, if you'll excuse me, I'm going to go find your ex and ask her why the devil she's here."

CHAPTER
TEN

"A speech is traditional at a Gathering," Valkyrie began, her voice carrying easily throughout the room without aid of a microphone. She stood on a stage at one end of the dance floor, rows of empty chairs behind her, the blush in her cheeks the only outward remnant of her earlier irritation.

"This year's speech should have been given by my father. As I am sure you all know of his disappearance, I trust you will understand that a heavy heart does not lend itself well to loquaciousness. So, instead of a speech, I will leave you with the words my father might have given you.

"The community here tonight is one that is built on trust and cooperation. That those with Aspect come together each year to renew our dedication to using that power for the betterment of others and not only for ourselves, to elect Council members who will further those ideals and root out those who would turn Aspect to darker uses, is a value to be cherished and nurtured.

"My brother and I thank you for your attendance and your friendship, and we open our home to you, in the same manner you would all no doubt open yours to us."

Valkyrie lifted her champagne glass, and she spoke her next words in the manner of a phrase that has been repeated so often that it has both gained meaning and lost it. "May your Aspect burn bright, may your hearts be true, and may your lives be full."

Guests raised their glasses and repeated the words back. Valkyrie left the stage and musicians filed in from a side door to fill the empty chairs.

"What was that?" Jace asked as Valkyrie rejoined them.

"What was what?" she clipped irritably.

"You had an entire speech planned. You worked on it for weeks. I know, because you made me listen to it in its entirety every time you added a comma or took out a word."

Valkyrie lifted her shoulders, let them fall. The move was too pointed and controlled to merely call it a shrug. "I didn't feel like giving it."

"But—"

"What are they all waiting for?" Siren interrupted. Although she *did* want to know why no one in the room had moved since Valkyrie left the stage, she mostly wanted to keep Jace from badgering his sister. He was so obviously clueless as to what was bothering her that he was likely to say something hurtful by accident.

"They're waiting for Jace," a dulcet voice said. Meredith had arrived, Random on her heels. He threw Siren an apologetic look.

"And for Valkyrie, of course," Meredith continued." It's traditional for the hosts to open the dance. Didn't Jace tell you?"

She smiled sweetly, looking for all the world like a helpful confidant.

"I think when Jace is around Siren he probably has more *intimate* things on his mind than talking about dancing, Mer." Random clapped her on the shoulder hard enough that she stumbled a little in her tall stilettos. "If you'll excuse us, we've one person more than is needed here, and the orchestra is getting impatient. Kyrie, I think you owe me a dance."

He held out his hand. Valkyrie glanced at it, glanced at the number of people staring at them, and clearly decided it would be more of a scene than it was worth to refuse him.

Meredith had not left, and people *were* starting to murmur about that. She spoke to Siren in a voice dripping with sugary sweetness. "If you don't know the dance, I can save you the embarrassment and take Jace off your hands."

Siren returned her syrupy smile. "So thoughtful of you, but unnecessary. What dance do you open with?" she asked Jace.

"Waltz." If his vocal cords got any tighter, they were going to snap the next time he spoke.

"Viennese or American?"

"Viennese."

"Oh, good. The American bores me." Siren slid her hand into Jace's, his warm calluses rasping pleasantly against her palm. Meredith did not immediately leave, and for one insane moment Siren thought she might cause an actual scene. Then she just smiled, inclined her head, and walked to join a group along the side.

"You waltz?" Jace asked quietly as they made their way to the middle of the floor where Random and Valkyrie waited.

"Don't sound so surprised. Years of cotillion. The dancing was the only part I liked."

He raised an eyebrow. "Debutante ball?"

"I'm afraid I never made it out into Society."

The orchestra moved into position and she took her proper starting pose with Jace.

"Why not?"

A memory surfaced of blood slicking her hands and face, of a body lying broken on the pavement, beautiful blue eyes open and unseeing. She swallowed hard and forced the memory back.

"Because I ran away."

The music started and she turned her full attention to dancing. The Viennese waltz was similar enough to the American, though much faster, and it would be easy enough to trip over herself as she hadn't danced it in over a year. In the larger cities she could usually find a venue that held free open dancing nights here and there. It was one of the few enjoyments she allowed herself, but the last three towns she'd lived in hadn't had an outlet for it.

Jace turned out to be an excellent partner, and she lost herself in the fast pace as they made a circuit of the dance floor, stepping and twirling, and passing near Random and Valkyrie.

"You might want to trade me to Random," she suggested when she was confident she had a good enough handle on the dance for speech.

"I don't think I want to do that at all, actually."

She grinned. "If you don't, I think Valkyrie might kill him."

"All right," he said, "but only for the sake of a friend." He caught Random's eye as they passed by again, spinning her free as Random did the same with Valkyrie. Siren and Valkyrie made one circle of the waltz on their own, until each came back to the opposite partner they'd started with.

"You are a godsend," Random said. "You know she was digging her nails in as hard as possible, and for Kyrie, that's *hard*."

"You poor thing," Siren purred.

"You have no idea. I think she drew blood. Will you marry me?"

Siren laughed so hard she almost stumbled when he spun her out and drew her back in. "I'll pass on the vows of matrimony, but when this dance is over you can show me where to find a *much* stronger drink than what the servers are passing around."

"Your wish is my command."

They passed the rest of the dance in silence, and when the orchestra drew its final notes, she humored Random and let him tip her back into a low bend that drew a fair amount of applause.

The opening sequence complete, other couples flooded onto the floor, and Siren gratefully followed Random off to the side. She might like dancing, but she didn't care for being the center of attention.

She smiled when she saw Jace walking to her, people parting naturally around him. He didn't carry the overbearing masculinity that some men exuded, as if they found it necessary to announce to everyone that they were just one step shy of a Neanderthal on the evolutionary chain. He just moved with brusque confidence and purpose.

For the first time in a long time, Siren was content to wait as he came to her.

Her patience was immediately tested when Jace was intercepted by a tall, distinguished Black man in a smart gray suit. Random noted her disappointment.

"You can expect that to happen all night. Jace hasn't been in Aspect Society in six years and everyone is dying to ferret out if he's here for Elijah's Council seat."

That got her attention. "His father was on the Council?"

Random nodded. "Still is, technically. If he doesn't turn up eventually the seat will go open to vote. Preference is given to descendants in filling a seat, but a vote can always swing towards someone else. The hordes will be all over him and Kyrie tonight."

"Does Jace want the seat?"

"Goddess, no." Random laughed. "The only reason he's even here is Kyrie begged him to help her find Elijah. He'd never have come home on his own."

Siren hesitated, wondering how far it was appropriate to probe. "Jace said his father disowned him. What was it over?"

"Oh, it's the age-old story. Father is disappointed his son is not as barbaric and warlike as he'd hoped he would be. Son turns eighteen, tells his father to shove it. Father cuts his son off from all financial support, expecting him to come crawling home with his tail tucked between his legs, begging for forgiveness. Instead, son does just fine out in the world and a cold distance grows between father and son, unbroken to this very day."

Siren digested this, worrying at her bottom lip out of habit.

"Whatever it is, go ahead and ask."

"It's just…Elijah sounds so harsh, but Valkyrie seems desperate to have him back." Realizing how that must sound she hastened to add, "I'm not suggesting she shouldn't want to find her father, just that she seems to have a very different view of him than Jace does."

Random sighed. "It's not really her fault. She came out of the womb with everything Elijah Winters wanted in a child. She is bold and fierce and deadly, and she does whatever he tells her to. She's never found herself at opposing viewpoints with him, so she's never had to learn if his love for her is contingent on her obedience.

"Jace and Elijah have spent their entire lives with opposing viewpoints."

Siren didn't have to try too hard to imagine what it felt like growing up and knowing you were not what your parent had hoped for in a child. She had always attributed that feeling in her childhood to being adopted. She had always tried to be polite and charming and acquiescent, to be the perfect daughter she had imagined Mark and Anne had wanted.

No matter how hard she'd tried, though, they had always been distant, as if they were more acting the roles of parents rather than being parents. And they had been, just not for the reasons she'd thought.

Jace ended his conversation and managed an entire three steps toward her before he was intercepted by a smiling, middle-aged brunette.

"Well, you've been in my business from the get-go," Siren said, opting for a change in subject, "so turnaround is fair play. What's up with you and Valkyrie?"

"I beg your pardon?"

Siren snorted. "Oh, please. Jace may be completely oblivious to putting you two together but I'm not. What gives?"

"Nothing gives," Random said finally. "That's the problem."

"And?" she prompted.

"And I'm going to need that stronger drink if you want these lips to loosen. I'm a gentleman. I don't ordinarily kiss and tell." Random snagged two champagne glasses off a wandering server's tray and handed one to Siren. "Start with this. I'll be back."

"Where are you going?"

"To raid Elijah Winters's whiskey stash."

"Aren't the house wards locking you in here with everyone else?"

He winked at her. "I'm Random. I'm never locked in anywhere."

Then he was gone, flitting through the groups of people and slipping out the ballroom door with no one seeming to notice.

CHAPTER

ELEVEN

If Siren had thought to blend in at the edges of the crowd, she didn't manage it. Random had been gone for all of two, maybe three, minutes when a voice behind her asked, "Have I seen you here before?"

She startled and spun to find a man in his mid-thirties with brown hair and a nose slightly too large for him. She was grateful the champagne glass in her hand was empty, else she would have spilled its contents all over the front of her dress. From the amused look on the man's face, he realized it, maybe even had been counting on it.

"I'm sorry, I didn't mean to startle you." He smiled, looking anything but sorry.

"That's the funny thing about strays, Julian—they startle so easily." Meredith's honey voice slid over Siren, sticky and false-sweet as she joined them. "It took me a moment to place you, but you're the new cashier at Hank's little store, aren't you?"

"Yes, that's right," Siren answered, refusing to acknowledge the condescension in the other woman's voice. This close, Siren could see her nose was just slightly crooked, but while it would have detracted from any other woman's beauty, it only made

Meredith look more approachable, kept her beauty from being a thing too far out of reach.

How, Siren wondered, was she supposed to compete with a woman whose *flaws* were adorable? Then again, Meredith appeared to have a complete lack of charming personality, so Siren definitely had the leg up on that account.

"Strange, then," Meredith said, "that you came here using the Savage name. I'm told you do look a fair amount like Mara, but considering the Savages were worth over two million at the time of their deaths, I wouldn't think their daughter would be working for minimum wage. Or showing up to the Gathering in one of Evelyn Winters's hand-me-downs."

Meredith gave her a deprecating smile. "You should have chosen a different dress. That one is a one-of-a-kind vintage Moravi. I recall Evelyn wearing it in this lovely little family photo in Jace's bedroom."

Siren had to give the woman credit for packing a strong verbal punch. If it hadn't been directed at her, she might have even admired the craftsmanship.

The nearby guests had formed an attentive circle around her and Meredith, and Siren didn't know how she was supposed to respond to the woman's layered insinuations without making herself look like an opportunistic imposter.

Two *million*? The mere thought made her sick.

"I like working," she said, like an idiot. "As for the dress, did you know that the fashion industry is one of the leading offenders of climate change? There's really nothing worse for the planet than a one-use garment."

A few of the onlookers openly snickered.

Okay, maybe using climate change in her defense hadn't been her brightest idea ever, but she really hadn't had any others.

"Charming," Meredith said drily. "But you will have to prove that heritage claim. I'm so looking forward to seeing the results."

"Would you like me to confirm it now, then?" Aunt Ella cut through the people around Siren, all of whom had ceased pretending to be engaged in other matters and were now avidly watching events unfold.

Meredith's eyes widened the barest fraction. Aloud, she just said, "If she wants to subject herself to a blood delineation in front of everyone in the room, far be it from me to stop her."

Aunt Ella pulled off one of the long white gloves she wore and held out her hand to Siren, asking permission.

Just rip it off like a band-aid, she told herself, and took Aunt Ella's hand. Power surged into her. It reminded her somewhat of the one time she'd had to have fluids pumped into her via an IV, coolness slowly creeping through her veins, chilling her entire body bit by bit. She felt Ella's power searching, creeping about, looking for something specific.

It was invasive, and it made her feel as if her insides were being pulled out, inspected, and then put back inside her. Unpleasant was too kind a word for it, but it did not feel cruel. While Ella's eyes were unfocused, seeing something that Siren could not, her hands were gentle, her power's searching careful and meticulous

Then Aunt Ella's power withdrew, leaving Siren empty and shaken, as if the things inside her did not quite belong entirely to her anymore. Her body's natural warmth had fled her, and she shivered, arms and legs covered in goosebumps.

Aunt Ella's eyes refocused. They were warm, and her smile was kind. "It's a pleasure to meet you, Siren Savage. Your parents were good people."

Excited muttering broke out around them. Siren didn't care. She just wanted to get away from them, away from everyone. Perhaps there was a strategic move to be made here, but she didn't know what it was and she didn't have it in her to figure it out. She'd done her part. She'd confirmed, in front of a crowd of strangers, that her parents were dead, and that was all they were getting from her for the evening.

She pushed her way through the crowd, ignoring several people who called her name, one of whom she would have sworn said he was from something called *The Aspect Tribune.* Apparently, secret societies had their own newspapers, because of course they did.

She was relieved to note that only a fraction of the ballroom had been privy to the recent drama, and if it looked like it would spread through the rest of the room soon enough, for the moment she found a small corner to hide in. When a figure appeared beside her, she nearly punched it before she realized it was Random.

"What the hell took you so long?"

Random winced. "Sorry, sweetheart, but I'm afraid Jace's enthusiasm for sinking power into the interior wards made them slightly more difficult to navigate than usual."

"But you were successful?" *Please, for the sake of my sanity, let him have been successful.*

He looked affronted. "Of course."

"Good. Then get me out of here."

CHAPTER

TWELVE

The porch on the east side of the Winters' house offered a stunning view of a lake by moonlight, made all the lovelier by the fact that it was gloriously empty of anyone save herself and Random.

She wrapped the jacket he had thoughtfully offered her tighter around herself and settled onto the wooden porch swing. As Random had explained it, chills were normal after Aunt Ella's rifling through her insides and should subside in an hour or so. Until then, she'd shiver in the jacket and allow herself to be pointlessly annoyed that this was the first time a man had ever given her his jacket—one of those hallmark dating moments she'd secretly thought she'd never have—and it wasn't a man she was romantically interested in.

"Does the jacket smell bad?" Random asked.

"No, it smells nice." It did, too. Clean and with a hint of after-shave. "Why?"

"Because you are curling your nose up at it."

"I am not."

"Are too."

"Fine, I'm annoyed it's not Jace's."

"Ah, *very* noble of you." Random settled onto the swing

beside her. "And I am sure it will fill him with barbaric pride to know you only accepted it for the sake of your health. Speaking of health, this ought to cure what ails you." He broke the seal on a dust-covered bottle and pulled out the stopper.

"This is a thirty-year-old Scotch which probably hails from some area known for its Scotch, and which Elijah Winters was no doubt saving for a special occasion." He handed her the bottle. "Ladies first."

"So gentlemanly of you." Siren tipped the bottle back and took two long, hard swallows. The spiced liquid warmed her mouth and a trail of fire bit down her throat to expand in her chest. She handed the bottle to Random.

"I am the consummate gentleman." He drank and passed the bottle back to her. "And because I am, even though we're both soon to be inebriated, I promise not to try and get into your pants. Or, more accurately, under your dress."

Siren snorted. Scotch went up her nose and tears of laughter filled her eyes. "You may be an incorrigible flirt, Random, but if I actually thought you wanted to seduce me, I wouldn't be out here with you."

Random sighed. "There was a time I would have. Wouldn't have given a second thought to *not* seducing you. You're a funny, sexy woman, and I am an exceptionally handsome, virile male."

Siren giggled, Scotch warming her veins. "Virile? Really?"

"You laugh now, but if I'd turned my smoldering gaze on you in my prime, you would have been out of that dress in ten seconds."

"Well then, let's see it."

"See what?"

"The smoldering gaze."

"All right." His eyes darkened, and he turned a sexy, smoldering gaze on her.

Siren's breath hitched. "It's not bad," she admitted. "But it wouldn't get me out of this dress."

"See, that's the problem. Three months ago, it totally would have. I think I'm broken."

"And that would have something to do with Valkyrie?" Siren prompted.

"Yeah." Random took the bottle of Scotch back and downed more of it than Siren privately thought was healthy. "Damn woman broke my damn heart." He swallowed another mouthful. "And the kicker is, she doesn't even care. Here I thought *I* was supposed to be the philandering, heartless asshole, and *she's* the one who doesn't give a good goddamn."

"I think she does."

"You think so?" Random lifted an eyebrow. "She hasn't spoken a civil word to me since..." He trailed off, shook his head. "She barely even looks at me now."

Siren considered how best to approach this subject. "She had an entire speech planned for tonight. According to Jace, she was obsessing over it."

"Your point being?"

"My point being that she was obviously too upset to give it after *someone*," Siren shoved a pointed finger at Random's chest, "decided to get all snippy at her in public. If she didn't give a good goddamn, it wouldn't have bothered her. Now stop hogging the Scotch." She retrieved the bottle from him with deft fingers.

"I am not the one hogging the Scotch. You're the one I'm starting to see two of, and if you're drunk enough to start separating into different people, I think you should give that bottle back."

"Uh-uh." Siren slapped his hand away, then took a long slow swallow she was certain she would regret in the morning. After, she was just drunk enough to ask, "Should I be worried? About Meredith?"

"Ah. Where to start there? Jace and Meredith were Academy sweethearts. The Aspect version of homecoming king and queen, I guess. Pretty, popular, everybody liked them. They were a good couple and frankly everyone expected them to get married."

"If they're so perfect for each other, why aren't they married with two-point-five children?" *And now I sound like a jealous teenager. Wonderful.*

"Meredith *used* to be nice, believe it or not. Sweet, really."

Okay, Siren had a hard time swallowing *that*.

"I think, buried somewhere underneath the layers of bitch and sophistication, she probably still is. Anyway, the last few months they were together she just turned into a different person. Always angry, didn't want anything to do with me or Kyrie. Then, when Jace and Elijah finally had it out and Jace left, he asked her to come with him. Thought if they got away from everything, maybe she'd go back to who she used to be."

"What did she say?" Siren asked quietly.

"She laughed at him. Told him a disinherited Winters wasn't worth her time, and if he wanted to go play at being a Null out in the regular world, he could damn well do it without her."

Ouch. "And he hasn't seen her since then?"

Random shook his head. "Technically, her family's name gets her into the Gathering, but I can tell you Kyrie didn't send her an invitation."

"She came because she heard Jace was back," Siren said dully.

"Yeah, reckon so."

If Meredith thought Jace was back for good, maybe she had decided he was worth her time again, and who knew what effect that would have on him? Siren had been involved with Jace for a handful of weeks. He'd spent years with Meredith, most of them happy, apparently. And if the woman had a good enough explanation for why she'd left him the way she had, maybe he'd decide she was worth *his* time again, too.

If Siren were honest with herself, she had no business becoming seriously involved with anyone. It was a rare night that she didn't wake screaming from nightmares, and simply being around her carried a certain level of risk. The harpies earlier were proof enough of *that*.

She had blood on her hands that would never wash off, and she'd tried to run from it only to find it followed her everywhere. She didn't like the things she had done to survive, but she had still done them. Would do them again, if she had to.

Jace was nice. Sweet. Smart. He didn't deserve to be swept up in the maelstrom that was her pointless, complicated life.

A long, loud snore interrupted her broody musings. Random's head rested against the back of the wooden swing and his mouth hung slightly open. He hugged the Scotch to his chest like a stuffed animal. Siren pressed the stopper into the bottle, then pulled the throw off the back of the swing and draped it over him for good measure.

She laid her own head back, debating whether she should sneak back inside and find an empty bedroom. Exhaustion from the day's events wore on her, and just when she had decided she probably *should* go inside, her own eyes closed, and sleep claimed her.

JACE STRODE for the ballroom exit, deciding that if one more person stopped him, he would snarl at them until they left. He was done answering questions about where he'd been, why he was back, and what his plans were. Let the bloody Society folk scramble their brains trying to figure out if he wanted his father's Council seat. They certainly didn't need his help to speculate.

He'd have been out twenty minutes ago if he hadn't done two circuits of the room looking for Siren, only stopping when Aunt Ella cornered him and told him what had happened between Siren and Meredith, and that Siren had left with Random.

"Jace. You're a hard man to get a word in with."

Meredith smiled at him. He marveled to see the difference between how she smiled now and the way she *used* to smile, back when she meant it.

"Possibly because I don't want to be spoken to."

Her lips pressed into a thin line before smoothing back out. "Can I talk to you? Privately?"

"Let me save you the trouble, Mer. I'm not back in Aspect Society, I'm still disinherited, and as soon as I help my sister find my worthless ass of a father, I'm going back to my unglamorous life out in the regular world. I'm still not worth your time, and I don't want to be. Now if you'll excuse me, I need to find my *date.*"

He left before she could say anything else. A heavy weight lifted off him as he left the ballroom and everyone in it behind. He hadn't realized until he'd come back just how much he had enjoyed being away from the whole mess. He didn't know how Val put up with it.

He searched the upstairs bedrooms, but he found no trace of Siren or Random. It wasn't until he'd checked the gym and the theater room that he thought to check the porches, and found the one on the east side of the house occupied.

Random was passed out on the wooden porch swing, a half-empty bottle Jace was pretty sure was his father's most-prized bottle of Scotch clutched tight to his chest, and a pink throw tucked around him. Jace would have laughed and possibly taken a photo for blackmail purposes if it weren't for the fact that Siren was nowhere to be seen. Given Jace was pretty sure Random hadn't tucked *himself* into a pink throw, she must have been here. But now she was gone, and she wasn't in the house, and the faintest traces of fear pricked at his chest.

A shimmer of moonlight caught on a pair of yellow heels, discarded in the grass at the edge of the porch. He walked to them, bent down, and pressed his palm flat against the ground next to them. Aspect pooled inside him, a cool river that rushed down his arm to connect with the grass and dirt. He felt the earth respond, sluggish and unhappy to be woken so late in the night when most of it slept. But it felt Jace's concern, and when he gave it Siren's scent, the way she walked, the way she laughed, the earth grumblingly stretched out its tendrils and searched for her.

CHAPTER

THIRTEEN

S iren stumbled as her bare foot landed on a rock, a long gash opening along the arch of her foot. Ahead, the dog whined, a high, pained cry that made Siren ignore the hurt and press on.

She'd woken on the porch to the animal's cries and seen it hunkered by a tree, twenty feet off. She'd approached cautiously, her stomach churning when she glimpsed the ruined mass of its left shoulder. She'd gotten close enough for it lick her hand before it ran off, hobbling on its three working legs and leaving a trail of blood on the moonlit grass.

Positive it couldn't get far with that kind of injury, she'd followed. Now her vision swam as Scotch still roared in her veins, and she swore if she made it to tomorrow morning, she would never drink again.

Two steps into the woods, power buzzed in her ears and she stopped. Her heart fluttered nervously behind her chest. Buzzing meant...something. What? She couldn't think straight, and she wasn't entirely sure that was the fault of the Scotch. She felt muzzy, drugged, and as she leaned against something to catch her breath, it took her far longer than it should have to remember the name for that something.

Tree. She leaned against a tree. There. That wasn't so hard. If she could remember what a tree was, she could remember what the buzzing meant. She'd heard it before, somewhere. Deep, deep down something screamed at her not to go farther into the woods. To turn and run back to the house, run to Jace, to anyone. The buzzing grew louder, painful now. She shook her head and tried to clear the noise but only succeeded in sending the world spinning.

Then it came to her.

Buzzing meant—

The dog gave a sharp, plaintive cry, and Siren forgot the noise in her head. The dog was hurt. It was hurt and it was all alone and if she didn't save it, it was going to die. Its pain called to her, whispered awake a soft flush of power that filled her veins. She pushed off the tree and went after it.

Getting Siren's location out of the earth had taken time. The ground didn't think like humans. It didn't see the world through an ocular lens and so couldn't merely show Jace an image of where it had found her. He'd had to extend his awareness out, to slip in with the dirt and roots, feeling for her footfalls, for the shape of the space she filled. He'd felt warmth dripping onto grass and into dirt when she'd stumbled and cut her foot, had felt her tremble through the bark of a large pine tree.

Then he'd realized she was heading straight for the nearest ward line on the property and he'd known something was wrong. Siren knew what types of creatures might be waiting for her on the other side; she wouldn't be foolish enough to leave the safety of the wards in the middle of the night for no reason.

He sprinted down to the paddock and pulled Marshmallow's halter off the gate. If he went after Siren on foot she'd reach the perimeter before he got to her. He haltered the little dapple-gray horse, tied the lead rope for a set of makeshift reins, and led the gelding outside the enclosure. A quick boost from the fence had him on the horse's back, and he'd never been more grateful to a creature for having the sort of disposition that meant he could be pastured for half a decade and still be trusted to carry a rider through darkened woods at a near-gallop with nothing but a globe of Aspect to light the way.

He wound his fingers into Marshmallow's mane for balance and leaned into the horse's gait. It took every ounce of his control not to urge him faster, not to ask more of the gelding than he could give. They already traveled faster than was smart. He'd ridden the horse through these woods every day in his youth, and only their combined familiarity kept them from crashing into the underbrush on the hairpin turns.

They thundered around the northern bend in the path, past the ancient oak that curled its huge branches toward the night sky, and he saw her. She ran in an awkward, broken gait, stumbling each time her cut foot hit the ground. She didn't turn at the sound of hoofbeats behind her, and she didn't so much as twitch when he called her name.

Jace eased Marshmallow to a stop, slipped off his back and tossed the lead rope over a low-hanging branch. He grabbed Siren by the shoulders and spun her to face him. Her gaze was unfocused, her eyes dull, and she gave no sign that she recognized him. She turned away and tried to continue down the path, but he held her shoulders.

"Siren, can you even hear me?" He cupped her face, turning it back to his. A flicker of awareness rolled through her irises, and she stared at him, as if trying with great difficulty to place him.

"Jace?" she said finally.

"That's right," he answered soothingly. "What are you doing out here?"

It was the wrong question. Her eyes darkened and she struggled against his hold. "Let go. He's hurt. I have to help him."

"Who's hurt?"

"The dog."

He was about to ask, "What dog?" when a soft whine carried to him. He pushed more power into the Aspect globe, extending its reach, and pale blue light touched on a dirt-covered mutt. It held one injured leg off the ground, its eyes as hollow and unfocused as Siren's. She struggled to move. The dog stayed perfectly still.

"Please, it's the first time he's stopped."

It was also, Jace was willing to bet, the first time *Siren* had stopped. Experimentally, he took two steps forward with her. Immediately, the dog hunkered forward, stopping when Siren stopped.

"Siren, did you touch the dog?"

"Let me *go*. He's *hurt*."

"And we'll help him, if you tell me if you touched him."

"I—he licked my hand. Then he ran off."

He lifted her right hand. "This one?"

She shook her head and gave him her left. He covered it with his palm and sent a pulse of Aspect into her, searching for the thread of foreign power he suspected he'd find. It was difficult, because normally he would be looking for the place where foreign Aspect hid within Siren's own Aspect, only he couldn't *feel* hers. The channels inside her where her Aspect should run were *there*, they were just strangely empty. She had power—he'd seen her use it, had felt the force of it when the spectral harpies had exploded—but wherever it lived inside her, it was not where it should be.

He shook the mystery off and focused, traced those empty channels until he found what he was looking for—a small mote of foreign Aspect, embedded inside her. It was Dark use, a tethering spell that had bound Siren to the dog when it had licked her. He followed that thin tendril of power to the canine, found the second tendril in the dog that slipped into the night and out through the tiniest of cracks in the ward wall.

As soon as he fixed this, he and Valkyrie would have a serious discussion about upgrading the wards.

Jace turned Siren's face into his shoulder and held her tight against him. "I'm sorry," he whispered, "but this is going to hurt." He grabbed hold of the Dark thread—it held the faintest tinge of familiarity, as if he'd felt the signature somewhere before—and plunged his Aspect into it.

Siren screamed and thrashed as his power burned through the Dark thread inside her. He clenched his teeth and held her tighter, locked his legs around her until he'd burned every last trace of Dark Aspect from her and the dog and she finally went limp.

He held her, ran his fingers through her hair and whispered comforting, nonsense things in her ear. She trembled violently, but when she finally stilled and lifted her eyes to his they were clear.

Then she looked to where the dog lay, unmoving, on the dirt. "No."

This time, when she pulled him toward the dog, he let her. Jace didn't have the heart to tell her it wouldn't live. Its shoulder was pared open down to the bone and its breath came in harsh, shallow gasps. She crumpled next to it, barely conscious herself, and laid her hand to its ragged side. A hiccupping sob tore out of her. Jace still had the faintest awareness of her, an after-echo from where his power had touched her, and through that tentative bond he felt the barren channels inside her flood with her Aspect.

The strength of it knocked him onto his heels. He only barely managed to keep hold of her hand, in awe of the sheer strength that radiated inside her. She was lit up like a lighthouse signal beacon, every inch of her aglow with power. He'd spent the entirety of his academic years studying Aspect—its history, its limits, how it worked, how it grew—and he had never in his life heard of anything like her, *felt* anything like her.

He didn't understand what she did next. She didn't work

power like he had been taught—forming it into predetermined patterns that would harness it to do what its wielder wanted—she just sent her Aspect blindly into the dog. The mutilated mass of its shoulder knitted back together. Muscle and sinew reconnected, blood vessels patched, and new skin crawled across the freshly healed insides. The edges of the new skin crept together and the area sprouted a thick, lush patch of new fur.

Then, as quickly as it had come, her Aspect disappeared from Jace's sight, the channels inside her as empty as before, and she collapsed. Jace held her against him, staring at the dog, at the perfectly healed flesh, and what it meant.

Before he could think about whether he *should*, he slipped his Aspect into her. It wound through her body, following the empty channels in search of the place her Aspect had gone to hide.

The faintest spark near her solar plexus caught his attention. He followed it only to ram into a wall that kicked him back out. Jace shook his head and dove back in, more carefully this time, his Aspect testing the limits of the wall inside her until he realized it wasn't a wall at all. It was more of a box, more of a…cage. Its edges dripped with Darkness, and he recognized the same power signature that had been in the foreign thread that had connected her to the dog. The same one he couldn't place the familiarity of.

Proximity to that Darkness turned his stomach, but he kept going, feeling at the edges of the cage until he found the spark of power that had first drawn him. He found what he looked for along one of the cage's seams, an infinitesimal fissure in its outline. Through that fissure leaked the faintest flicker of Siren's Aspect. Hesitantly, he reached for the crack and felt along its edges, then beyond those edges to the inside of the cage.

The second his Aspect moved beyond the fissure, Dark power sprang from the cage, grabbed his Aspect, and spat it out of Siren's body. His power rebounded into him with a snap akin to whiplash, and for a moment Jace sat, stunned. Then a low, cold fury roiled over him as he realized why he'd first thought the Dark Aspect felt familiar.

John's and Mara's murders. Siren's kidnapping. The cage. The lengths someone was currently going to in order to find her.

He pulled out his phone and texted Valkyrie. Then he lifted Siren onto Marshmallow's back, clicked to the dog to follow, and took them home.

CHAPTER

FOURTEEN

"What is the point of having a famously paranoid father if his supposedly infallible wards can't keep anything off the property?" Jace growled at Valkyrie. He paced the floor of his old bedroom, glancing every five seconds or so through his open door into the room across the hall, where Siren slept. The mutt she had healed kept guard at the foot of her bed.

"I'll set up new wards tomorrow."

Jace stopped pacing and really *looked* at his sister. "Why haven't you done it already? And don't give me that bullshit about it being a redundancy since Dad's were already up. You're nearly as paranoid about security as he is but you've left practically the entire estate in the care of wards you aren't keyed into. Why?"

She shrugged. "You know how touchy he gets about things like that."

Jace couldn't believe what he'd heard. "You didn't enact new warding because you thought he'd get angry? The man's been gone for five months, Val."

Her left hand trembled, then stilled. "I don't expect you to understand."

"You keep telling me that every time I push you on anything. I *want* to understand. What's going on? What are you not telling me?"

"Nothing," she ground out between clenched teeth. "There's nothing you need to worry about. I am sorry for what happened to Siren, and I will fix it so it doesn't happen again, but when I previously chose not to install new wards, I wasn't expecting to have an actively-hunted individual in the house.

"Now, do *you* want to tell me what's really bothering you about what happened? Because you weren't this on edge even after the harpies attacked her."

Jace tried and failed to come up with a delicate way to say it. "It involves Mom. And what happened to her."

Valkyrie stiffened. "What does our mother's kidnapping have to do with Siren?"

It was that kidnapping that had produced Valkyrie, and she never handled the reminder of it well.

"I asked her about it once. She told me that the people who held her were deranged. That they didn't have a purpose in taking her other than to hurt her."

"And?" Valkyrie bit off the word.

"And I think she was lying. Right before she died, I accidentally touched one of her scars. I *felt* old traces of Dark Aspect, and it hadn't been used for torture." His mother's Aspect had been Empathy, and he'd inherited a shadow of that gift, if not enough for it be considered a secondary talent. "It felt like whoever used it was trying to *change* Mom's Aspect—either how it worked, or turn it into something fundamentally different altogether."

He waited, letting the words sink in.

"You took an interest in Aspect Theory right before she died." If Valkyrie had possessed weather Aspect, her voice would have frozen everything in the room.

"Yes. What I felt in her was very specific. I memorized everything I could about it, every twist of Aspect, every nuance. I thought if I could learn enough about Aspect Theory then I could figure out what they'd tried to do. If I could understand that then maybe…"

"You could have stopped her from dying?"

Jace nodded. His voice was down to a hoarse whisper. "What they did broke her. She never tried to hide that she was going to die. But I thought if I knew what they'd done to her, maybe I could reverse engineer it and undo the damage."

"Why didn't you ever tell anyone?" Valkyrie's voice was heated now. "If you thought it could save her, we could have asked someone who already knew about Aspect Theory."

Jace laughed, one harsh, short bark. "I did tell someone. I told Dad. *He* told me that I wasn't half as smart as I thought I was, and that if I ever repeated my theory to you or Mom or anyone else and, as he put it, 'made dying harder for her,' he'd cut out my tongue."

Valkyrie blanched.

"Then he told me that if I'd really wanted to save her, I never would have been born, because having me was what ripped the life out of her."

"You know that's not true."

It was—her health had been too fragile to have a second child, but she'd done it anyway—but he nodded.

"What does this have to do with Siren?"

"I looked into the Council file on Mom's kidnapping, when I was older. They caught a few of the people involved, but not everyone, and not the person she mentioned the most in her testimony."

"The one who raped her," Valkyrie said flatly. "My father. They didn't catch my father."

"Sharing DNA with him doesn't make him a father, Val."

She waved his words away. "Get to the point."

"The Dark Aspect signature I felt in Mom—it took me a while to recognize it, but it's the same one I felt in Siren tonight." He explained about the cage he'd felt inside her, the reason her Aspect was so impossible to recognize when she wasn't actively using it. "If I was right about Mom, and the person who held her was experimenting with altering Aspect, it makes sense for the same person to be involved with what happened to Siren."

"An experiment," a voice said.

Jace's gaze jerked to the door. He hadn't heard Siren get up but she stood in the doorway, the mangy dog pressed against her legs.

"You think I'm a fucking experiment?"

JACE WINCED. "I didn't mean it like that."

Siren curled her fingers into the dog's fur, grateful for its silent support, and reminded herself that Jace hadn't done this to her.

"Were you going to tell me?"

"Of course." He stepped toward her.

The dog shoved himself in front of her and growled. Jace stopped.

"I was going to tell you as soon as you woke up. I don't know how much you heard, but this has some personal relevance for us, too."

The anger went out of her. It was Jace's default to talk about things in a scientific manner, and if that made the words sound cold, well, maybe it would be better if she could have that same sort of detachment regarding what had happened to her.

"I heard enough." Most of it, she thought. Valkyrie's closed-off nature made more sense to her now. Siren's own childhood made more sense to her now. Her foster parents had said things about her the night she ran away, had spoken about her as if she were some kind of investment. "What did they do to me exactly?"

"The cage I said I felt inside you? It's been storing your Aspect since you were born. Keeping you from accessing it. You said you never felt your power at all until you were sixteen, and your first experience was in a bad situation?"

She nodded, numb.

"A sufficiently traumatic event could have made your pull to your Aspect overcome the cage's containment and crack it—"

Sufficiently traumatic, she thought. Well, that was one way to describe it.

"—but it wouldn't have been strong enough to destroy it. Since the cage's default setting is to trap your Aspect, when you don't have a pressing need for it, it remains inside that cage instead of flowing readily through you like it does in everyone else. It's why I didn't recognize you had Aspect at all before the harpies attacked you."

"And what would be the point of that? What was it all for?"

"I don't know. But I do know it means you have over twenty years of nearly untapped Aspect built up inside you. Aspect generates daily, like new blood cells, and some people can store it for a few days, a few weeks, but years? Aspect *wants* to be used. We're incapable of not using it.

"The amount you have at your disposal is unprecedented. So I'm not surprised the person who did that is willing to go to extreme lengths to try and retrieve you."

"You also have no idea how to control it," Valkyrie said. "If that cage inside you gives? You're a ticking time bomb waiting to explode, and goddess save anyone in the vicinity when you do."

Jace stiffened. "Valkyrie."

"I'm only telling her what the Council is going to say at her hearing."

"They can't blame her for what was done to her."

"They shouldn't," Valkyrie corrected. "They *can* all they want. The more afraid people are, the more badly they react." She turned to Siren. "And they are going to be very, very afraid of you."

Siren's heart thudded and nervous sweat prickled at her skin. "Jace?"

"They may be," he conceded. "But I also don't think they'll do anything to harm you."

"What makes you so sure?"

"Because I know what type of Aspect you have. Life."

CHAPTER

FIFTEEN

ife. The word echoed in Siren's head the next morning as she showered. It didn't make any sense to her. Not when every time she'd used her power, it had been to cause the opposite of life.

According to Jace, it hadn't manifested on record in over a century, and because of that no one had a clear idea of the extent of its abilities, though healing was clearly a part of them.

As if to underscore the fact, the dog chose that moment to stick his nose through the shower curtain and then clamber in. He immediately slipped on the sloped plastic sides and went sprawling. Dirt, odor, and matted fur went everywhere. He scrambled to get his paws underneath him and nearly tore the shower curtain down.

"Okay, easy buddy." She grabbed the wriggling dog, who finally found his feet and managed to sit down without destroying anything. Tufts of fur came off as Siren let him go, and she wrinkled her nose and reached for the strawberry-scented body wash.

"There's no help for it, pup. You're going to smell like fruit."

It took three washes and half the bottle of soap to get the dog clean. Once she finished he slunk to the corner and hunkered down, staring at her with big, betrayed eyes.

"Hey, you jumped in here with me, remember?"

He whined and looked, if possible, even more betrayed. Cleaned up, he was adorable, with creamy tan fur and wide chocolate eyes. He looked mostly cattle dog mixed with something else—pit bull, maybe?—and if he weren't half-starved she'd guess he would weigh around sixty pounds. A big, handsome dog and there he sulked in the corner, like she'd stolen his favorite toy.

She'd just gotten dressed, and was on the floor trying to dry the dog off, when someone knocked on the door.

"Siren?" Jace asked.

"Come in."

He did, and the dog immediately growled at him.

She swatted him gently on the nose. "Hey, none of that."

He ceased growling and gave her a piteous look.

"Are you sure that's the same dog?"

"Mmm. There's about three pounds of dirt and fur that may never come out of that shower that can attest to his transformation from mongrel creature to adorable pup."

Now that he'd been reprimanded, the dog decided it was time to go from suspicious of Jace to curious, and he stuck his nose out toward him as far as he could get without moving from Siren's side. Jace took pity on him and crouched next to them both, and after two ear scratches the dog decided Jace was his new best friend.

Jace had a faraway look in his eyes, like he was in his head instead of really being present, and the fact he hadn't said much of anything since he came in made Siren worry.

"Is something wrong?" When he didn't say anything, she prompted, "Jace?"

"I got word from the Council a few minutes ago. They set your hearing."

"Okay. That's a good thing, right? It means they accepted the petition?"

"Yes. But they set it for three hours from now."

"Oh."

"Everything will be fine," he told her.

"Will it? I know a setup when I'm being asked to walk into one."

"It means someone on the Council is being difficult, but it's nothing we can't handle. Nothing will happen to you."

Siren shook her head. "You can't know that."

"Hey." He cupped her face in his hand. His thumb stroked across her cheek. "Nothing will happen to you, because I will not *let* anything happen to you."

They were just words. Anyone could say them, could say what they thought a person wanted to hear. They shouldn't have wrapped around her like warm comfort, and she shouldn't have believed them.

But the woman inside her who longed for normalcy, for acceptance, the woman Siren kept so far buried she rarely ever made an appearance, heard those words and clung to them. *That* woman arched into his touch, and when he leaned closer, that woman raised her lips to his and kissed him.

It was nothing like the kisses she'd shared with him yesterday, when her only thoughts had been on getting him undressed. This was slower, deliberate, and somehow more intimate because she *wasn't* thinking about having sex with him. It scared the hell out of her, but it was Jace who pulled back first.

"We should probably talk about this," he said, gently.

"Right."

"It's just that a lot of things have changed since last night, and—"

"Of course. I get it." He wasn't wrong, but it felt like a rejection, and her emotions, still on the never-ending rollercoaster that was the last twenty-four hours, weren't ready for it. "Can we talk about it later, though? After the hearing?"

"Sure." They sat in awkward silence for a few seconds before he said, "I think breakfast is happening downstairs, if you're hungry."

She wasn't, but she'd take any excuse to extricate herself from this awkward moment. The dog beat both of them to the kitchen and Siren ran after him, a new mother's worry at the dog being out of sight beating behind her chest. That worry vanished when she found him sitting patiently by Random's feet, his big brown eyes filled with the hope and yearning of a dog who really, really wanted bacon.

Bacon that Random was frying in a skillet. Siren blinked and looked again. Yes, that was still Random, standing barefoot in Jace's kitchen, his white dress shirt rumpled as he turned slabs of bacon in an enormous pan, a pastel-blue apron with frilly lace edges tied around him. A large plate of perfectly fluffed scrambled eggs waited on the counter, complemented by a plate of toast and a small platter of cut fruit.

Random whistled while he flipped the bacon pieces over, looking alert and far, far too chipper for a man who had drunk more Scotch than she had last night.

She must have been glaring because Jace gave her an amused look and said, "It *is* obnoxious, but he can't help it."

"Can't help it at all." Random grinned. "I'm Random."

"I didn't get so drunk last night I forgot your name."

Random sent sorrowful eyes heavenward. "Alas, if only half the women I've known had possessed such fortitude."

"Perhaps if you didn't bed every attractive one that came along, half of them would." Valkyrie glided into the room, black hair drifting around her shoulders. Last night's curls had loosened into waves that softly framed her warrior's face.

Random's jaw clenched, but he didn't respond to Valkyrie's jab.

"He means his Aspect is random," Jace explained. "He can't control what it does. It just randomly does what it thinks he needs."

"Like cure hangovers?" Siren guessed.

"Like cure hangovers," Random confirmed.

The dog whined, pawing at Random's ankle. Random reached for a piece of bacon.

"Oh, no, you don't." Valkyrie fixed Random with a pointed glare, and he immediately dropped the piece of bacon back onto the plate. She retrieved a bowl and a bag of high-end dog food from the pantry. "I didn't drive all the way into town last night to get this just for you to ruin him with bacon."

"Yes, ma'am?" Random offered meekly.

"Thank you," Siren said, taking the bowl and bag. The bag was open. Valkyrie must have fed the pup last night. Siren felt a rush of gratefulness that the dog hadn't gone hungry all night, that Valkyrie had cared enough to go buy him things. Ridiculously, tears welled at the backs of her eyes.

She was a bigger mess than she'd thought if someone buying dog food made her cry.

Siren set the food bowl on the counter. The outside of the dog bowl was a chocolate brown that matched the dog's eyes and was decorated with tiny bones. On the inside, engraved on the bottom of the food dish, was a large skull and crossbones, underneath which were the words, *Bad to the Bone*. Siren couldn't help but wonder if Valkyrie had picked it out herself or if a salesperson had been involved.

Siren read the feeding chart on the back of the bag, found a measuring scoop inside, and transferred the appropriate amount into the bowl. At the first sound of kibble on metal, the dog scampered around the side of the kitchen island and reached up to place his paws on her hips. It was adorable now. Later, when he had more energy and weighed twenty pounds heavier, he would probably knock her over. So she put on her sternest face and looked the dog in the eye.

"Good puppies get their breakfast when they stop jumping all over people."

Jace raised an eyebrow at her. She ignored him.

The dog sat, an oh-please-oh-please whine trilling in his throat. Siren picked up the food dish. The dog's tail thumped frantically against the floor. She lowered the food dish. For one brief moment, she thought he would lunge for it before she placed it on the floor. Then her Aspect flickered inside her, linking to the connection she'd built with the dog when she healed him, and beneath her power's touch, the dog sat quietly until she placed the food on the floor.

It wasn't that her power actively restrained him—it didn't—it just connected them long enough to let her need for calm wash over the pup.

She placed the dish on the floor and withdrew. He lunged for the bowl, scarfing—no, inhaling, she decided—the kibble down. She watched incredulously as six, seven, eight seconds later the bowl sat completely empty. She hadn't heard him chew even once.

"I think we're going to need a bigger bag of kibble."

Jace reached for the dog food bag, but Siren shook her head. "It doesn't look like he's eaten with any regularity lately. If he eats more right now, he'll just get sick."

"Speaking of people who need to eat, you two, sit." Random pointed fingers at Siren and Valkyrie. Jace, already seated at the kitchen bar, did not get treated to Random's glower. Siren dutifully sat. Valkyrie waited just long enough for her behavior to be considered properly resistant to command and then settled herself on the stool next to her brother.

Random passed out plates and silverware, his familiarity with the kitchen items' locations making it obvious he'd spent a great deal of time in the Winters' residence. It was another one of those moments that sent a stupid pang of longing through Siren's chest. Even with whatever was going on between Random and Valkyrie, even with Jace having been gone for years, Random was still comfortable here, still accepted.

What did that kind of acceptance feel like?

Siren shrugged the wondering away as Random passed the

platter of bacon around. One damn day in this house and all of her carefully constructed emotional walls were crumbling. She needed those walls back, needed them stronger. Because watching Jace laugh at something Valkyrie said, his eyes sparkling and his hair still mussed from sleep, made Siren happier than she'd been since she'd started running.

He was so warm, so alive. She wanted to curl up against that warmth, press her mouth to his lips and taste that life. His eyes caught hers and she looked away, trading the platter of bacon to Random for the one piled with scrambled eggs.

She wanted to stay here. But if things went badly at the Council today…

"Something wrong?" Jace murmured quietly.

Siren looked up to find him frowning.

"No." He didn't look like he believed her, so she added, "I was just thinking about him." She nodded at the mutt, who was lying down and staring mournfully at his empty food bowl. "I know things about him. Three of his left ribs were hairline fractured when he was six months old. Probably someone kicked him, I'd guess, from the angle. The bits missing out of his right ear are from another dog chewing on it. The wounds he had last night, someone did that to him. Intentionally."

She swallowed, fighting off the rising anger. "Is that—I was wondering if knowing things like that is normal for people with Life Aspect?"

Random dropped his fork.

"You have *Life* Aspect? Are you kidding me?" He turned to Jace. "Is she kidding?"

"No," Jace said.

"You don't look surprised," Random said to Valkyrie. "What did I miss last night?"

Succinct to the point of being abrupt, Valkyrie told him.

"Damn." Random whistled. "I can't believe I slept through all of that."

"After the amount of Scotch you ingested, I can't believe you're awake right *now*," Siren pointed out.

"What were the two of you doing out there, anyway?" Valkyrie asked.

"Sharing long, poetic thoughts about the emotionally turbulent states of our lives, obviously." Random threw her a deep, brooding look.

Valkyrie scowled. "Fine, don't tell me."

"So is it?" Siren asked. "Normal?"

"I really don't know. I wasn't exaggerating when I said we don't know much about it. Theoretically? It makes sense that to heal him on the physical level you did, you'd have to forge a link with him, and that link might confer the sort of information you have."

"This is so exciting," Random said cheerfully, adding another two strips of bacon to his plate. "Aunt Ella will be thrilled."

"Why?"

"Because she's the only living person with Death Aspect. Opposite sides of the same coin and all that. I'd give it ten minutes once the Council meeting concludes before she asks you to tea."

Jace's face blanched of color. "Do not, under any circumstances, agree to have tea with Aunt Ella."

Siren paused, her fork halfway to her mouth. "Why not?"

"I—" He shook his head. "Just don't do it, okay?"

Siren shrugged. She wasn't a huge fan of tea anyway. "Okay."

"Anything else I should know?" Random asked.

"The Council decided I'm having a hearing in," Siren glanced at her watch, "two-and-a-half hours."

"And no one told me?" Random asked.

"The Council only informed *us* half an hour ago," Valkyrie responded.

"Then I should have been told half an hour ago."

Siren tried, she really did, but she couldn't come up with a single reason why Random would care when her hearing was. "Why would you need to know?"

"Because I am your legal counsel."

"*You're* the lawyer Jace mentioned?"

Random bowed. "At your service."

"Aren't you a little young to be a lawyer?"

"The joys of private academies are that you can skip multiple grades if you feel like not having a life. I've been practicing for five years and I'm very, very good at what I do."

Siren heard the sound of a screen door opening and a bird—the falcon—flew into the kitchen. It landed on the back of a chair and sent the dog into a frenzy.

"Uh-uh." Siren fixed the dog with a meaningful stare. He gave one last excited yip at the bird and settled onto his haunches. The bird cocked his head at the dog and gave a low screech that set the dog to whining again.

"Nelsen, don't antagonize him," Random admonished. "We have work to do."

The bird quieted.

"I'll meet you all at the Council House." Random removed the pastel-blue apron and hung it on the stove rail. "Jace, text me any details you haven't told me that I should know." He looked Siren over, frowning. "And find her something to wear."

Then he and Nelsen were gone, leaving a half-eaten plate of food behind.

Siren glanced down at her clothes. Sure, the shirt and lone pair of jeans she'd found in Evelyn Winters closet didn't fit the best, but they were ten steps in quality above anything she normally wore.

"What's wrong with my clothes?"

"They don't scream high-society bitch," Valkyrie answered.

Jace sighed. "I'll call Mabre."

CHAPTER

SIXTEEN

Siren sat in the passenger seat of Jace's truck, trying not to tug at the soft ivory pantsuit that fit her as if it were stitched to her body. She didn't know how she was going to get the damn thing off.

"You look great." Jace told her.

"I look like the sixteen-hundred dollars this getup cost," Siren muttered. Valkyrie had paid for it and given Siren a look that dared her to argue about it.

Jace turned the truck from the main road onto a narrow dirt lane that was soon swallowed by old-growth forest. The treetops were lost from her sight to the skies, the lane cloaked in that peculiar darkness that could only be found in forests in the day. The call of a bird she didn't recognize echoed through the leaves, high-pitched and angry, as if sensing an intruder.

The truck trundled over a wooden bridge not much wider than the dirt lane. A shallow creek flowed underneath, hissing and burbling, the river rocks shrouded in moss. The furor and madness of the civilized world fell away, replaced by an entirely different madness, one cloaked in calm and quiet.

"You aren't actually a very normal-seeming psychopath

whisking me off to your creepy cabin in the creepy woods to turn me into your sex slave, are you?"

Jace tapped his thumbs on the steering wheel. "It's a very nice cabin. I should think any woman happy to live out her days as a sex slave there."

Siren punched his arm. Jace grinned at her.

"In all fairness, we are sort of going to a cabin, and it is sort of creepy. It just isn't *my* creepy cabin."

The truck rounded a corner, and the cabin came into view. Built of ash-gray wood that time had darkened to near black, it nestled against a ridge. Only the very tip of the shingled roof rose above the crest of the land behind it. Kudzu climbed the cabin's sides, curling around the brick fireplace jutting from the roof. The greenery had been trimmed carefully from the windows and lone door, but it had been left to flourish elsewhere, trailing around the posts and rails of the cabin's small porch.

Jace pulled the truck off the dirt lane and parked in the first place he found room, next to a sporty Volkswagen sedan. Odd, to see another car in a place that felt so old.

"Care to enlighten me on why the Council holds its meetings in a creepy cabin in the woods?" she asked, hopping out of the truck and giving the cabin a skeptical once-over. It didn't look big enough to have more than one room.

"This," he said, grandly indicating the cabin, "is the original meeting place of the Council. It dates back to the late seventeen hundreds. Aspect Society is snobbish, and there is nothing more snobbish than heritage."

Right. Sure. "There's no way that building has been standing for over two centuries."

"You might be surprised what Aspect can hold together."

"Might be," a voice agreed. "But in this case, I think it's gone through a few modifications since the original build."

Random walked toward them, and Siren had to lock her teeth together to keep her jaw from dropping. He looked like a—well, like a *lawyer*. He wore a tailored black suit that fit him like a glove, designer shades he couldn't possibly need in the density of the forest, and carried a perfectly respectable black briefcase.

In retrospect, he looked less like a lawyer and more like he'd escaped the set of *Men in Black*. His ink-black hair was tamed back, and Siren was really going to have to ask him what he'd done to make his complexion so…perfect. He came by the beautiful skin naturally, but she was quite certain the perfectly even, not-a-pore-in-sight-anywhere glow he gave off now hadn't been *that* perfect two hours ago.

"He's probably right," Jace admitted, "but it's not what you can see that matters."

"Ooh, cryptic. Just what I needed."

"We do cryptic real good too, darlin'," Random drawled, voice taking on a cowboy twang as he slid his shades down the bridge of his nose. "Just come with us and don't ask any questions."

Siren snorted.

"Will you stop messing around and get inside before we're late?" Valkyrie swept past them, gliding up the short steps into the cabin.

In between wondering how she'd never heard Valkyrie's Jeep pull up and whether she was walking into her impending doom, Siren noted that Valkyrie wore a black suit that could have qualified her to be Random's partner on the movie from which they'd obviously escaped.

"What are you thinking?" Jace asked as they walked up the steps.

Siren sighed. "That I should have taken Mabre up on the black suit."

Stepping inside the cabin was like stepping through a portal into a different part of the world. If Siren hadn't known she was in a forest in the middle of nowhere, she would have thought she'd just entered the reception area of a posh office that catered to the wealthy.

A sleek, curved obsidian desk sat in the left-hand corner of the small room, the woman behind it a short, polished blonde in a mint-green dress that probably cost more than Siren made in a month. Aside from the desk, the room only featured two wing-backed waiting chairs, a coffee table, and an ornately carved wooden door on the back wall of the room. If she were anywhere else, Siren would have thought the carvings decorative. Here, she wondered if they had some arcane meaning or hidden power.

The receptionist was intent on the computer screen in front of her, rose-pink fingernails flying across the keyboard as if she and it were one. She glanced up as they walked in, her gaze sliding off Siren and Valkyrie, then lingering a moment on Random before zeroing in on Jace. Her lips—painted the exact same shade of pink as her fingernails—broke into a flirtatious smile.

"Jace Winters," she purred, her voice as soft and pretty as the rest of her and lacquered in Southern charm. "I haven't seen you in years. I bet you don't even remember me." She looked up at him through her lashes as he approached a sign-in sheet on the desk.

The confused expression on Jace's face before he said, "Angela Winthrop, right?" made Siren painfully aware he was one of those men who wouldn't recognize a woman coming on to him until she shoved her tongue down his throat. On the one hand, Siren found his cluelessness utterly adorable. On the other hand, it made her want to slap a sticker on him that read, "Property of Siren Savage."

Only, he wasn't hers. He wasn't even *close* to hers, and if his unpromising "We should probably talk about this" statement earlier was any indication, their brief flirtation might be ending soon.

Angela beamed at him. "You *do* remember. I was going to say hi at the ball last night, but you disappeared an hour in."

Jace made a noncommittal, "Hmm," and continued filling out extensive paperwork.

"So, what brings you back after all these years?"

"Family matters."

"Oh, that's right." Angela's voice softened, and she sounded genuinely consoling when she said, "I heard about your father. It's so awful, him disappearing like that. Has there been any news?"

"I'm afraid not." Jace snapped the lid on his pen, placed it back in the inside pocket of his blazer, and handed the paperwork to Angela.

"That must be so difficult. If you ever need anyone to talk to, I've always got an open ear." Once again, Angela sounded like she actually cared.

Genuine, concerned flirting was so much worse than ditzy flirting. It had a higher chance of a positive outcome.

Siren ground her teeth together and reminded herself that Jace *did not belong to her.* If Angela wanted to offer him a shoulder to cry on, it was well within her rights to do so. Hell, if he wanted to accept, that was also well within *his* rights. It might be rude of him to do it in front of her, but...

"Uh, thanks." Jace did not sound eager. He sounded as confused as he looked. Next to Siren, Valkyrie snickered.

Siren leaned over and whispered, "Is he always this..." she floundered, trying to find the right word.

"Oblivious?" Random supplied.

Siren nodded.

"I'm afraid so," Valkyrie answered, her voice breathy with the laughter she held back. "I'd forgotten how amusing it is to watch."

Amusing was not the word Siren would have chosen, but then, that probably had something to do with the irrational jealousy consuming her. Angela looked at the paperwork and turned businesslike, much to Siren's relief.

"You're here for the Savage hearing?"

"That's right."

Angela's gaze flickered back to where Random and Valkyrie stood beside Siren.

"You're all here for it?"

Random smiled. Valkyrie glared. Siren shrugged.

"I believe I listed everyone on the form," Jace offered.

She glanced down at it. "So you did. I'll need her to sign this." Angela opened a drawer, pulled out a fresh form and pen, and nodded at Siren.

Siren took the form and read over what turned out to be a basic non-disclosure agreement. The unnecessary amount of legalese and flowery wording essentially stated that she would not speak about the details of her hearing to anyone not present in the room at the time of it, until she was released from such restrictions by the Council, and that she would not mention Aspect or anything related to it to anyone not already a part of Aspect Society.

Siren signed on the dotted line and handed the form back

"You'll be in the Warded Room. And honey? Good luck."

CHAPTER

SEVENTEEN

Angela's words echoed ominously in Siren's mind as she stepped into a narrow stairway of dark-gray stone. The steps led down, the path illuminated by wall sconces set into stone crevices.

"*There* you are," an irritated voice came from the bottom of the stairwell. A moment later, Aunt Ella appeared on the landing. She wore an elaborate ceremonial robe with gold filigreed symbols that strongly resembled the carvings that had been on the door at the top of the staircase. "You're late."

Random looked at his watch. "We're fifteen minutes early."

"Don't argue with me, boy. I trust you'll be on your best behavior?"

"Aunt Ella, I live to please you." Random executed a little bow.

Aunt Ella sniffed. "You don't, but I wouldn't mind the pretense every now and then. Now, you three wander along. I need to speak with Siren for a moment." She shooed them along. "Go on, I won't bite her."

Siren shot a pleading look at the three of them, but none would meet her eye and all promptly abandoned her.

Cowards.

Aunt Ella linked arms with her and held their pace to something slightly slower than the movement of glaciers. "You don't seem like an idiot, so I'll be frank with you, dear. The Council is looking for any reason they can find to discredit you. They can't deny your heritage—*my* word is irrefutable in these halls—but they can grill you on every other intimate detail of your life."

"I don't understand," Siren said, when it became apparent Aunt Ella wasn't going to continue. "I wasn't expecting a welcome wagon, but why would they already dislike me?"

Aunt Ella sighed. "It doesn't reflect well on them, you popping up after all these years, and them never having a clue what happened to you after poor John and Mara died. It opens up questions about certain...failures of the Council's."

"I see." She didn't. "Your advice?"

"Let my dear nephew take the lead. He pretends to be useless so no one expects too much out of him, but he is smart, and quite good at his job. Mind you, don't tell him I said so. Follow his lead and he'll keep you out of any real trouble. And don't let Meredith rile you like she did last night."

Siren stopped walking. "Meredith? Meredith is on the Council?"

"Not on the Council itself, dear. She's their Truthfinder."

"Truthfinder," Siren repeated blankly.

"Yes. Once she establishes a connection with a person, her Aspect allows her to determine if they answer a question truthfully. An odd talent, that," Aunt Ella said, absently. "Everyone puts such faith in it. But truth is a slippery thing, I should think. For a person, it all just comes down to belief. Ah, here we are."

They stood before a set of black stone double-doors, every inch of them covered in symbols of glittering gold and silver, some of the smaller symbols woven together to form larger ones. Through the muddled entanglement of it all, Siren felt the power in them, the purpose: to contain. To ward the outside world from anything and everything that might be on the other side of that door.

"They haven't opened this room in years. Overkill, if you ask me, but then people rarely do anymore."

"Why not?" Siren asked, before she could help herself.

"Because my answers are usually right and they're never the ones people want. At any rate, I'm afraid this is where I leave you. Best not to arrive arm-in-arm." Aunt Ella lifted the stone ring on the door and paused. "You know, you really must come over for tea sometime."

"Oh, I—well, it's very kind of you to ask," Siren began, remembering Jace's warning about tea.

"Say tomorrow evening around four? The late afternoon is such a lovely time for tea. And I've another guest I think you'd enjoy meeting."

"But—"

"It's settled, then." Aunt Ella smiled, revealing perfectly even white teeth that put Siren in mind of nothing so much as a dragon in human form. "Random can give you the address. Give it thirty seconds or so, I'd say, and then follow me in." Aunt Ella opened the door and disappeared inside the Warded Room.

Siren counted to thirty in her head, then tugged the great doors open and walked inside.

The door had only just been the beginning of the symbols. Inside, they were everywhere: the floors, the walls, the furniture. There were no windows since they were underground, and no pictures broke the monotony of the stone walls. The room lived and breathed symbols, and the people in it appeared mere casualties of its greater pattern.

She felt the pulse and echo of the room's power sweeping around her, squeezing, already attempting to cage anything that might break free of her control. It made her skin itch, like her body was covered in chigger bites.

Jace sat behind a long, low table, Random and Valkyrie beside him. Twenty feet away and sitting on a raised dais facing them stood a table of the same length but with more elaborate carvings. Five robed figures sat behind it. One was Aunt Ella.

The second Siren recognized as Julian, the man who had been with Meredith at the Gathering last night. Wonderful. She'd already spoken to a member of the Council and hadn't even known it.

Siren didn't recognize the other three. The one to Aunt Ella's right was a balding middle-aged white man gone slightly to fat. Next to him a dark-haired woman of indeterminate heritage sat with the most perfect posture Siren had ever seen.

Last was a tall Black man with a straight nose and high cheekbones, his eyes like golden coals. Despite the intensity of his gaze, Siren couldn't help but find him the most approachable, probably because, despite wearing the same black robe as the others, she could just make out a tie that rather prominently featured the Wonder Woman symbol.

Then her gaze landed on the woman standing next to the dais. Meredith wore an ice-blue dress that clung to her figure, her long blonde hair pulled into a neat chignon. Her fingernails and shoes were the exact shade of her dress, and the stilettos added a good four inches to the five feet ten she came by naturally.

Meredith smiled at her, and the expression was anything but welcoming. Perhaps this was why Jace made a point of standing up and pulling Siren's seat out for her, though as she took it Siren couldn't help but think the act would only make things worse.

When she was settled and Jace had reclaimed his seat, the balding man spoke.

"The Council will now hear the petition of Siren Savage to join the Society of Aspect." He glanced at a form in front of him, and Siren was dead certain it was the sheet Jace had filled out in the lobby, though she couldn't say why, or how it had gotten to the room ahead of them.

Only the furious scratching of a pen—no, quill—made Siren realize there was another person in the room, one she had missed entirely because he sat in the far corner, his nondescript clothes and desk seeming to blend into the wall behind him. He was young and thin, with wavy brown hair and ink stains on his shirt cuffs. He never looked up from his paper, even when he finished transcribing what the man had said. He simply paused, quill hovering over the page, waiting for someone to speak again.

Like a marionette on a string. The thought made Siren shudder.

"Council members bearing witness are I, Martin DuPont," the balding man said.

"I, Ella Tremayne."

"I, Julian Astor acting in place of Elijah Winters."

"I, Kara Barrow."

"And I, Theodore Bronte." As he said his name, the man with the Wonder Woman tie gave her the briefest of encouraging smiles. It steadied her, though it did nothing for the thudding of her heart.

"Who speaks with the petitioner?" Martin asked.

"Jace Winters," Jace said. "Witness."

"Valkyrie Winters, second witness."

"Random Tremayne, legal counsel."

The woman—Kara—frowned. "Is there a reason the petitioner feels she needs legal counsel?"

"No. However, my client is unfamiliar with our laws and customs. I offered myself as legal counsel to guide her through the waters."

"How generous of you." Kara's lips curved into the slightest twist of a sneer.

"Siren Savage," Martin began, "you are petitioning to be recognized by the Council as a person possessed of Aspect and to be formally recognized as a member of Aspect Society, being fully subject to its laws?"

"Subject to its laws, and privy to the law's protections," Random amended.

"Of course." Martin smiled pleasantly.

"I am."

"This petitioning will seek to determine three things. One, that you applied for inclusion into Aspect Society within twenty-four hours of learning what you are. Two, that you have never used your Aspect to cause injurious harm to anyone who has not first attacked you. And three, that you are in control of your Aspect and not a danger to others. Do you swear to answer any questions asked of you with honesty and integrity, the truth of which shall be judged by a person possessed of the Aspect of Truth?"

"I swear to answer questions truthfully. If those answers being checked by one with Truth Aspect is standard procedure in such petitions, then, yes, I agree to that stipulation."

Random gave her an approving wink.

"Meredith Townsend will serve as Truthfinder for this petition. She will require an initial physical connection to forge a link, which shall hold until she either releases it, or one or more parties leave this room. Is this acceptable?"

Siren nodded.

"Ms. Townsend." Martin gestured and Meredith approached Siren, her heels making delicate, pointed clicks on the stone floor.

Physical connection. Siren sincerely hoped they weren't going to have to hold hands.

Meredith covered Siren's left hand with her right.

At least it wasn't *quite* holding hands. When Meredith dug her fingernails in, all while holding a pretty smile on her face, it was nothing like holding hands.

Siren gave no reaction to the pain, even when she felt something wet and warm well up and trickled down her hand. A second later, power riddled through her, Meredith's Aspect cold and foreign as it looked for places to burrow in and latch onto. Siren gritted her teeth against the invasiveness, determined not to let Meredith see her squirm.

When Meredith's power had found enough footholds, the woman smiled and lifted her fingers, two long nails bloodied, and walked back to the side of the Council table.

"We're ready."

Martin nodded. Neither he, Kara, nor Julian appeared the slightest bit bothered by the blood trickling down the back of Siren's hand, despite her being quite certain it hadn't been standard procedure. Theodore, at least, wore a slight frown, and Aunt Ella remained as inscrutable as ever.

Jace's rage was a quiet, fierce energy that practically vibrated the table. Given his affinity for the elements, Siren thought it might actually *be* vibrating it.

"For the sake of simplicity," Martin continued, "unless Ms. Townsend voices an opposition, your words will be taken to be truthful for the duration of this meeting. When did you first become aware of Aspect Society?"

"Last night."

"Prior to that you had no knowledge you were the child of John and Mara Savage?"

"No."

The tiniest of shivers ran through her, so light Siren almost missed it, or mistook it for a quickening of her pulse. Meredith's Aspect, running through her, searching. She resisted the urge to scratch her arms.

"How did you become aware of that connection?"

"Aunt Ella—I mean, Mrs. Tremayne—thought I looked like Mara. I'd always wondered who my parents were so she offered to verify it."

"Ella, you officially confirmed the heritage?"

"Indeed. The girl is a Savage, through and through."

"Very well. What affinity of Aspect do you claim?"

"I—" She swallowed. "Jace says it's Life."

The room went still and silent, her own breathing the only sound she could hear. Siren wished she had a watch so she could at least listen to the seconds tick by. As it was, she didn't know how many passed before Martin cleared his throat.

"Ms. Townsend?"

Meredith's Aspect tugged at Siren, as it had been doing since she made her announcement. Finally, it stilled.

"She is telling the truth as she believes it," Meredith ground out.

"Theodore." Martin gestured at the man.

Theodore straightened his Wonder Woman tie. "Ms. Savage, with your permission, I would like to read you. I have an Aspect called Clarity, which, among other things, allows me to determine what type of Aspect resides in others, and how strong it is. It will be painless, though it may feel a bit…invasive."

Invasive? Meredith's Aspect already writhed beneath her skin. The urge to scratch herself bloody had risen to a fever-pitch. The last thing she wanted was someone *else's* Aspect crawling around inside her. But if she said no…if she said no, the Council wouldn't believe her. If they didn't believe her, they wouldn't help her. She thought of the dog, waiting at the Winters' for her to come back. Thought of Hank, and the job she didn't hate going to.

Thought, stupidly, of Jace's arms around her while they danced.

"Okay."

"There is something you should know, before you read her." Jace's hand slipped beneath the table and took hers, the squeeze he gave her almost apologetic. "Her Aspect isn't entirely normal. I believe someone has tampered with it."

"What do you mean 'tampered with'?" Julian asked.

"When I first met Siren, I thought she was a Null. I couldn't feel Aspect in her. Can any of you feel it now?"

One by one, each face on the Council took on a look of concentration that soon melted into a frown.

"The first time I realized she had Aspect was during the attack I reported by the two spectral harpies."

"Alleged attack," Kara qualified.

Siren had no intention of putting up with words like "alleged" when Meredith's power invaded her for the express purpose of determining the veracity of her words. She looked directly at Meredith. "I was attacked yesterday on the Winters' property by three spectral harpies. True or false?"

A muscle ticked along Meredith's jaw. "True."

"I didn't know I had Aspect at all, nor did I use it, before I was sixteen years old, which I'm told is impossible. True or false?"

Meredith didn't answer. Her Aspect twisted through Siren, painful in its insistence to find a lie that wasn't there. Siren had never wanted to punch someone quite as badly as she wanted to punch Meredith right then.

"Ms. Townsend?" Martin asked mildly. Still, silence. *"Ms. Townsend."*

Meredith's Aspect ceased its search. "True."

"Most of the time, I can't feel my Aspect or access it, which I'm told is unusual. True or false?"

The look on Meredith's face said she did not like playing this game, but when Martin looked at her, she answered, "True."

"When I am in situations causing heightened emotional stress, such as when I am being carried into the sky by supernatural creatures, I am able to use my Aspect. True or false?"

"True."

Siren turned back to Kara. "Should I continue playing True/False with Ms. Townsend, or do you want to let Jace take it from here? I confess, I don't really understand Aspect and I can't explain to Mr. Bronte what Jace feels he should know before he goes digging around inside me."

The look on Kara's face said she would as soon skewer Siren on a hot pole than answer her. Somehow, she managed. "You were saying, Mr. Winters?"

"The channels that in any of the rest of us continually flow with Aspect are normally barren inside her. The whole of her Aspect is centralized in what I believe to be a containment field built around her Aspect's Source. I believe situational stressors have induced cracks in that containment, which is the only reason she is able to access her Aspect at all."

"What you are describing is impossible." Julian's face was a pale mask. "And I, for one, didn't come here to have my time wasted by some—"

"Why don't you let me be the judge of what is impossible?" Theodore cut in mildly. "I can determine quite easily if Mr. Winters is mistaken."

Theodore stood, descended from the ridiculous dais, and took the chair next to Siren when Valkyrie vacated it. Up close, the perfectly straight fall of his nose, the high, prominent cheekbones, put Siren in mind of an Egyptian god of old. It wasn't the face alone, wasn't even the golden eyes that burned like hot coals. It was the quiet, terrifying power she felt when his hands took hers. Yet his grip was gentle, his hands warm and kind.

"I like your tie," Siren blurted out.

A smiled ticked at the left corner of his mouth. "Thank you. My daughter bought it for me. She has excellent taste." He paused, and she felt his Aspect gather in him. "I'll be as gentle as I can."

CHAPTER

EIGHTEEN

At first, it didn't feel like much at all, just a steady, liquid cold seeping through her body, much as Aunt Ella's power had done the day before. Theo's eyes glazed over, and she wondered what he saw, if he saw inside *her*. Did he see the empty channels, the cage Jace spoke of? Could *she* see those things, if she wanted to? She drifted, drowsy on the cold river trickling through her, and thought that this wasn't nearly so bad as Theo had made it out to be.

Then pain bit without warning, skeletal fingers tearing open her skin, their edges rimmed in fire. Siren jerked, eyes flying wide open, all sense of drowsiness, of safety, gone. She didn't scream, but only because her lips had glued shut, teeth locked together. She caught Theo's gaze and willed him to see her, to stop, but his eyes were vacant, the burning golden orbs unseeing.

The skeletal fingers clawed at her skin, scrabbling and flaying until enough of her lay open. She looked at her arms and couldn't understand how she wasn't bleeding, how the so obviously violated flesh appeared unharmed. Her stomach gave a sickening twist as she realized no one would stop him. She

117

couldn't move, couldn't give voice to her pain, and outwardly she appeared quite intact.

Of a sudden, the skeletal questing fingers stilled. The relief lasted a mere second, perhaps two, and the fingers morphed, shuddering and jerking until they became something smaller, more agile. Was it better that she couldn't actually see them, or worse?

Still rimmed in fire, the things slithered through the gaps in her torn flesh, wriggling into her with wet, squelching sounds that made her gorge rise. Inside her, they swam through the empty channels her Aspect should fill. She recognized those spaces, recognized them now that something foreign filled them, and the overwhelming desire to have the wriggling things out of her made her throw herself recklessly at the invisible bonds that held her.

The more she flailed, the hotter the fire inside her grew, the little maggots swimming through her veins, bouncing against the confines of the channels inside her, each contact an electric jolt. Her heart hammered against her chest, adrenaline coppery-sweet against the back of her throat.

The maggots swam deeper, through the bend inside her shoulders, dropping down, down, over her ribs, slithering inward to where her heart would be if it resided in the right half of her body. She felt the exact moment they halted, fetching up against a barrier that was both of her and not of her, because the pain she felt as they slammed into it was a half-pain. A steady pause, a few seconds of relief before the maggots collected, shuddering and twisting to reform the two skeletal hands, fingers probing at the barrier.

The pain as they searched was muted, and she became aware, as the fingers mapped the thing inside her, that it was a cube, of sorts. For a moment, she let herself relax, the half-pain a welcome reprieve from the whole. Then the scuttling fingers ran across a hairline crack in the cube, and as bony fingernails dug in, clamping onto the edges of the crack, Siren felt beyond it to where her Aspect waited.

Hesitantly, carefully, she reached out and touched it.

Instantly, the probing fingers stilled.

Siren's Aspect curled against her touch, warming to her as if she were its lover and had been gone far, far too long for its taste. It stretched, slipping out of the crack in the strange cube, and moved for the empty channels inside her, the channels, she understood, it was meant to inhabit. Before it could reach them, her Aspect brushed up against Theodore's skeletal hands. As it did, those fingers grasped the edges of the cage's fissure and *pulled*.

Pain howled through her, as did a fury that was both her own and her Aspect's, and though her Aspect was of her, the two were nonetheless separate. She felt her Aspect's intent a moment before it struck, and she was powerless to stop it as it latched on to the invading hands inside her, enveloped and consumed them.

JACE THREW himself in front of Siren, a shielding ward blazing to life around him a half second before Martin DuPont's Aspect slammed into it. The shield, hastily constructed, buckled under the assault. Jace poured Aspect into it, fortifying its construction even as Valkyrie alighted on the floor in front of him, the ward she snapped around them far more powerful than anything he could create.

Water Aspect did not take easily to warding, but Battle Aspect was born for it, and his sister was never quite so much in her element as when her Aspect blazed around her.

Martin DuPont stepped out from around the Council table, his face livid. "I might have expected this from your brother, Ms. Winters, but not you."

Valkyrie shrugged. "People can surprise you, Mr. DuPont."

"You are in direct defiance of the Council."

Random stepped in front of Valkyrie. "Precisely how do you claim Ms. Winters is in defiance?"

The look on DuPont's face said he couldn't believe he had to answer this question. "She has directly interfered in the apprehension of a woman who just attacked a member of the Council *with Aspect.*"

"What passed between Ms. Savage and Mr. Bronte is unclear. To call it an attack would be premature."

Incredulity painted DuPont's face. "*Look* at him."

Random did not, but Jace did. He hadn't had a chance, before, had only felt Siren's Aspect ignite, seen Theo's eyes roll back into his head a second before he fell to the ground, convulsing, his hands writhing like possessed things. And Siren—Siren stared into nothing, her eyes empty.

"I *have* looked. I see an unconscious man and a catatonic woman, and no clear picture of how either of them came to be that way. Under Section III Code VI of the Laws of Aspect, instances of Aspect use in which the intent and/or result of use are unclear as to intended harm shall be deemed benign until contradictory evidence is obtained. As such, you have no grounds for attacking Ms. Savage and both of the Winters are well within their rights as witnesses to the petitioner to defend her."

DuPont's hands curled into fists. He looked over to the man who sat in the corner, transcribing the hearing. As if sensing eyes on him, the man looked up and met DuPont's questioning gaze.

"Mr. Tremayne's articulation of the Code is technically correct, sir. Until either Mr. Bronte or Ms. Savage awakens, we cannot proceed."

As if brought to wakefulness by the words, Theodore Bronte moaned, pitching onto his side. His hands, still twitching madly, came somewhat under his control, enough that he placed one on the floor and shoved up to a sitting position. His eyes snapped open, the golden fire in them dimming until the orbs looked almost normal as they swept from Jace and Valkyrie to Martin DuPont.

"Martin? What seems to be the matter?" Theodore asked mildly, as if he hadn't just been lying unconscious on the floor and his hands weren't dancing in his lap like bewitched things.

"You tell us. We felt Ms. Savage's Aspect manifest and you went into convulsions."

Theo muttered a curse under his breath, turned about until he saw Siren, still in her seat, body perfectly still save for the rise and fall of her chest.

"Help me to her."

SIREN STARTLED INTO WAKEFULNESS, cold clawing at the palms of her hands. Those hands went to her chest, searching for the pain she had felt, for the cage she had discovered inside her and yet could not feel from outside.

"Siren," a voice said gently, "are you all right?" Theo's golden eyes looked at her, reassuring in their warmth, their lack of duplicity.

"I...think so?" Her head felt stuffed with cotton, but the pain was gone. "Are you?"

He smiled, hands twitching. "I will be."

"And now that Ms. Savage is awake, perhaps you would condescend to explain this mess, Theodore?" Julian's voice was cool and empty.

"As Mr. Winters said, Siren's Aspect channels are empty. I followed them to her Source and found the cage he spoke of. As he suspected, it is a containment field, built around her Aspect's Source, meant to trap it there, to keep her from accessing it. It would explain why she never managed to use Aspect before her sixteenth year."

"How is such a thing possible?" Aunt Ella asked, curious rather than challenging. "Her body should reject a containment field, and the instinctual need to use Aspect and be unable to do so should have driven her mad." She stated it simply as if being driven mad were nothing at all unusual.

Theo patted Siren's hand, as if he knew his next words would hurt. "It was placed in her when she was only a few days old. Because she was so young, her body accepted it, and likewise because she never grew accustomed to her Aspect, if she suffered any withdrawal from being unable to connect with it, it would have been minimal, and she incapable of remembering it."

"And her ability to access her Aspect on occasion? How is that possible?"

"The containment cage is cracked, allowing her to pull small pieces of her Aspect from it instinctually in times of heightened emotional distress. I believe that with training, she could learn to pull from it of her own will."

Kara's fingers drummed rapidly on the table. Aunt Ella looked morbidly interested, DuPont furious, and Julian incredulous. Only the last spoke.

"You mean she has over twenty years of untapped Aspect inside her? Of *Life* Aspect?"

Theo looked reluctant to answer, and it wasn't hard to guess why. Julian stared at Siren with a newfound hunger, like he'd been on the brink of bankruptcy and discovered a chest of gold.

"Yes," Theo said.

"Can you destroy the containment cage?"

"No. I attempted to widen the crack in the containment field to give Ms. Savage greater access to her Aspect. This was a mistake, as I had failed to understand the nature of the containment field itself. Siren's body did not simply accept it, it bonded with it. It is as much a part of her as any other organ. Attempting to widen the crack was akin to splitting open her heart. Her Aspect defended itself. The entire incident was my fault, and I will accept all blame for it."

"If the testimony of your own councilman is sufficient, may I trust my client can resume her petitioning without fear of retaliation?" Random asked.

DuPont sighed. "Yes. Ms. Winters, you may release your warding and take your seat. This petitioning will continue with the second question."

Just like that, as if nothing unusual had happened, the room returned to the formalities of bureaucracy.

"Ms. Savage, have you ever used your Aspect to cause injury to someone who was not immediately placing your life in jeopardy?"

Siren's heart fluttered. Blood splattered her vision, took her back into memories she didn't want to relive. She thought of the man who had pushed her into the bathroom stall, how her Aspect had poured out and she'd felt his heart stop. She thought of the policeman who had liked to hit his wife, how her Aspect had pulsed one day as she handed him his order, of his death a week later.

"Ms. Savage?" Kara prompted, one eyebrow raised.

Siren swallowed. If she never heard another "Ms. Savage" it would be too soon. *Truth is a slippery thing*, Aunt Ella had said. *For a person, it all just comes down to belief.*

Belief. She needed only to answer the question in a way she could believe. "I have never used Aspect to harm an innocent."

DuPont glanced at Meredith, perhaps because Siren had taken so long to answer. Meredith shrugged, a graceful rise and fall of her shoulders.

"That brings us to the final question, of whether you are in control of your Aspect and whether you pose a danger to others."

"A question I should think the answer to is obviously 'no'," Julian drawled. "If she cannot access her Aspect when she is not ragingly emotional, she can hardly be said to be in control of it."

"On the contrary, the very fact Ms. Savage's Aspect *is* largely inaccessible to her should be tantamount to proof that she is not a danger to others," Random countered.

"Until she becomes emotional, in which case her inexperience will lend her no ability to control her Aspect whatsoever. Unless, of course, you're suggesting no woman is ever emotional, Mr. Tremayne?"

Random gave Julian a withering look. "Mr. Bronte, was it not your opinion that with proper training, Ms. Savage could learn to access her Aspect without need of an emotional trigger?"

"Yes, I believe so."

"And if she is given such training, might she not gain the experience Councilman Astor suggests she lacks, so that in the case of an emotional trigger, she would be quite capable of controlling her Aspect?"

"I see no reason why she should not, with training, be as capable as anyone else," Theodore said pleasantly.

"It is common for petitioners who have had no formal training in their Aspect to be assigned inclusion into Aspect Society on a probationary basis along with an instructor to help them better understand their abilities. I see no reason Ms. Savage's inclusion ought to be any different."

"The consequences of possible failure are much higher in this case, wouldn't you say?" Kara suggested. "Two decades of untapped Aspect. We've never seen anything on that scale. If she loses control, we haven't the slightest notion of how much damage she could do. I motion to hold Ms. Savage in custody until the extent of her Aspect can be determined."

Panic welled in Siren and she surged to her feet. Or would have, if Jace's grip on her arm hadn't held her down. She glared at him, but he only shook his head, tilted it slightly in Random's direction.

Have a little faith, his nod seemed to say.

"On what grounds?" Random challenged.

"The Council has the right to detain any individual within its borders which it believes to be an imminent threat to the Aspect community."

"You have no grounds for imminent threat. Clause IV of

Amendment III to the Aspect Constitution states that for an individual to be classified as an imminent threat they must be possessed of Aspect of significant ability, intent to use such Aspect to do the community harm, and the Council must have evidence that said individual has already committed an act of violence against a member of the Aspect community.

"To start at the end, your own Truthfinder has verified Ms. Savage has harmed no one, and she has exhibited no words or actions which could be construed as intent to do harm. The very nature of her Aspect—Life—goes against harming anyone. And while Ms. Savage will undoubtedly wield significant Aspect someday, she cannot be said to be possessed of it at present, as even if she does learn to harness it at will, only a fraction of her Aspect is available to her for use."

"The potential for disaster in this instance is too great to ignore."

"I was not aware it was this Council's job to hold an individual responsible for *potential* failures, Kara." Aunt Ella flashed a set of bone white teeth. "What the girl might do is not under question, only what she has done. As a senior member of this Council, I motion to vote on approving Siren's petition to join Aspect Society. Will anyone second me?"

"I second the approval," Theo said.

"Kara?" DuPont asked.

"Deny."

"Julian?"

"Deny."

Siren gripped Jace's hand, wouldn't be surprised if she was cutting off his circulation, only she couldn't bring her gaze away from DuPont long enough to find out. One vote. It all came down to one vote.

If they said no, how was she going to escape this room? Her pulse ricocheted. Coming here had been a terrible idea. She had no easy way out. She was surrounded by people who understood their power, had years of training with it.

A cage. She was going to end up in a cage. A real, physical one, not unlike the one inside her. Sweat trickled down the inside of her neck, and she couldn't focus on anything, couldn't really see anything.

Run. Run, run, run. She inched her toes back.

"While I agree in spirit with Ella and Theo, the possibility of the threat posed cannot be ignored. I am willing to grant Ms. Savage probationary entry into Aspect Society."

The thudding of Siren's pulse receded. Not a cage.

"Provided," DuPont continued, "she has an instructor whose full-time responsibility she will be. Given the severity of that responsibility, I am unwilling to assign anyone the position. They must volunteer."

"I'll do it," Jace said.

Martin sighed again, He didn't strike Siren as malicious. It was more as if he was simply tired, and her case held too much excitement for him.

"I suspected you might. You understand, Mr. Winters, that she will be your responsibility twenty-four hours a day? She will live under your roof. If she leaves your residence, for any reason, you will be with her. If any harm comes because of her, you will be responsible."

"I understand."

DuPont rubbed wearily at his forehead. "I will expect weekly progress reports on her training, as well as reports on anything unusual that may occur."

"I'll keep you apprised as necessary."

"Ms. Savage, do you agree to be bound by these terms?"

Siren's hand, still clenching Jace's, trembled. She would have to live in his house. If she went anywhere, he would be a constant shadow. It was another kind of imprisonment, another way of losing freedom. But it wasn't a jail cell, and she knew enough to know she had no options if she didn't agree.

"Yes."

"Wonderful." Random said. "That brings us to the matter of

the harpy attack itself, which is only the latest in a string of attacks against my client."

"An investigation will be opened," Kara said, "but Dark Aspect constructs are notoriously difficult to trace back to their makers. Especially when there is so little of them left."

"Then there is the matter of her safety."

"She has already been assigned to the Winters' household. Ms. Winters herself tested more highly than anyone in the history of Battle Aspect. Is she not sufficient protection for your client?"

"I have my own work," Valkyrie said. "It's unreasonable to expect me *or* my brother to be her only protection."

"What do you want?"

Random smiled. "Given that, by your own admission, Siren's power would be a valuable commodity in the wrong hands, I should think you'd want to protect it with a rotating guard of at least two individuals at all times."

"While the harpy attack is unusual, we have no clear evidence that Siren was the intended target and not merely a convenient one. And while she may *believe* she has been pursued, we have no physical evidence of any previous attacks to lend credence to her assertions.

"Childhood trauma can manifest itself in strange ways. Unless she is attacked again, this Council does not recognize the need to spend resources on a constant guard. If there is nothing else?"

"There is. I will take this moment to remind you that was done to Ms. Savage's Aspect is a tier one violation of Aspect law. Add to it that whoever did this to her is likely also responsible for murder and kidnapping, and I should think you ought to be far more concerned with finding *that* person than with worrying about my client.

"I will expect, as she is now a preliminary member of Aspect Society, that you will reopen the investigations into her parents' murders and her initial disappearance within the week. Your investigators will, of course, need to speak with her regarding her memories of the persons who raised her, who may well be connected to these events. Those interviews will be scheduled through me, and she will only be questioned in my presence."

Random stood. "Now, Mr. DuPont, that is all."

Jace swept more than pulled Siren out of her seat and she followed him, a little numbly, to the door, Random and Valkyrie flanking them. They crossed the threshold of the Warding Room and Siren felt the link Meredith had forged with her snap.

Siren couldn't find any humor in her as they exited the cabin and climbed into Jace's truck but somehow,*he* did.

"So, baby," he said casually, "want to move in with me?"

Improbably, *impossibly*, she laughed.

CHAPTER

NINETEEN

"Everything is going to be all right," Jace said for at least the third time since the meeting. "You're smart, you'll learn to control your Aspect, and we'll figure out the rest of it as it comes along."

He drove them into the south side of town, and she found the now-familiar rumble of the old truck's engine oddly soothing.

"They don't even want to look for the person following me." They basically thought she'd hallucinated being hunted for years. "And I can't even tell them anything useful."

"Maybe they do, and maybe they don't. But they *will* look for them. Random will make sure of it. And if they can't break the curse that keeps you from talking about it, we'll get creative."

"And you're just okay with the rest of it?"

"The rest of it being…?"

"I know you said you didn't mind training me, but they put a lot more on you than that. You're fine with being responsible if I step a toe out of line? I mean, you're going to have to come to work with me and I have no idea how I'll explain that to Hank."

He coughed. "Uh, Hank shouldn't be an issue."

She turned to him. "Hank? Seriously? *Hank* has Aspect?"

Jace gave her an apologetic nod. "It doesn't run terribly

strong in his family, but yeah. Seclusion *is* the heart of Aspect territory. Not many families here *don't* have at least a trace."

She remembered Hank telling her yesterday that there wasn't a lot of trouble Jace couldn't get her out of, and his words suddenly made a lot more sense now. The old bastard.

"And, obviously, being your constant shadow is a lot to ask from either of us, but I can work anywhere as long as I have a laptop, so we'll manage."

"What exactly do you do for work?"

"Uh, just freelance stuff, mostly."

He looked oddly embarrassed so she didn't push it.

"Any other concerns you would like to air?"

"I'm sorry they're making me move into your house."

"Technically, not my house."

"I don't want to be an imposition."

He gave her a sideways glance. "You remember the house, right? Pretty sure if we get sick of each other one of us can move to another wing. There's a suite with a kitchenette on the second floor if you get really desperate for privacy."

"Of course there is," she muttered. "Turn here."

"You could just tell me where your apartment is. I'm pretty familiar with Seclusion, you know, growing up here and all."

"No doubt, but then, it would ruin the surprise."

The surprise in question was the Everglade Apartment Complex, more colloquially known as "The Glades," and over-grandly named in either case. It was a single-level strip of six apartments in varying stages of disrepair, though from the outside at least number four, her very own, had the advantage of looking *slightly* less decrepit than the others, mostly because her door contained no visibly-patched holes.

She pulled the truck's door handle, stopped when Jace reached for his.

"You don't need to come in."

"I don't mind helping."

"All right, then, I'd prefer if you didn't come in."

"Going back to the whole shadow thing—I technically have to come in."

Right. He's responsible for me. The very idea of anyone being responsible for her was ludicrous.

"It doesn't matter to me where you live," he said softly.

And what about how *I live?* She shook her head and jumped out of the truck. She'd only been gone a day, but it felt strange coming back. The difference between the three deadbolts she unlocked on the front door and the security camera-watched gate at the Winters' home couldn't be further worlds apart. She unlocked the last bolt, putting her shoulder into the door when she turned the handle because the door liked to stick.

She felt the wrongness even before the door swung to a halt midway through opening, fetching up against something on the floor that shouldn't have been there. Siren shimmied through the open space between door and frame, then stopped so abruptly that Jace walked right into her.

The small apartment lay in shambles. Every cupboard in the kitchen was thrown wide, their meager holdings scattered. Food boxes were torn open, contents strewn about the countertops, the sink. The few dishes she'd owned were broken, sharp edges glaring at her in the sunlight that streamed through the front window. The item the door had tangled itself in was a pair of her jeans. Her clothes were everywhere, pulled out of the two duffel bags she kept them in. They looked as if someone had taken a knife to them at will, little more than strips of ragged cloth. The mattress bore great gashes, its stuffing torn out, the bed pillow rent.

Her print of *The Scream*, that stupid print she'd bought because she'd *wanted* something, something normal, was destroyed. The books that had been piled on the floor—every single one of the JC Morden books, the only ones she couldn't bear to part with from town to town—were torn apart, pages littering the ground like day-old confetti.

A strangled noise, half-sob, half-animal fury, rose in her

throat, and with a panicked thought she ran for the bathroom, leaping over shredded clothes. It was as bad as the rest of the apartment, the shower rod pulled down, broken into pieces, the shampoo and conditioner bottles opened and poured out, bath towels sliced to ribbons. The doors to the sink's vanity hung wrongly off the hinges.

Heart thudding, she dropped to her knees, relief singing through her as she found the drainpipe from the sink intact. She reached up to the connector on the u-bend and gently unscrewed it. The inside of the pipe was dry, as she hadn't used the sink since she moved in, and her trembling fingers felt about. They latched on to a plastic bag and pulled it out.

She stared at it a moment, not quite willing to believe it. Her emergency cash and two spare IDs, good ones she hadn't burned yet, stared back at her. She didn't know how long she sat on the floor, clutching the plastic bag, tears of anger and frustration burning her cheeks. At some point, Jace settled on the floor next to her, the strong fingers of one hand working at the knots in her back.

"I'm sorry," he said. "I guess there's no point in asking who did this?"

Siren shook her head. It took her a moment to find her voice because her throat was thick with tears she refused to shed anymore, because crying never fixed anything and it was embarrassing, besides. "It's never going to stop."

"It will," Jace said. There was steel in his voice, but it didn't matter now. He might mean it, but he hadn't lived with this as long as she had. He didn't know how pointless determination could be. "It's a terrible way for it to happen, but this means the Council has to look into it now. *This* is the pattern of proof they asked for."

As if that decided him, he pulled out his phone. Siren was close enough, practically leaning into him, that she could hear the two rings before the line connected and a tired voice answered, "Yes?"

"You wanted to be apprised of any unusual developments, Martin. Siren's apartment was broken into and vandalized. There are traces of Dark Aspect inside. I trust you'll have someone here to look at it within the hour."

"I—"

Jace ended the call.

She suddenly wanted to be far away, wanted to be anywhere but *here*, in her dingy, now-destroyed apartment."Do we need to stay until he sends someone?"

Jace shook his head. "I'll text Random. He'll handle it."

Part of her felt she should protest, that she should stay, as if being here were somehow required. But she had no influence with these people, and she hadn't been here when it happened, besides. Jace was right; Random could handle it. She nodded and picked herself up off the bathroom floor. In the living room, Jace paused, looking at the mess.

"Is this—was this everything you had?"

Siren looked away. If there was pity in his gaze, she had no interest in seeing it. "Yeah."

She waited for his response, braced herself for pity or disgust.

"We'll get you some things on the way home."

She looked at him then and found no pity, no disgust. Only anger, and for that she was grateful.

CHAPTER

TWENTY

A brief argument had ensued over precisely where Siren needed to go clothes shopping. She thought Goodwill was a perfectly respectable option. He objected in favor of an actual clothing store. In the end, they compromised on Target.

Few things, she discovered, were as awkward as clothes shopping with a man you had been—dating?—for a few weeks, especially when she realized she also needed to buy intimates and he was supposed to be glued to her side by Council edict. She rushed through it as quickly as possible and did the same with the hygiene section. She only slowed down when she hit the pet aisle.

So what if she already had more money's worth of clothes in her cart than she'd spent in the last year combined? Her dog deserved nice things. And he was, she decided, *her* dog. She grabbed a black collar with little white paw prints on it, a tennis ball, a dog-bone chew toy, an adorably soft cloth turtle, something called a Kong you were apparently supposed to fill with peanut butter, a new bag of dog food, and the largest bag of dog treats she could find.

Then she had to buy peanut butter for the stupid toy. By the time she finished, Jace stared at the cart in semi-amazement.

"Are we starting a dog rescue?"

She glared at him. "I can always go back and get the dog bed, too. And now that I think about it, maybe he needs a cute sweater. And a toy that squeaks. And—"

Jace lifted his hands in defeat. "I'm sorry, I take it all back."

"He's been through a lot. He deserves nice things."

"Sounds like this woman I know. My main point being, I think the dog will own more things than you, based on this cart selection."

"I'm on a budget."

"Siren, you know I can—"

She shook her head. "Don't. I can take care of myself." And because something suspiciously akin to hurt crossed his face she added, "I *need* to take care of myself."

Gods knew she'd done too little of it in the last day. It didn't take much, she reflected, to soften that iron core of self-reliance inside her. She could take care of herself. She always had. Always *had* to. Having a brief taste of what it was like for someone to share that burden made her crave the help, the companionship. But she had already accepted too much, and the more she accepted, the more difficult it would be to live without it.

She hadn't forgotten they were going to "talk" at some point today.

Jace didn't argue with her any further. She hit the checkout line and ignored the cashier's suspicious glances at her plastic bag full of money. She counted out enough bills to give her chest contractions and decided it was a very good thing she wouldn't have a rent bill next month.

Siren had just finished putting the last bag behind the seat in Jace's truck when the sound of buzzing flies filled her ears. She jumped into the cab, slammed the door closed and locked it. She left her fingers on the lock because she didn't trust it not to pop open.

"Is everything okay?"

"Get us out of here."

Jace did not, bless him, question her. He slammed the truck into reverse, pulled out of the space, and peeled out of the parking lot. The buzzing in her ears, the hunger, the pressure, rose to a crescendo. Jace yelled something she didn't hear and jerked her down a half second before the passenger side window exploded. Glass flew inward, raining down on her body, her hair, on the hand Jace held up to shield her eyes and face.

The truck revved, RPMs climbing higher and higher until Jace finally took his hand away long enough to shift into the next gear. Siren pushed herself up, glass tumbling.

"What the *fuck*?" she screamed, rage replacing terror.

Jace flew through the last two gears, and the truck shot down the road at a speed that didn't even come close to legal. The buzzing in her ears faded into nothingness.

"My thoughts exactly." Jace looked grim. "I take it this isn't usual behavior for your stalker?"

"No, h—" Siren choked. Oh, for fuck's sake, she couldn't even say the pronoun *he*. "The *asshole*," she corrected, "hasn't ever attacked me in public before yesterday. And yesterday, they backed off when you were around. A *lot* of things are happening that haven't happened before."

She didn't like it.

"It's Seclusion," Jace said, finally. "We have the highest concentration of Aspect users in the country and the seat of the Council is here. He or she, whoever they are, is getting desperate."

Siren chose her words carefully. When she spoke, she very pointedly thought about anything other than the gray-eyed man. "That first gender you mentioned," was all she said, all she *could* say. Even adding "was correct" would have choked her up.

He looked at her sharply, and she nodded.

"He, then, *he's* getting desperate. Your apartment—I don't think he was looking for something in the apartment. I think he went there looking for you, and when he didn't find you it drove him into a rage. He wanted to leave a message, scare you."

Yeah, well, he succeeded.

Jace sat tensely, his grip on the steering wheel tightening until the leather creaked underneath his hands.

"What aren't you telling me?" she asked.

"Nothing, it's just a hunch. I don't have any proof."

"I happen to prefer being let in on hunches, especially when my life is involved."

"Some of the Council can be difficult, but they don't usually take a near-unanimous dislike to someone they've never met. I think someone pushed them in that direction where you're concerned."

"And?"

"And I think that that someone is involved with the person stalking you." He pulled up to the gate in front of the Winters' house, rolling down the window to punch a code into the small box. "He didn't attack you in public until *now*, which means someone gave him information on the Council meeting, probably told him you were under twenty-four-hour watch from this point on. I'd guarantee he's discovered Val redid the wards on the estate, and whatever holes were in the old ones I can guarantee hers don't suffer from. He'd want to get to you before we returned to the house."

Siren took hold of calm, logical thought. Logic was good. Break the situation down into small, manageable chunks. "Why not just wait at the apartment for me? Stands to reason I'd come back for my things."

"For the same reason, I think, that he didn't come anywhere close enough for me to get a location on him. Identification. Which means I would either recognize him, or if I sketched him for the Council *they* would recognize him."

Jace pulled through the security gate and up to the house,

parked in front of the double front doors and killed the engine. Siren made no move to get out. She didn't want to take the conversation indoors. If she thought about this mess the rest of the day, she'd go insane, and there wasn't anything she could do about it anyway. She needed to finish what could be finished and leave it here.

"You seem pretty sure. That there's a connection to the Council."

He didn't answer her unspoken question directly. "When Val and I were talking last night, did you hear the part about my mother?"

"Yeah."

"My father has spent every waking day of his life since my mother's death trying to find the person that held her. He'd disappear for weeks at a time, searching. My father is smart, he is a Council member, and he has a lot of money. Those three things can get a person almost anything they want, and he has never found this man. I don't see how that's possible unless this person has connections high in Aspect Society."

"You think he's working *with* someone on the Council?"

Jace rubbed his eyes. He looked tired, she realized. Realized also that she didn't like it, didn't like knowing it was because of her.

He shook his head. "Julian and Kara can be infuriating, but I don't see them for it. DuPont tries to be fair even if he frequently fails. Theo's practically a saint and Aunt Ella would never. No, I think it has to be someone close to the Council, someone with influence, just one step removed."

"And this influential person is theoretically in contact with the person who's after me?"

"That's the idea."

"Does Aspect Society have a newspaper or some other kind of publication?"

"Several. Why?"

"Because I'm going to need to go through the back issues, if you can find copies for me. If this guy's connected that high up, it stands to reason a picture might have made it into the newspaper at some point."

Jace stared at her.

"What?"

"I can't believe I haven't thought of that. The library upstairs has a backlog of issues going back to the eighties, I think."

"Right. Great. Tomorrow, though. I'm all done with plotting and people trying to kill me for the day."

She opened the door and hopped out, levering the seat forward to grab the plastic shopping bags behind it.

Jace hopped out of the truck and came over beside her. "I can get those."

Siren started to refuse, the habit of rejecting assistance ingrained in her. Then she stopped and gave him a tired smile. "I suppose you could help."

He took half the bags while she grabbed the others, along with the twenty-pound bag of dog food she stubbornly insisted on carrying herself, gods-alone knew *why*. But the weight of the bag on her shoulder was comforting. Not the weight itself, necessarily, but her ability to bear up underneath it.

She bore up, Siren told herself. She bore up, and no matter how bad, how rotten things got, she made it through. This time would be no different.

As they walked to the front door, she found another smile, this one easier, more genuine. "Let's go see if the dog destroyed the house."

CHAPTER
TWENTY-ONE

S iren managed to drop her bags to the ground before forty-five-odd pounds of manically happy, wriggling dog bounded into her and knocked her down. He apparently thought he was a lap dog, attempting to fit every inch of his considerable bulk onto her legs. His tail whacked against the floor as he licked all over her face and neck.

"Okay, Percy, calm down boy."

"Percy?"

"Short for Perseus," Siren explained, and extricated herself from beneath the dog. She scratched behind his ears and he flopped onto the floor, rolled over and demanded belly rubs.

"Funny," Jace said, crouching down to rub Percy's ears, "he doesn't look like he's been rescuing maidens from sea monsters."

"Sometimes names are earned, and sometimes names are indicative of potential. And this guy has lots of potential, yes he does." She said the last part to the dog, her words devolving into mushy puppy-speak.

Jace rose and began methodically unpacking grocery bags while she continued to praise her dog on all of his adorableness. *Her* dog. She decidedly liked the sound of it.

Jace cleared his throat. "So, uh, about that talk I said we should have."

Siren tensed. It wasn't as if she hadn't known this was coming, but she still wasn't ready for it. She'd thought—she'd thought he *liked* her. Realistically, her strange Aspect, her being hunted by nightmare creatures, and her hot mess of a life were a lot to ask for anyone to get involved with. Especially when they hadn't known each other that long.

Still, when he hadn't run away screaming after the harpy attack, when he'd offered to help her, she'd hoped. But everyone had to draw a line somewhere, and clearly he drew his at her being the result of kidnapping and experimentation. He was helping her because he was a nice person, and she should just be grateful for that, even if it hurt, and—

"I don't ever want you to feel pressured."

"What?" It was so far from what she'd expected him to say that she didn't have a clue what he meant.

"It was bad enough when I thought I'd just be training you to use your Aspect. In retrospect, I never should have—" he broke off, and she was absolutely certain he was thinking about what they'd almost done yesterday. "But now that you're living here, now that it's my progress reports to the Council that determine your probationary status in Aspect Society, you might feel pressured to continue this" —he waved a hand between them— "whether you actually want to or not."

"Oh." She absolutely *should* have considered that, but she hadn't. Because Jace was *Jace*. Because she always felt safe around him. Imagining him trying to pressure her into something felt ridiculous. The very fact they were having this conversation was practically a guarantee he was the type of man who would never do it. Maybe some people were good enough actors to say everything Jace had said and not mean it, but she didn't think he was.

He looked away from her. "And I also don't want to be the thing you use and discard after you get what you want."

Ouch. It would have hurt more, except she knew that was exactly what Meredith had done to him.

"I said I'd help you, and I will, regardless of whatever is or isn't between us."

His entire body was tense, as if he were a Jenga tower and he expected her to pull out the fatal piece and send him tumbling apart. She walked over and touched him lightly on the shoulder. He jerked and turned to face her.

"Look, I'm sure we both have some unusual hang-ups, and I wouldn't blame you if you didn't trust me."

"It's not that I don't—"

"Just let me finish. I like you, Jace. I did from the start. I should have left town after work yesterday, but I texted you instead because I'm an idiot."

That got him to smile, at least.

"I like *this.*" She rocked onto her toes and kissed him, a light, quick kiss. Or at least she'd meant it to be. He leaned into her, his mouth soft and sweet against hers, and she wrapped her hands around his neck and pulled him closer. She made herself break away before her hormones could entirely erase her ability to think.

"I sense a 'but' coming," he murmured.

She swallowed. "But there are things you don't know about me."

"I'm sure there are a lot of things we don't know about each other. That's half the fun, isn't it? Getting to know someone?"

Why did he have to be so perfect? And why did she have to be so fucked up? "I'm not talking about what kind of tea I like or what my favorite book was as a kid. I'm talking about things I've done. Things I'm not ready to talk about." She breathed in his scent and took a step back from him. "Things that might change the way you think about me."

"I didn't exactly miss the turn of phrase you passed off on the Council. You've never used Aspect to harm anyone *innocent.*"

Siren flinched.

"I don't know what happened to you. I don't know what you've been through. But I know you're not the kind of person who would hurt someone if you had another option."

"How could you possibly know that?"

"Because, even when you were drunk and drugged on Dark Aspect, your only concern was for a hurt dog that was trying to lead you to the one thing you've been running from."

She sniffed. "Maybe I just like animals better than humans."

"I wouldn't blame you if you did. My point is, when you're ready to talk about it, I'm not scared of anything you have to tell me."

She believed he believed it. But she could barely live with the things she'd done, and she'd *been* there, immersed in the fear and the panic and the hopelessness. But there was always a chance, and as long as there was, she wasn't going to throw it away. "So what do we do until then?"

"Until then, we take things slow."

Slow. Right. "What does that mean?"

"It means," he said, brushing a kiss across her temple, "that I find out what kind of tea you like and what your favorite book was as a kid."

A hint of a smile ghosted across her face. "Earl Grey and *The Black Stallion.* You?"

"Not terribly fond of tea, and the Sherlock Holmes adventures."

Her smile widened. "Did you want to be a detective?"

Jace laughed. "No. I liked the idea that if you were smart enough, people had to put up with you despite your flaws."

He turned back to unpacking the Target bags. "There is something I'm curious about. You don't have to tell me if you don't want to. Back at your apartment, you don't—didn't—own anything."

"That's not exactly a question."

"How many times have you moved?"

She shrugged. "As many as I needed to."

"That's not exactly an answer."

"I don't know, really." She'd kept a log of the cities when she'd first started out. She'd thought it would keep her sane until, one day, she'd realized that the list would never end. "Thirty, maybe?" Closer to forty, more like.

"You left when you were sixteen and you're twenty-two?"

She nodded.

"You've lived in thirty cities in *six years*?"

"I wouldn't really call it living," she joked. He didn't laugh. "I wasn't always in them very long. Sometimes I'd move and it would feel weird, so I'd leave after a couple days or weeks."

"Weird how?"

"Just weird." *Flies buzzing in my ears, under my skin. Hunger in the wind.* Things she'd choke on if she tried to say them. "I ignored it the first few times."

"What happened?"

"A pack of wolves ripped through my apartment door in Baton Rouge. Well, not wolves exactly. They had four red eyes and their teeth were black. They dragged me halfway down the block before I kicked one in the face and got away." It was a relief to say the words out loud to someone who wouldn't think she was crazy.

"Purple eel-snake things invaded my hotel room in Texas." They'd swum up out of her toilet, of all places, and *that* had caused an interestingly difficult phobia of bathrooms for the next year. "Things like that. I caught on pretty quick that if things felt weird, it was best to move on."

"But you didn't feel that here?"

"Not until yesterday. I should have left the second it happened. If I had, you wouldn't be mixed up in all this."

"Hey." He caught her hands in his. "I'm *glad* I'm mixed up in all this."

She gave him an incredulous look. "I'm pretty sure the first day we met you told me you'd rather eat hot nails than be in Seclusion for any longer than you had to."

"That was before this really hot woman moved in with me."

He leaned forward.

Her phone buzzed.

She gave him an apologetic look and frowned at the six texts from an unknown number.

"Did you give my number to anyone?"

"No. Why?"

Siren didn't answer immediately. She pulled the texts up and read from the beginning.

Hey.

Are you guys home yet?

I took care of everything, call me.

??? It's been like an hour.

You guys aren't making out, are you?

She hazarded a guess and typed, *Random?*

The response was immediate. *Obviously. What took you so long?*

Siren rolled her eyes. "Apparently, your best friend is as emotionally needy as a preteen and his Aspect felt the need to find my phone number."

Jace snorted. "I'll tell him you said that." He frowned and pulled out his own phone. "Why is he texting you and not me?"

Siren sighed dramatically and leaned back against the counter, fanning herself. "Well, we did have a moment last night."

"A moment?"

"Oh, you know. He gave me his jacket, told me of his exceptional male qualities, and turned his sexy, smoldering gaze on me."

"Did he?" Jace settled his arms on the counter to either side of her, effectively trapping her. "Remind me to kill him later."

A zing of heat flared through Siren. It might not be rational to get turned on by the primal possessiveness in his gaze, but it was definitely happening.

"Just to clarify something on the taking-it-slow front," he

said. "I don't see more than one person at a time, and I know myself well enough to know I can't date someone who does. If exclusivity isn't something you can do, you should tell me that now."

"I have absolutely no problems with that."

"Good." He kissed her, a quick, hard kiss that sent her pulse leaping into her throat. "I'm still going to kill Random."

"There's really no need." Siren danced away from him because if he kissed her again she had the decided feeling that they would not end up taking things slow. At all. "He doesn't like me like that. He just feels broken."

"Broken? I can think of a lot of words to describe Random. Broken isn't one of them."

Siren let her shoulders rise and fall. "He hides it well but he's not in a great place right now. You're his best friend. You should talk to him." She brightened as an idea hit her. "Take him out tonight. Make him have fun."

"I can't tonight. I sort of promised Val that movie night and she doesn't take cancellations well."

"Then invite Random. He's practically family, right?"

Maybe that was the better option, anyway. She had a feeling Random was the type to find distraction on his own, and distraction clearly hadn't worked. Maybe she just needed to throw him and Valkyrie together at every possible moment until they worked out whatever had happened between them.

Because all joking aside, she *was* worried about him. He'd had that dead look in his eyes last night, the one she'd seen in the mirror the first year she'd started running, the one that said something had hurt him bad enough that he wasn't sure how to keep going.

"Just say yes," she told Jace.

"Okay, yes, if you come, too."

"You don't think Valkyrie will mind?"

"I don't, but if she does, she'll get over it."

"Okay. I'm taking Percy outside and I'll call Random." If the incessant buzzing coming from her phone was any indication, she already had a fresh dozen text messages from him.

"Just out of curiosity, what exactly is it you think is wrong with Random?"

"He's in love."

"Random doesn't fall in love."

"Everyone falls in love at some point."

"Okay, who is he in love with then, and why is it a problem?"

"It's not my business to say, and it's a problem because she broke his heart." She motioned to Percy, who eagerly trotted up to her side, and dialed Random's number as they slipped outside, leaving a baffled Jace behind them.

TWENTY-TWO

Siren hurled a handful of popcorn at Random. Most of it missed because the Winters' theater room was ridiculously large.

"Ow." Random rubbed in mock hurt at his cheek where a lone piece of fluffy popcorn had succeeded in bouncing gently off him. "All I'm saying is that if Flying Snow had been a little more understanding of why Broken Sword made certain choices, things might not have ended so tragically."

"Perhaps," Valkyrie answered icily, "if Broken Sword hadn't been so cavalier about a decision that was obviously important to Flying Snow, things wouldn't have *had* to end so tragically."

"He wasn't being cavalier. He was thinking about the greater good, and about how he was losing his relationship with Flying Snow to an unattainable vendetta."

Siren only barely managed not to groan. She did bury her face in Percy's fur. *Hero*, apparently, was not the best choice of movie night flicks for a quarreling would-be couple. At least, not *this* quarreling would-be couple. It had sounded safe enough. Martial arts. History. An emperor bent on conquest and unification of countries. Then came Flying Snow and Broken Sword's relationship, which Random and

Valkyrie were clearly finding a little too much to identify with.

Just when Siren was afraid Valkyrie's head might explode in an impressive array of flaming sparks, Percy intervened. He gave a wide yawn and shook himself up off Siren's lap, jumped off the couch, and trotted across the room to lay a paw on Valkyrie's knee. He whined adorably.

"Why is it you always think *I* should take you outside, pup? She's your mother, not me."

Siren laughed. "I'll take him."

Valkyrie waved a dismissive hand. "It's fine. He'll just guilt me later if I don't." She swept out of the room, Percy prancing happily at her heels.

Random stood. He looked irritated and forlorn at the same time. "Guess I'll be heading out, then."

Jace made a noncommittal noise. Siren elbowed him in the ribs. When he gave her a *What the hell?* look she inclined her head slightly at Random.

"You can crash here, if you want," Jace offered. "I think half of your high school wardrobe is still in the corner room."

Random brightened. "Yeah? Maybe I will."

"If you stay," Siren prompted, "I will let you make me breakfast in the morning."

A hint of Random's usual smile returned. "Clearly I can't turn down such a generous offer from a beautiful woman."

"Clearly," Jace said dryly.

"Well, I'm beat." Siren gave a long, exaggerated stretch. "And unlike some people here, I have to go to work in the morning."

She and Jace said their goodnights to Random, who was slowly sinking back into a zombie-like state, and though she didn't like it, she figured he was better off being here in that state than being at home alone in it. At least, that was what she hoped. She didn't have a great deal of experience in the kind of emotional suffering he was going through, but she'd suffered a different, though equally painful, kind of loss. Enough to know that being around other people could keep the bad thoughts at bay.

Jace insisted on walking her to her room, even though it was a whole ten feet down the hall from his own. Then he stood in her doorway, like he was standing on her front porch after a first date, and kissed her.

"Goodnight, Siren."

"Goodnight, Jace."

And because she liked her little fantasy, she stood in her open doorway and watched him until he disappeared into his own room. Inside hers, she crawled into the absurdly large, fluffy bed, and wondered how the hell she was supposed to sleep knowing he was one room over from her.

She bet he looked incredibly sexy with sleep-mussed hair. Did he sleep naked? Did he—

No, she told herself firmly. *Sleep. You have had a long day, and you are going to sleep, and you are not going to have sexy dreams about Jace Winters.*

She fell asleep, and though she did dream, those dreams were quite the opposite of sexy.

CHAPTER

TWENTY-THREE

Siren's first morning of "training" essentially boiled down to meditation, wherein she tried unsuccessfully to "feel" her Aspect inside her. After an hour of her mind wandering all over the place, she'd finally felt the faintest flicker that could have been her Aspect, or could have been indigestion, when her phone alarmed, reminding her she had a job to go to.

She tried again on the drive to Hand Me Down Sound, but if she *had* felt anything, it was gone now.

Jace parked and they walked up. The darkness behind the glass storefront made her stop.

"Everything okay?"

"No. Hank always opens the store. It shouldn't be dark."

She tried to fit her key into the lock, but the door swung inward at the slightest touch.

Concern punched her and she lunged forward. Jace's arm snaked around her waist and pulled her back.

"Let me go first." Aspect built around him, ready to answer his call. It frustrated Siren that she couldn't do the same, that Hank could be inside, hurt, and she couldn't summon anything to help him at will.

Jace stepped inside and flicked the lights on. After a minute, he motioned Siren inside.

"Does anything seem wrong to you? Out of place?"

The cash register was untouched and the cases of CDs and DVDs were still lined up orderly in rows. Nothing was overturned and no merchandise littered the floor to suggest a break-in.

"No, it's all—" She broke off as her gaze snagged on the northeast corner of the store where a single black door listed open an inch. The door opened onto the stairs that led to the little above-store apartment where Hank lived. It locked automatically upon closing and it was never, ever left open.

Jace followed her gaze and walked to the door. It took all of her self-restraint to let him go up first, to not run past him when they hit the landing and she saw the door to Hank's apartment hanging open. She'd never seen the inside of Hank's apartment before, but she doubted the man whose khakis were always starched and pressed, whose hair was always perfectly combed, lived in a mess like *this*.

Clothes and paper were strewn about the floor. A teacup had spilled over on its side, dripping liquid down an antique coffee table. She cautiously followed Jace inside, growing bolder when she felt none of the telltale signs of the gray-eyed man's presence. She moved from the entrance into the small living area, righting the overturned teacup as she went, and saw him.

Hank sprawled on the floor, motionless. She saw no obvious sign of struggle or abuse on his body, no bleeding wounds, no bruises, and yet he lay so *still*. She watched, holding her breath, and *there*—she felt more than saw the soft rise and fall of his chest.

She lunged forward and, once again, Jace caught her around the waist. She fought him, forgetting *why* he held her back, forgetting everything as the desperate need to get to Hank overwhelmed her. Aspect brimmed inside her, spilling out to fill the empty channels in her body. Hank was hurt and she needed to help him, like she'd needed to help the dog the other night and—

Remembering what had happened with Percy broke through the primal part of her brain to the logical side. There was something *wrong* hovering over Hank. The same something she'd felt around Percy when she'd followed him into the woods. Dark Aspect. If she touched Hank, what would happen to her this time?

"Back with me, then?" Jace asked when she quit struggling.

She nodded and he let her go. Her Aspect still flowed inside her. It tingled the edges of her fingertips and she held on to it tentatively, willing it to stay.

"It would seem," he said, "that you have an injury trigger. Does this happen to you a lot?"

"No. Not before Percy." A memory rose to put lie to the words, reminded her of that first night her power had torn out of her. After the nightmare hounds had exploded, her power had turned to the body at her feet and sunk itself in to flesh and bone, trying to fix something that couldn't be fixed. Because *death* couldn't be fixed.

At the time, she hadn't understood what she'd been trying to do—what her power had been trying to do. She'd just been terrified and grief-stricken. It was worse, now, knowing that maybe she *could* have fixed it, if she'd reacted quicker, if her terror had cracked the cage inside her even a minute earlier.

She forced the thought out of her mind. It might be true, but it wouldn't fix anything now. It wouldn't help Hank. "Is he going to be okay?"

"I'm sorry, Siren, I don't think—"

"He isn't dead. I can feel it."

Jace was quiet for a moment, then, "Without touching him, you'd have a better chance at finding out if he's okay than I would."

"What do I do?"

"Don't think about it, just feel. How do you know he's alive?"

"I can feel his breathing."

"Okay, good. Focus on that."

She did. She closed her eyes and felt the rise and fall of his chest. "Okay."

"Now focus past that. What else do you notice? Can you feel his heartbeat?"

She listened, strained, felt the odd sensation of slipping out of herself and into someone else. Her breath changed, gained a regularity that was not her own. Then came the weak but steady heartbeat behind a chest that was not hers and the feeling of being trapped in a body that couldn't move. She felt heat next, sweaty and achy, like the week she'd spent holed up with the flu in that shitty apartment in Birmingham. Beyond that there was nothing, no thought, no panic, just the blank, quiet space of a dreamless sleep.

"I think he's in a coma." She wasn't a medical professional by any stretch of the imagination, but it *felt* right. "He has a fever, but I can't sense anything else wrong." She hesitated. "Do we take him to a hospital?"

"They won't know what to do for him. Call Random. Tell him everything."

She paused, her finger hovering over the "Call" button. "What are you going to do?"

"I'm going to call the Council."

CHAPTER

TWENTY-FOUR

Random arrived first, pulling up to the curb on a sleek black motorcycle. Siren had been keeping a lookout since she'd called him. The Council had told Jace they were "sending someone." Looking out the window was better than looking at Hank, at the way he just sprawled unmoving on the floor. Her throat felt constricted, something hollow and hurt inside her like it hadn't since before she'd started running.

She cared, Siren realized. Cared what happened to Hank. He was crotchety and set in his ways, but he was also sweet and patient. He'd given her the closest thing to a family she'd had in a very long time, and knowing that he was hurt—that he was hurt because of *her*—cut a place deep inside her she had thought long-ago armored over.

Jace was downstairs waiting for the Council and, she suspected, guarding the entrance. Without another moving presence in the room, the air felt still and dead. On the other side of the window, another car pulled up, this one a sleek, silver Porsche Spyder. The driver's side door opened, and a pair of three-inch silver stilettos landed on the sidewalk, followed by a pair of black designer jeans that hugged curvy hips and thighs, a lacy silver halter top, and a long fall of silver-blonde hair.

The door opened, and Random walked in.

"Why is Meredith here?" she asked.

Random turned a long-suffering face to the heavens and imitated Siren's voice, "Thank you *so much* for coming, Random. You were the first person we called. How good of you to get here on such short notice."

Siren folded her arms over her chest. "Thank you for coming, Random. What is Meredith doing here?"

"The Council sent her. She has dual Aspects. Truthfinder and Tracker. If the trace is fresh enough, she can track the person who attacked Hank." His eyes swept over the room, lingered a moment on Hank, then returned to her. "Did you touch anything? Touch him?"

Siren shook her head. "It's all how we found it."

Siren breathed in through her nose, held it, let it out in a rush through her mouth.

"And the Dark Aspect? Can she remove it? So he'll wake up?"

"Not her area of expertise." He crouched down, studying the floor and the room as if he could see something she didn't. "Besides which, she'll need it to do her thing. The medical team will be on her heels, though. If they can help him, they will."

Siren swallowed, her throat tight. "And if they can't?"

What he might have answered, Siren never found out. The door opened again, and Jace and Meredith walked through.

"Did you touch anything?" Meredith demanded.

Siren shook her head.

"Good." Meredith crouched next to Hank and splayed her fingers on the floor beside him. Power built in the air around her and her eyes slipped out of focus.

Meredith's poise, her elegant beauty, had made Siren think of her as a fragile, perhaps useless thing. As Aspect slicked the woman in waves, Siren realized she had been completely, utterly wrong. Meredith was beautiful, certainly, but at the moment that beauty shone in the strength of the Aspect that wove around her.

The determination in the lines of her face as she concentrated power made Siren think that the search was not going well, but Meredith dug in her heels, resolved, and Siren couldn't help but admire that. Couldn't help but admire it so much she felt her own Aspect surface and stretch out across the room to dance across Meredith's skin.

Siren felt, as she often did when her Aspect took this urge, a light feedback of Meredith's emotions. She felt the obvious things first—Meredith's focus on the task at hand, and the woman's genuine concern for Hank—but underneath that, behind the mask of perfect beauty, the woman was tired. More than tired. Her body spoke of a bone-deep exhaustion born not of recent irritations but of months of sleeplessness and chronic stress.

What did Meredith have to be stressed about?

Siren's Aspect dug deeper, slipped past the surface. It found a pain so systemic that Meredith's body remembered it and remained constantly tense, on guard for its return. Siren recoiled, bile rising in her throat. She'd never, *never* felt anything like that in another person.

The patterns and traces of harm were etched into every twist and turn of Meredith's body, consistent with years of abuse, and yet it had left no exterior trace on her body. No scars marred the flawless pale skin, no bones showed the crookedness of repeated breaks, save for her slightly crooked nose. From the outside, she looked as if her life had been a shelter from disaster, as if she'd never so much as suffered a scrape from falling off a bicycle as a child.

The memories beneath Meredith's skin told Siren a different story, one she was so engrossed in she did not realize at first when Meredith spoke.

"They Scoured the scene. Did a hell of a job, too, I can't read anything." She stood, pulling her Aspect back in. As she did, her eyes refocused, snapping to Siren with ice in their depths. "What the hell are you doing?"

Siren was too horrified by what she'd found to heed the warning in Meredith's voice. "Who did that to you?"

Meredith went from cold to glacial. "I don't know what you're talking about."

Random and Jace both looked from Meredith to Siren, twin expressions of confusion on their faces.

"Someone hurt you," Siren insisted. "Are they—"

"Shut. Up." Meredith's voice was like a blizzard in June, ice sizzling in the height of summer.

"But I—"

"I said *shut up*. You don't have a clue what you're talking about." She took a step back, only the slightest tremble in her posture revealing how rattled she was. "The medical team will be here soon. There's nothing more that I can do."

"Meredith?" Jace stepped toward her, but she slipped past him.

"Leave me the hell alone. All of you," she snapped and walked out.

Siren knew she should leave her alone. It was none of her business. But she'd *felt* Meredith's pain. Only a fraction of it, but a fraction had been horrible enough. The most recent scar was six months old, but that only meant that whoever had hurt Meredith had been gone recently. What if they came back? What if she needed help?

Siren ran after her. Jace tried to grab her arm but she dodged past him. She bounded down the stairs, ignoring Jace and Random as they yelled after her, and burst out the front door. Seeing that Meredith had already slipped behind the wheel of the Porsche, Siren sped up. She slid around the front of the car and jumped into the passenger seat, grateful for the retracted convertible top. The car moved before her ass fully landed in the seat, and she clutched to any handhold she could find as Meredith roared through gears and the speedometer edged past sixty before they even hit the end of the block.

Siren couldn't bring herself to look at the speedometer after that, the scenery whizzing by too fast for her to follow. Meredith turned to stare at her.

"Please watch the road," Siren managed to squeak out.

A slow smile spread across Meredith's face, and she took a curve at who-knew-what speed without ever taking her gaze off Siren.

"You're going twice the speed limit." Siren had finally caved and checked the speedometer again.

"I had no idea you were so concerned with rules, considering you haven't even made it twenty-four hours without breaking the ones the Council laid down for you."

"I haven't—" Oh. But she had. Jace yelling after her, *running* after her. She wasn't supposed to be out and about without him, and she'd left him behind. There was no way his old truck was catching up with *this* thing, even if he knew where they were going, which he didn't. Siren didn't even know where they were going. She'd just impulsively jumped in the car. Maybe Meredith wouldn't tell the Council. Of course, considering she looked furious and sort of had every right to be, the odds were not in Siren's favor.

"I'm sorry."

Meredith snorted. "For what?"

"I shouldn't have said what I did in front of everyone. I didn't mean to, I just—"

"You shouldn't have been digging around inside me in the first place."

Siren winced. "I didn't exactly mean to do that either. It just...happened."

Meredith didn't respond. She pushed the car through its final gears, and the speedometer edged toward triple digits. Siren managed to take her hands off of their death grip on the car's seat to fasten her seatbelt, then went back to clutching at the car's interior for dear life. She had put herself in this car. She would sit here in silence and pray she didn't die.

The world turned gritty and rural outside the car window

and then Meredith angled the car into the gravel parking lot of an enormous dive bar, arriving in a thundercloud of dirt and sliding tires. Siren thought for sure they must be turning around, until the car slipped into a parking space and Meredith flicked off the ignition, opening her door.

"What are we doing here?" Siren asked.

"Getting a drink."

"Umm." Siren stepped out of the car and looked at their surroundings. They were not ones that necessarily made *her* uncomfortable. She had been in too many dive bars to count, *lived* near too many of them, but glamorous, high-society Meredith? "I don't think you want to leave a car like this here."

"A car like what?"

Siren turned to gesture at the Porsche and found herself staring at a late-nineties Toyota Camry, the paint job faded and the passenger-side fender slightly dented. *Huh.* "Neat trick."

"Yes, I like to think so."

The bar was a converted warehouse with a giant neon sign proclaiming it to be Savado's. Siren followed Meredith inside, past a cadre of men in flannel shirts playing pool, past the giggling bottle blonde in faux-biker clothes who laughed as her game of darts went badly—and intentionally, Siren suspected— astray as her date, in serious biker gear, attempted to "educate" her on the finer points of dart-throwing.

Meredith settled onto a barstool as if she'd spent her entire life in rough-and-tumble bars as opposed to country clubs, and Siren couldn't help but envy the woman her chameleon nature.

Siren blended in because she had to and, *because* she had to, there were certain places she didn't go because she *wasn't* good at blending into them. Meredith looked like she could go anywhere, be anyone, and be as comfortable in one skin as in another.

"Double gin and tonic," she told the barkeeper, "and a shot of tequila." Meredith glanced at Siren. "Better make it two."

"Of each?" The barkeeper looked to be in his early thirties

with a linebacker's frame and a wealth of red hair that just brushed the tops of his shoulders.

"Yeah."

The barkeeper returned with a speed Siren herself had never been served with in a bar— granted it *was* eleven in the morning, so there weren't many customers—and placed a gin and tonic and a shot of tequila in front of each of them.

"Anything else?"

Meredith shook her head, waving him off with a style only she could manage without being offensive.

"I don't think—" Siren began.

"If you're sitting here with me, you're drinking." Meredith picked up her shot glass and raised it.

Siren eyed her own tequila shot. *In for a penny, in for a pound.* She raised the shot glass, clinked it to Meredith's, and tossed the whole mess down. She chased it with a swallow of the gin and tonic. Liquid fire burned down her throat, hit her stomach, and spread through her veins.

She hadn't done tequila shots since she'd spent the entirety of her eighteenth year and its attendant fake ID pretending to be twenty-one and making Very Bad Life Decisions. She'd thought, being on the run with no end in sight, that the decisions she made didn't matter. If she drank until she couldn't remember her own name, then that was a relief, because who was she, anyway?

But she could only wake up in unfamiliar surroundings with unfamiliar people so many times before she'd realized it didn't fill the hollow places inside her.

Emboldened by tequila, Siren turned her full attention on Meredith, though the woman didn't meet her gaze. "The person who did that to you...do you need help?"

Meredith laughed. "If I did, why ever would you want to help me?"

"No one deserves to be treated like that."

"How would you know?" Meredith swirled the ice in her

glass, the gin and tonic already halfway gone. "Maybe I've done terrible things."

"Everyone's done terrible things at some point or another. It's why you do them that matters."

"Is that how you justify it?"

"Justify what?"

Meredith laughed again. "I didn't miss your little evasion to the Council's question yesterday."

Siren was beginning to wonder if anyone had. "Why didn't you say anything?"

Meredith shrugged. "Maybe I felt guilty."

"For what?"

Meredith waved at the half-moon circles her nails had left on Siren's hand. "I saw a different side of myself yesterday. Maybe I didn't much care for it." She downed the rest of her drink in two long swallows.

Siren wrapped her hands around her own drink, wishing it were something hot and comforting and nonalcoholic. Trickles of sweat ran down the sides of the glass and slicked against her skin.

"I know it's not really my business," Siren began, "and I won't ask you much more, but your newest wounds are six months old. The person who…" She trailed off, not sure what to say, not sure if she wasn't just making things worse.

"Brutalized me?" Meredith offered. She motioned to the bartender for a second round of gin.

"Yeah. Is there any chance they're coming back?"

What the hell did she think she was going to do for this woman? *I can try. I can do* something.

Meredith waited for her new drink to arrive and knocked half of it back. Finally, she said, "They're dead."

"Did you kill them?"

"You're very blunt." Meredith considered her, blue eyes fringed with ice. "It's oddly refreshing. No, I didn't kill them. Though I wish to gods I'd had the guts."

Siren felt an odd relief at the news. She'd felt many things after people she'd been around had died: panic, anger, sadness, even merely the cessation of fear. She'd never felt relief. She decided it was a shitty world where she'd seen enough death to have varied reactions to it, a shittier one where a woman was abused by her own family. Had to be family, because some of the scars inside Meredith were old enough that whoever hurt her had started when she was very young.

Though it hadn't been her intention, Siren suspected it was her silence that got Meredith talking again.

"Do you know how I ended things with Jace?"

Not the question Siren had been expecting. Not even on the *list* of questions she'd been expecting. She nodded.

A tight smile stretched across Meredith's lips. "Who told you?"

"Random."

"Ah. No doubt the most flattering version, then." The bartender refreshed Meredith's drink again—Siren sincerely hoped he wasn't still doubling the gin—and she took a reflexive drink. "You must think me quite shallow."

"At first, I did." She was beginning to see the woman went to a lot of trouble to make people see just another beautiful, self-involved heiress when they looked at her. Underneath that, she was something different. "But I don't think Jace would have cared for someone who wasn't more than that."

A noncommittal noise in the back of Meredith's throat. Another swallow of gin.

"You should talk to him. Jace." Siren felt just as surprised she'd made that pronouncement as Meredith looked at hearing it.

"This is not the stay-away-from-my-man speech I was expecting."

Siren wrinkled her nose. "I never really saw the point in those. Obviously I'm insanely jealous any time the two of you are in the same room together but...I'm assuming you have a reason for what you did to him? And I'm assuming it wasn't the one you gave him?"

Meredith tipped her head slightly in a nod.

"Then I think he deserves to hear it."

"And you aren't concerned that if I smooth over the predominant thing that destroyed our relationship, he might come back to me?"

Of course she was concerned. She'd be an idiot not to be, but… "Do you actually want him back?"

Meredith swirled the ice in her glass. "I don't know."

It wasn't the flat-out denial Siren had been hoping for and it must have showed on her face.

"Still think I should talk to him?"

"Yes," Siren moaned.

"You don't make any sense to me."

"I don't make any sense to *me*. I just—I don't want to be with someone who'd rather be with someone else."

"How heroically logical of you. But it's a wasted effort. He doesn't want to talk to me, and I can't blame him."

"Have you tried calling him and asking?"

"Asking what?"

"To talk to him."

"*Ask* to talk to him?" Meredith's lips twisted into such an expression of perplexity that Siren had to turn laughter into a choking cough. She was willing to bet Meredith had never had to ask for something she didn't already know would be given to her.

"Ask," Siren repeated. "Call him, tell him why you want to talk to him, and ask him to hear you out."

"And you think that will work?"

"I do."

"All right." Meredith pulled out her phone. Siren snatched it out of her hands before she could dial anything.

"Maybe try calling when you're sober?"

"You take all the fun out of everything. I can see why Jace

likes you." She hiccupped. "He always was *way* too serious for his own good."

Right. Boring and responsible. That's me. Siren pocketed Meredith's phone. "You will thank me later."

"Don't hold your breath."

The long, wailing country song that had been playing faded out in favor of something upbeat that Siren didn't recognize, but Meredith obviously did.

"I *love* this song. We should dance." Meredith looked positively aglow at the idea, and it made her seem younger, happier.

Siren shook her head vehemently. She already didn't like the way one of the guys playing pool—a six-foot-something man wearing a backwards baseball cap—kept glancing at Meredith, and while a woman *ought* to be able to dance in a bar in the middle of the day if she damn well felt like it, Siren knew exactly how the men would view it.

"Come *on*." Meredith's voice took on a whiny note, and the attendant rise in volume told Siren the alcohol was starting to kick in, full force. "You're no fun. I haven't had fun in a long time, and I'd really, really like to have fun."

"I can show you how to have fun, baby," Baseball Cap called, much to the amusement of his friends.

The barkeeper glanced up sharply, a hard line pulling at the corners of his lips.

Siren was going to ignore the guy—ignoring was usually better, easier—but then Baseball Cap was walking over.

"Hey, baby, you wanted to dance?"

"She doesn't want to dance with you," Siren snapped.

He laughed, but there was nothing happy about it. "Wasn't asking you, was I? What do you say, baby?"

Meredith was looking at the floor, her shoulders hunched and trembling. "I don't want to dance," she said softly, all of her earlier excitement gone.

"You heard her, Craig, the lady doesn't want to dance." The barkeeper's voice was relaxed, but a muscle ticked along his jaw, and the way his hands moved as they polished a glass spoke of a preparedness for violence.

Craig flashed the barkeeper a smile that was all teeth. "No problem, Matt. Just askin'." He walked away, and only when he had picked up his pool stick and was once again focused on the game did Siren's shoulders relax.

"I think maybe we should go."

"Yeah." Meredith nodded, coming out of her haze, and fumbled for the clutch in her hands. She pulled a one-hundred-dollar bill out, dropped it on the counter, slid off her stool, and headed for the door. Siren scrambled after, ready to catch her when the inevitable stumble happened, but Meredith walked as if intoxication and four-inch heels went together like bread and butter.

Meredith fumbled for her keys, and Siren realized they had another, bigger problem.

"You can't drive."

Meredith paused, then nodded and thrust the keys at Siren. "You're right. You drive."

"I can't drive."

"You had one drink like an hour ago. You're fine."

More like twenty minutes ago. "No, I mean I don't know how."

Meredith's meticulously plucked eyebrows drew together. "Don't know how to drive stick?"

"Don't know how to drive at all." Technically speaking, she'd had her learner's permit at fifteen and driven under supervision for a year, but she'd never gotten her official license and hadn't been behind the wheel in over six years, regardless. "I can call Jace, or Random..." Those were literally the only two phone numbers she had.

"No, definitely not. Jace will be all concerned and disapproving, and Random will spend the next two years laughing at me. You want your unsupervised excursion kept between us, you don't call them."

Siren still had Meredith's phone, and she looked down at it.

"Say, you're a normal on-the-grid person with phones and credit cards. You have Uber, right?"

Meredith looked horrified. "You want me to climb into some random person's car? Ugh, no. Give me the phone, I'll call my driver." She scrolled to a contact, hit call, and said nothing but the name of the bar before hanging up.

"You have a driver? You couldn't have led with that?"

"I hate being driven around like I'm a child."

The door to the bar swung open and Baseball Cap—Craig, she supposed—stepped out.

Siren's hackles went up. Despite Meredith's refusal of him and the bartender's not-so-subtle warnings, Craig was walking over to them.

"If you need a ride, baby, I can give you one." The way he said the word made it clear just what sort of "ride" he had in mind. He reached for her but Siren slapped his hand away, anger burning in her veins.

"She doesn't need a ride. She doesn't want to dance with you, she doesn't want to *talk* to you."

Craig's lips twisted into a sneer as he looked between Siren and Meredith.

"Oh, I see what's going on here. You her bitch or something?"

Right, because that was the *only* possible explanation for a woman not wanting him slobbering all over her.

The sneer went away, replaced by an unpleasant desire as he looked Siren over. "Course, I could take you *both* for a ride."

"Go fuck yourself," Siren said, ignoring years of experience that told her antagonizing was never the best option. "Neither of us is going to."

"You fucking cunt."

He grabbed her wrist in a bruising grip and jerked her forward. Aspect poured out of her, rushing down her veins in an uncontrolled torrent.

Craig stumbled back—*would* have stumbled back—only his

hand was stuck to her like he had his hand on a live power line, trapped in the current. He sagged to his knees, coughing and wheezing. His free hand clutched at his throat as if he couldn't breathe.

Siren's hand tightened on his wrist and his wheezing intensified. His eyes bulged, his face flushed and angry. A faraway part of her said that she should pull her hand free and let him go, let him run. But her heart pounded in her ears, the world was cast in the red sheen of her anger, and it felt *good* to tighten her grip, to let her Aspect slip inside and crush the finger bones that gripped her.

He cried out as they broke, and that—that felt good, too.

In the distance someone called her name, the voice vaguely familiar, almost panicked and yet still elegant.

Meredith.

A hand tugged her arm, trying to break her contact with the man, but Siren didn't budge. She'd seen the look in his eyes, and she knew what it meant. He would have taken what he'd wanted from Meredith if given the chance, and it wouldn't have mattered what she said. It happened all the time. They got away with it all the time. But it wasn't happening *now*. He wasn't getting away with it *now*.

Her Aspect warmed, and she knew that if she wanted, if she *asked*, it would crush his heart as easily as it had crushed his bones. She let it slide inside him, deeper, refusing to feel the feedback of his emotions. Her Aspect curled around his frantically beating heart and gave a single, gentle squeeze.

"*Siren.* Hells, we're in *Seclusion.* You kill him here, there's no hiding from the Council."

The words gave her pause. She should heed them, she knew, she really should. She just wanted to hear him scream one more time. Just one more flicker of his heartbeat, one more moment of terror, and then maybe, if he begged, she'd let him live.

Something hard hit Siren on the left side of her face and the surprise of the impact made her drop the man's wrist. He didn't linger. He scrambled to his feet and ran away as fast as his legs would carry him. He jumped into an old lifted Suburban and peeled out of the gravel parking lot.

She turned to find Meredith cradling her right hand, her knuckles red, and sense rushed back into Siren. Meredith had punched her. Because she'd been about to...gods, not again. Her stomach tumbled over, threatening to reject the earlier tequila shot. Siren forced it down. She would not throw up. She would not admit how close she had come to ending someone's life again, or how easy, how good, it had felt to hold his heart in the palm of her magic and consider taking it all away.

She made herself meet Meredith's gaze, and couldn't read whatever was in the woman's ice-blue eyes.

"Thank you," Siren said.

"No problem. You're...kind of scary, you know that?"

"Are you going to report me to the Council?" How could she have been so completely, utterly stupid? She'd just used her Aspect for all the things she wasn't supposed to use it for, right in front of someone who worked for the Council and probably hated her.

"After what he was going to do? No. Just...maybe try meditation or something."

A smile pulled at the corners of Siren's lips. "I'll think about it."

A black town car pulled into the parking lot and the driver jumped out to open the back door. "Let's get out of this place," Meredith said.

CHAPTER
TWENTY-FIVE

After seeing Meredith safely inside the monstrous white confection she called a house, Siren let the woman's driver take her back to Hank's because she didn't have any other means of transportation. She found Jace and Random sitting on the lowered tailgate of Jace's truck. Random leaned on the edge of the bed, his hair artfully disheveled while he stared out into the distance, looking once again like he belonged on the cover of a romance novel. Jace stared, equally moodily, at the ground, his legs swinging idly back and forth. He stopped when he looked up and saw her.

He slid off the truck, something angry tugging at his lips as he came to her and put his hands on her shoulders. His touch was gentle whereas the look on his face was not.

"Are you okay?"

Siren frowned. "Why wouldn't I be okay?"

"You pissed off Meredith in an exchange I still don't understand and then you ran after her. Without me, I might add."

"I'm sorry. I wasn't thinking."

"Obviously. Is she going to cause you problems over it?"

"No. We…talked."

"About?"

"Stuff. Look, umm, I know it's not my place, but she's going to call to see if you she can talk to you. I think you should."

A muscle ticked along his jaw. "You're right. It's really not your place."

"I'm sorry." She took a step back and looked away from him. "I know it's none of my business."

He let out a long breath. "It's fine." After a moment, he reached out and tugged her to him. "Do you want to tell me *why* you think I should talk to my ex? You know you're supposed to discourage that, right?"

She hesitated, not wanting to tell Meredith's story—especially since she didn't really know it. "I think it would be good for both of you. And I don't have anything to worry about. Right?"

A throat cleared before she could get an answer to that question, and Random walked up.

"Would you care to tell me why Aunt Ella just called to say you're late for tea?"

Tea. Right. She'd forgotten all about tea.

"I thought I specifically said *not* to go to tea with Aunt Ella?" Jace asked.

"I didn't exactly say *yes*, she just said we should have it and then told me when to show up. There wasn't time to say no."

"Sounds like Aunt Ella," Random conceded. "Very well, I'll take her over."

"But I—" Jace began.

"Have a lot of paperwork to fill out at Council headquarters. Aunt Ella asked me to bring her. Something about me never stopping by anymore. So enjoy your break from shadowing duty and don't make a fuss. Let's go, sweetheart."

"Wait. Hank." Siren's stomach twisted into knots. "Is he okay?"

"He's stable," Jace said. "Whether or not he wakes up, I'm afraid, is up to him."

"Where is he?"

"At a Council medical facility. I can take you to visit later, if you want."

Siren nodded. She did want. "Did they find anything on who did this?"

Jace shook his head. "When Meredith said they Scoured the place...a Scouring burns up all traces of a caster's Aspect. Whoever did this covered their tracks well. They'll keep looking, but..."

But they won't find anything. She shouldn't be surprised. Had she really thought some almighty Council was going to swoop in and solve the problem she'd been running from her entire adult life? The world didn't work that way.

"So about this tea thing. If it's such a problem, can I just cancel?"

The horrified look on Jace's face was outdone only by Random's.

"No," they said in unison.

"You don't *cancel* on Aunt Ella." Random's face blanched of color, only the natural caramel of his skin keeping it from looking like freshly fallen snow. "No one does that."

"Well, Dad did. Once." Jace shivered. "He didn't sleep for a week."

"On that cheerful note, maybe we should go?"

"Call me when you're finished at Aunt Ella's and I'll pick you up." Jace leaned over and kissed her, a quick brush of the lips, like he'd been casually kissing her goodbye their entire lives.

Siren watched him walk back to his truck and only resisted the urge to put her fingertips to her lips because Random stood beside her.

"You're blushing."

"Am not," Siren retorted, but she could feel the heat in her cheeks as she followed Random over to the motorcycle parked at the curb, a sleek black Honda Fury.

Random picked his helmet up, looked from it to her. "Looks

like you're going to need…" A second helmet, flame red and metallic, popped into his hand out of nowhere.

Siren stared at it as he plunked it into her hands. "Do you get whatever you want?"

"Alas, no. Since my fourth birthday, all I've truly wanted was a bright pink unicorn." He swung a leg over the bike. "Sadly, one hasn't shown up yet."

"My heart bleeds for you." Siren worked her way into the helmet and slid onto the back of the bike, putting her feet where Random instructed.

Random brought the engine to life, and as the motorcycle revved beneath her, Siren couldn't help playing the conversation with Meredith back in her head. It wasn't her business. It really wasn't, but, "Hey, Random? Did anyone in Meredith's family die recently?"

"Her mother passed away."

"How long ago?"

She felt him frown. "A few months ago. Why?"

"No reason." Siren secured her arms around Random's waist. "We should go, before Aunt Ella mauls me for being late or something."

Random toed the motorcycle into gear, and Siren was glad he couldn't see her face as they flew down the street. The scars she'd seen in Meredith's body, all that pain—in all likelihood her own *mother* had done that to her. It was a good thing, Siren decided, that the woman was already dead. Otherwise, she'd be far too tempted to drive to a different woman's house right now and finish what she'd started with Baseball Cap Craig.

CHAPTER

TWENTY-SIX

Siren stood in Aunt Ella's bright, sunshine-yellow kitchen while they waited for the teakettle to whistle.

"Not quite what you expected, dear?"

Siren had expected to arrive on the doorstep of a Dracula-esque castle and been greeted instead with a quaint cottage. Trellises leaned over each window, grown high with morning glories and kudzu—apparently Aunt Ella had a thing for invasive species—and cheerful flowers cascaded out of colorful pots on the front porch.

"How did you guess?"

"Everyone expects a Death Aspecter to be all doom and gloom. I tried to conform once, but the older I get, the more I don't see the point. What's life without a little color?"

Color, Aunt Ella had in abundance. The tea kettle was a soft seafoam green and a white tea tray painted with green vines waited to the side, already holding three mismatched cups. The window curtains were a soft pastel purple, the floor a mosaic of multicolored tiles. In the hands of anyone else, the room would have ended up looking like a rainbow-based disaster, but Aunt Ella had tied it all together in a way that made it look homey and cheerful, like each piece had been carefully selected for how it would interact with the whole.

"Honestly, I'm just relieved that someone lives in a normal-sized house."

The little two-bedroom cottage was comfortable, personal in a way that large houses never could be. Siren was accustomed to studios and one-bedroom apartments, and the smaller space of Aunt Ella's made her feel at home, where she hadn't realized she felt out of place before.

"It's easier to keep a small space tidy," Aunt Ella agreed, pulling the kettle off the stove and adding the tea leaves to steep. "And now that Random's moved out, I finally get to have the second bedroom entirely for my knitting projects again."

"Random grew up here?"

"He didn't mention it?" Aunt Ella tsked. "You'd think I raised him feral the way he acts. His mother, my niece, passed away when he was just a little thing, and his father was long gone before that. The boy was a hellion, mind you, and far too much for an old woman like me to keep up with, but I did my best."

Siren tried to imagine a smaller version of Random running through the cottage, terrorizing the place, and found she could imagine it quite easily.

"Speaking of my great-nephew, how is the boy? He used to visit every Sunday, but lately I can scarcely get ahold of him, and when I do, he's all glum and glower."

"I don't really know him that well, ma'am."

Aunt Ella waved her hand. "No 'ma'am', just Aunt Ella's fine, and I'd wager you've seen more of him recently than I have. It's that Winters girl, isn't it?"

"I—"

"I told him not to go getting mixed up with her. She's a good girl, mind you, but she's got emotional walls a battering ram couldn't bring down. Do me a favor and keep an eye on the boy, would you? He acts as tough as Valkyrie, but inside he's got the heart of a kitten."

Siren managed not to snort at the image of a tiny baby kitten curled up in Random's chest where his heart should be, but it was a near thing. "I'll try, ma'am—Aunt Ella."

Aunt Ella finished preparing the tea.

"Why were Jace and Random so terrified of me coming to tea?" she blurted out. Aunt Ella didn't *seem* that scary to Siren, Death Aspect or no.

Aunt Ella laughed. "They're convinced any time I invite someone over for tea it's because I have nefarious plans for meddling in their life." She gave a long-suffering sigh that was so like the one Siren had heard Random give that she understood immediately where he had learned the art.

"Really, you make one or two attempts to push people in the right direction and they start assuming you're up to no good all the time. Just because I tried to set Random up with that nice Ariel girl over oolong." She shook her head. "And if I talked Jace into planting the entire back gardens over a pot of jasmine green, well, the poor boy needed direction after Meredith tromped all over him. Physical labor is good for a broken heart, you know. It gives one plenty of time to think without being mired in self-pity."

Uh-huh. "How extensive are the back gardens?"

"Oh, three acres, give or take. And perhaps I made him replant the lilac garden twice, but the spacing really just wasn't right." Aunt Ella opened a package of shortbread cookies and artfully scattered them onto the tea tray.

Three *acres* of gardens. "How long did that take him?"

"Oh, a few months or so of constant work. He stayed here for a short time, after the fiasco with his father. I needed a gardener, and there was really no point in him finding other accommodations when there was so much work to be done."

In other words, Siren thought, *you gave him a place to stay and kept him distracted while he got his feet underneath him again.* She was beginning to have warm, fuzzy feelings toward Aunt Ella and wondered if that was dangerous for her health.

"We'll have tea on the back porch. Would you mind carrying the tray? I'm afraid my hands aren't quite as steady as they used to be."

Siren dutifully picked up the tray.

"Our other guest is already outside, and he's very excited to meet you."

That's right, she said someone else would be here. Apprehension enveloped her.

"Why would he be excited to meet *me*?"

"He was very close with your parents, dear."

They stepped out of a sliding screen door and onto a white stone patio as abundant with flowerpots as the front porch had been. A round glass-and-green-metal table rested in the center of the porch, three matching chairs scattered around it. In one of those chairs sat a man. He had dark, ebony skin and short-cropped, curly white hair, and he looked to be around Aunt Ella's age.

He wore a gray t-shirt and green cargo paints, everything about him utterly normal, save for his eyes. They were milky white, luminescent from lid to lid, no pupils in sight. The whiteness of his eyes wasn't solid, wasn't still. It swirled and shifted within the confines of his eye sockets, as if looking for something.

Siren forced herself to quit staring, because staring was *rude*, and she didn't want to offend this man. A calm sort of energy emanated from him, and the gentleness in his posture made Siren feel at ease despite having never met him before.

Aunt Ella placed the tea tray on the table, next to a gray folder. The man stood as she set it down, extending his hand. His luminescent white eyes looked out at Siren and she had the impression that he wasn't blind, but neither did he see the world quite like she and Aunt Ella did.

"Siren, it's wonderful to meet you. My name is Charles."

She shook his hand, her Aspect flaring to the surface—it was doing that more and more often, of late—and she picked up his essence, cream and cinnamon.

"Charles. You're the one who fixed my shoulders? What was that stuff?"

Charles didn't answer. His face had taken on a distant expression, as if the questions had overwhelmed him.

"Why don't we sit down and have some tea," Aunt Ella suggested, "and take things a little more slowly." She tugged Charles into a seat before taking her own, then poured tea into three cups and doled them out. "I'm afraid questions can be a bit disorienting for Oracles like Charles. It's their natural inclination to *search* for answers. It can throw them out of the here and now."

Siren took the tea cup handed to her. "I'm sorry. I didn't know."

"How could you? I should have mentioned it, but it's been a long time since I've needed to explain these things to anyone. The 'stuff,' as you so eloquently put it, was silkweb. Making it is an arduous process Oracles keep to themselves. They give it to very few people, and then typically at exorbitant prices."

"Is—" she cut off, remembering she wasn't supposed to ask questions.

"You can direct questions to *me* without disrupting him."

"You said he's an Oracle. Like, telling the future?"

"In a way, though it isn't nearly as straightforward as all that. When asked a question, they see everything related to both the question and the answer. Everything that is, and was, and every-thing that *might* be. It's extraordinarily disorienting, I'm told, and the majority of them go mad before they ever reach adult-hood. Of the ones that don't, only a few ever learn to interpret what they see to any effect. Charles is one of those few."

Siren sipped her tea—it was a lovely white jasmine, not too floral, with a creamy undertone. "Is it a branch of Aspect?"

"No. Aspect is, in simplest terminology, power a person

creates merely by existing. There are common uses that anyone with Aspect can access—wards and various other spells—and then there are specialized uses particular to an individual, such as Jace's affinity for elements, or your own for healing. An Oracle's ability is not like that. Their power is not a malleable thing that can be harnessed to a specific will. They cannot make wards or cast spells with it. It is simply a part of who they are. An extra sense, perhaps, as opposed to an extra limb. The origin of the ability is unknown to us, but there are a great many who believe it was born from a curse."

Charles reached out a slightly trembling hand and pulled his teacup to him.

"Back with us then, Charles." Aunt Ella carefully phrased it as a statement rather than a question.

He nodded, reaching for the little pitcher of cream on the tray.

"I'm sorry," Siren said. "I'm afraid I don't really know much about…any of this. You, umm, that is, Aunt Ella said you knew my parents." It was more difficult than she'd expected to keep her voice from lilting up at the end in that manner that asked a question without asking it.

He smiled and took a sip of tea, seeming more grounded after he did. "I'm sorry, too. I'm afraid I don't interact much these days. The older I get the easier it is to stay in familiar surroundings. Yes, I knew your parents. I was very fond of Mara. And John, though I knew your mother first.

"She and my own daughter grew up together. I searched for you for a long time but…" He lifted his shoulders, then let them fall. "An Oracle's visions are never precise. And there are ways to muddy our vision further. I knew you were alive, but I never could see where you went."

"Thank you. For looking. I don't—I don't know if I can hear about them, right now." She wasn't ready for charming anecdotes and nostalgic stories. She wasn't ready for her parents to come to life, to be real people that she would then have to mourn. She didn't even know what they'd looked like, save that she apparently looked like her mother.

"I understand. Their estate has been in my care since their deaths." He slid the folder she'd noticed earlier across the table. "The information you'll need to reclaim the estate is here."

Siren brushed the edges of the folder, but didn't look inside.

"Random can walk you through the legalese, dear," Aunt Ella said.

"I'd like to give you something else, but I'm afraid gifts are unwise for my kind. They tend to have unfortunate results." He and Aunt Ella exchanged a grim little smile, as if in shared remembrance of just such an unwise act.

Charles slipped an item from his cargo pockets, this one a small book, about the size of a deck of cards. Its cover was soft black cloth, the edges tipped in silver. Embossed in silver lettering across the cover were the words *Life Aspect: Its History and Methods*.

Aunt Ella let out a short bark of surprise. "Charles. You've been holding out on me. The Council's been after a copy of that book for the last century."

"What they don't know won't hurt them, Ella darling." Turning to Siren he said, "I understand Jace is teaching you about Aspect. He knows a great deal about how Aspect works, but after what Ella told me about how yours has been altered, I'm not sure the traditional instruction will be all that useful to you. This might help you at least understand your particular branch of Aspect, since there is no one living to teach it to you."

Siren reached for the book, paused with her fingertips hovering above. "But you said you can't give it to me."

"Not safely. I propose a loan, instead."

Siren leaned back in her chair, and picked up her teacup so she wouldn't be tempted to grab the book. It called to her physically, and she yearned to take hold of it.

"A loan," she repeated, working her next phrasing to avoid a direct question. "A loan would have terms."

"Indeed. You may keep the book for however long you need to read every line. Once finished, the book must be returned to me within three days' time. Upon its return, you will perform a service for me. If, for any reason, you are unable to return the book, I will come collect it."

"I would be interested to know what the service you require is."

He smiled broadly. "I assure you it is one you will have no moral qualms with. One you cannot yet perform."

Siren frowned. "But I could finish the book before I'm able to do so."

"I trust you won't do a foolish thing like that. These things tend to work out."

Aunt Ella gave Siren a sympathetic look. "Oracles. They could simply tell you what they mean, but they never do."

"If you tell people too much, you risk changing the outcome," Charles said.

"And I'm sure the fact it's more fun this way has nothing to do with it."

"A little, perhaps, but you're one to talk. You play more games than a trickster god."

"Well," Aunt Ella replied, a coquettish glint in her eyes, "a lady has to keep nimble."

Siren glanced between the two of them. Charles smiled, luminescent eyes dancing. Aunt Ella looked up at him artfully from beneath her lashes, head tilted just-so. Yes, Siren decided, they were definitely flirting.

Adorable as it was, the book's call to her had intensified to the point her skin itched with such fierceness she had to set her teacup down or she'd drop it.

"One service and I bring it back within three days of finishing it or you're allowed to come get it. That's the deal."

"That's the deal."

"Then I'll take it." She swiped the book off the table. With it in her grasp, the itching beneath her skin mercifully subsided, and she had a moment to wonder if the book had been doing it to her, or if it had been Charles. Then again, seeing the satisfied look on Aunt Ella's face, it might well have been *her*.

In the end, it didn't matter. The book was hers for the time being, and the way her Aspect flickered out from its cage in little pulses told her just how satisfied it was with that fact.

CHAPTER

TWENTY-SEVEN

"Good." Jace leaned over her shoulder. "Now add a circle here, and here."

Siren stood in the middle of the Winters' training room, a glowing mass of symbols in front of her. She'd finally managed to reliably summon her Aspect—though sometimes it still snapped back inside her like a too-taut rubber band—and it turned out that had been the easy part.

She added a small circle to the first place he'd indicated, her fingertip trailing a line of white Aspect. Making her Aspect visible was something children did, she'd learned when Random had cracked a joke about it a week ago. But since she hadn't had spell designs drilled into her brain since she could talk, she needed visibility.

"Perfect," he said, when she'd finished the second circle.

She *felt* it as that last symbol made the entire design come together, and the shielding ward blazed to life in front of her.

"I still don't see how this would be useful in a combat situa-tion," she said, letting the ward fade. "It took me five minutes to get all the details right. Even if it only took a few seconds that's plenty of time to die in."

"Drawing it is still sort of kindergarten level." He still stood behind her and his breath whispered against the outer curve of her ear.

"So what's the college graduate level?"

"Knowing the pattern well enough that you can do this." He held his hand out in front of them. Aspect pooled into it, visible for her sake, and immediately coalesced into the tangle of circles and lines that comprised the shielding ward. He formed it whole in the blink of an eye and it snapped into place around them, maybe half a second after she'd felt him call it.

"Show off," she muttered.

She felt him grin. "I'm not showing off. I'm inspiring you to greater heights."

"I have so many greater heights, you don't even know."

"Oh yeah?" His arms came around her stomach and tugged her against him, her back meeting the flat, hard wall of his chest "Like what?"

Like the things she'd tried from Charles's book. Growing a plant from seed to maturity in a span of minutes. Nicking herself and healing over the small cuts. Creating an illusion, a simulacrum, of a living thing. Magics that were instinctual to her affinity and didn't require she draw them into existence with complex symbols.

But she couldn't tell him any of that. If she did, she'd have to tell him about the book.

"Like this." She tilted her head up and kissed him.

His arms tightened briefly around her, then loosened as he spun her to face him. He took her bottom lip in his mouth and rolled it between his teeth, nipping lightly. Her hips jerked forward of their own accord and she kissed him again, harder, ran her hands up the broad muscles of his back.

His fingers teased at the slice of bare skin between her shirt and jeans, then slid underneath the fabric at her encouraging moan. His hands skated over her stomach, up her ribs to cup her breasts. The material of her bralette was far too thin to be any real barrier to sensation as his thumbs grazed over her nipples, stoking the flames inside her to bonfire levels.

His hands left her breasts to grab the hem of her shirt.

Yes, she thought, *take it off. Take* all *of it off.* She wanted him. Badly. Hadn't wanted anyone this much since—

—since Thomas.

The thought was a bucket of ice water dumped over her head. Fear and panic and regret lashed through her all at once. She put her hands on Jace's chest and shoved. They stumbled apart. Confusion spread across his face and he *looked* at her. She didn't know what he saw, but it made him straighten and take a step back.

"I'm sorry," he said. "Clearly, I misread the situation."

"No, you didn't."

His lips tightened into a thin smile. "You look terrified, Siren. I meant it when I said I'm not interested in doing anything you don't want. And if you don't want this at all, that's okay, too."

"I *do* want you. That's not the problem."

His gaze sharpened. "Did something happen to you?"

"No. At least, not the way you're thinking. Not that no one ever tried, but well" —she called up her Aspect, let it fade again — "they didn't get very far."

This news didn't seem to relax him any. "Then what is it?" he asked softly.

Her heartbeat thudded in her ears. "You don't think it's been too quiet? No attacks. Nothing."

"I don't." He looked like he wanted to reach for her, but shoved his hands into his pockets instead. "A great many powerful people know exactly who you are and what you're dealing with, now. Coming after you in the middle of all that is a very bad idea. And I don't understand what that has to do with this."

But she did. It echoed in time with her heart, one name, over and over again.

Thomas. Thomas. Thomas.

What if it ended just like Thomas all over again?

"It has to do with those things you don't know about me."

"The things you don't want to tell me?"

"Yes. I think—I think I need to. If we're going to do this, I need you to know."

Once he did, he'd likely never look at her again. Not like he had moments before, anyway, all desire and heat and like she was the only person in the world that mattered.

"Hey." He did reach out, then, and took her hand. "Whatever it is, you can trust me."

She wanted to believe that. "Can we do this somewhere else? And I'd really, really like a drink."

CHAPTER

TWENTY-EIGHT

S iren sat on Jace's bed, a glass of whiskey clutched in her hands. She'd pulled the blackout curtains in his room closed, casting the room in darkness despite the afternoon hour. She wasn't sure why she was more comfortable talking here than in her own room, except maybe for the fact that it wasn't hers. There was something comforting in how thoroughly male the room was, in the way the bed smelled of Jace.

He hadn't asked her any awkward questions, just found her the drink she'd wanted and asked her where she wanted to go. Now he looked at her expectantly and, caught in his gaze, she wanted to run.

This was a terrible idea.

"I don't really know where to start."

He settled onto the bed, his knee brushing hers. "I think the beginning is usually best."

She wanted to laugh, could only think of Lily Bart's words from *The House of Mirth*: "*Why, the beginning was in my cradle, I suppose...*"

She could only hope her fate did not end quite as tragically as Lily's.

The beginning, then.

"Before all this started, before I knew I was different, I had a boyfriend. Thomas." His name caught in her throat and she took a sip of whiskey and let it sit on her tongue, as if the spice and bite could burn the taste of the words she spoke from her mouth. She swallowed and fire trailed down her throat. "I'd been over at Thomas's the night it happened. Anne and Mark, my foster parents, said I could stay out until midnight if Thomas walked me home. It was weird, because they were usually pretty strict on late nights, but I was sixteen, it's not like I was going to argue, and Thomas didn't mind walking me."

He'd never minded anything she'd asked him, and she'd asked him for quite a lot of things when they'd first started dating, just to see if he would do them: to walk her to class, for him to carry her books, take her to see a romcom, take her out for Chinese food even though she knew he hated it. When she'd realized he *would* do them all, she'd stopped asking, had eventually discovered he was that rarest of creatures, a teenage male with sincerity and a conscience as well as hormones.

Not, of course, that he hadn't had the latter as well. But then, so had she, and things had gone well enough in that department as teenage love went. She swallowed whiskey past the tightness in her throat. He'd deserved better than what being with her had gotten him.

"He only lived a couple streets over from me, and we were maybe halfway home when they leapt out of the bushes. I thought they were dogs at first, six of them, only they weren't. They weren't skeletons, but they weren't whole, either. They didn't have any fur, and it was like their flesh had started rotting off their bodies while they were still alive." She could still picture it, ribs peeking out through putrid tatters of flesh, ragged, moth-eaten ears and their breath like rotten fruit.

"Carrion hounds," Jace said, softly.

She stumbled on and the words tumbled out of her. If she

didn't say them now, she never would. "They circled us, like they were waiting for something, and that's when I saw my stalker for the first time."

The gray-eyed man had stood ten feet away, silver glasses and black coat, looking more like a part of the night than like a human being. She'd screamed at him for help anyway, and the slow smile he'd given her, more a drawing back of lips than a smile, still haunted her dreams.

"He whistled and the hounds attacked. They went straight for Thomas. They didn't come after me at all until I tried to pull them off him. One of them grabbed my leg and pulled me away." She traced her fingers over the thick, raised scars on her ankle, remembered the pain of jagged teeth cutting into her flesh.

Remembering how that had felt was easier than remembering what she'd seen.

"They tore him apart. The way he screamed—" She broke off. She could still hear those screams, the terror in them. They haunted her dreams, but she'd never talked about it before. She felt like she was trapped in that moment again, Thomas's blood spreading across the asphalt, slicking the tips of her fingers where they dug into the street as she fought the hound's hold and tried to reach him.

She downed the rest of the whiskey, but it didn't help.

"I was so scared, and angry, and it felt like something punched a hole right through me, like everything inside me was coming apart. Then I felt this." She summoned her Aspect, let it spill through her body. "It felt so good. Like I'd spent my entire life paralyzed and now I could walk, and it was angry. Maybe even angrier than I was.

"The hounds exploded. Like the spectral harpies, but worse." She remembered chunks of rotting flesh, splinters of bone falling on her like raindrops in a thunderstorm. "My stalker didn't explode but they looked... Well, I thought they were dead.

"Thomas was. I tried to help him but—" She didn't know

how long she'd sat in the street, as she dumped power into him. She hadn't known what she was trying to do, then. She understood, now, that she'd been trying to heal him. "I didn't know what to do. I thought about calling the police, but I knew they wouldn't believe me. I ran home, snuck in through my bedroom window. I couldn't feel the power anymore, and only the wound on my ankle convinced me I wasn't entirely crazy.

"After a while I convinced myself we'd been attacked by a pack of wild dogs and I'd cracked under the stress. I could go downstairs and tell my foster parents what had happened, and the police could find Thomas and he wouldn't be dead.

"Only I heard them talking, saw them before they saw me. My stalker was in our kitchen. Anne sounded happy. She said that I was stronger than they'd thought I would be. Mark was angry that I'd gotten away, but Anne told him not to worry, that I wouldn't get far in my condition and even if I went to the police, they wouldn't believe me, and I'd be easy enough to collect from local law enforcement."

The gray-eyed man hadn't said a single word the entire time. To this day, she'd still never heard his voice.

"Anne ordered my stalker to go back out and search for me. Then they were just standing there in the kitchen, talking about me like I was some kind of investment. They said they were glad the sixteen years they'd spent raising me hadn't been a waste, and they might have pulled the short straw getting this assignment but *he* would be grateful enough, given how I'd turned out, that it would be worth it."

"He?" It was the first thing Jace had said since she started, and he asked it softly.

"They didn't say a name. I don't know who they meant. I should have left then. I know I should have, but power was spilling through me again, and I was just so *angry*."

She looked up and found Jace's gaze, because he needed to know, needed to understand. "I killed them. Both of them." She hadn't *meant* to, but the power had burst out of her again. Her foster parents hadn't exploded, like the hounds. They'd simply collapsed, and after she'd finished vomiting her insides up again she'd just left them there, taken all the money in the house she could find, packed some clothes, and ran.

"If you're waiting for judgment, I'm not going to give it."

She scraped her hair back from her face, resisting the desire to pull at it. The pain of reliving it all was fading, shuttering back inside the closed box she kept buried beneath so many other boxes in her mind. The temptation to stop talking was strong, to take his apparent willingness to accept what she'd told him without judgment. But if she didn't go on, it would always be there between them in her mind. She would always wonder if he would stay by her if he knew everything she'd done, and eventually it would destroy anything they might build.

"They aren't the only ones. It's ironic that you call my Aspect Life. Most of what I've used it for involves taking life."

So she told him. Each incident had its own box in her mind, and she carefully pulled them out, one by one. They had a theme, born of the necessity of the life she had led—under-the-radar, poor, and female. The type of life that attracted men who preyed on women without any apparent means of protection. The type of woman society and the courts did not care about.

Her association with those types of women had led to several incidents, because some of the deaths she had caused were a result of her inability not to interfere in the lives of others. She could only hear her neighbor's husband beating the woman so many times, watch the police show up when she called them and then leave without doing anything so many times, before she did something herself.

Sometimes, women had been grateful for her interference. Most of the time, they had not. In the end, it didn't matter. She'd made the choices she could live with.

"Siren, I can't blame you for the things you've done. I haven't lived your life. I haven't seen the things you've seen. I've never had to make the choices you've had to make."

"I'm not looking for blame," she said, finally. "And I'm not looking for forgiveness, either. I don't regret the things I've done. I don't like them, and I don't go looking for opportunities to do them again, but I don't regret them, either.

"I would rather have not had to do them, and if we lived in a world where courts didn't let rapists and abusers go free with pathological regularity, maybe I would feel differently—that I should have left them to legal justice. But we don't, and I don't feel differently.

"*That's* the kind of person I am. I need to know if you can accept that." She met his gaze without flinching, searching for the answer in his eyes. She needed to know, when he gave her an answer, that it was a true one.

He extracted the empty glass from her, set it on the nightstand, and took her hands. "I can." He didn't waver, didn't look away from her.

"I'm not naive enough to think the world is always a fair place. No one should have to go through the things you've gone through but, sinister Aspect users aside, people live through them every day. You did what you had to do to survive and be able to live with yourself at the end of the day. That's not just the kind of person I can accept, that's the kind of person I want."

She eyed him skeptically. "You *want* a borderline serial killer?"

He winced. "I think vigilante is probably more accurate, and that's not what I meant." He paused, looked up as if collecting his thoughts, and then back at her. "Some people live their entire lives without ever having to confront the darkest parts of themselves, the things they'll do if they're pushed far enough. They have inklings of those feelings, of what they *might* do, but they never really know.

"You do. You've confronted that part of yourself, but you didn't get lost in it. Some people might look at the things you've done, but I'm looking at the things you haven't done. I know Aspect, Siren. I know how it calls to you, especially when you're angry, or terrified. I know what it can promise, and I know what it can deliver, and I know, from what I've felt in you, that yours is capable of more than ten of the rest of us combined.

"You have enough power to do almost anything you want, but you've never tried to use it for your own gain. You use it when you have to. Even under mandatory training you aren't trying to use it. You're only trying to control it.

"The point is, I like the person you are, dark pieces and all."

She wanted to leave it there and pretend that it was only her guilt, only the fact he hadn't known everything, that had made her push him away earlier. But it wasn't.

"I've thought a lot about that night lately, Jace. The extended curfew, the condition that Thomas walk me home. You told me it would have taken sufficient trauma to make that first break in the containment around my Aspect. They waited until I had someone I cared about enough to be sufficiently motivated and then they set the dominoes up and watched them fall.

"What if that's what's happening now? What if the attacks stopped because my stalker is waiting for me to have a sufficient trigger to break the containment more?"

She couldn't say aloud what she truly meant. *What if he's waiting for me to love you, so he can take it away again?*

"Then he's made a very bad miscalculation."

"I'm serious."

"So am I. I understand why you're afraid. But Siren, I'm not sixteen, and I'm not a Null. I understand exactly what is happening here, and exactly how dangerous it is." He cupped her face in his hands. "Nothing is going to happen to me."

"But—"

He kissed her. She leaned into it and kissed him back, want and need a river coursing through her. Part of her couldn't believe she could be turned on again after everything she'd just talked about, but those were old memories, old nightmares. Jace was here, now, his warmth and touch a shield against the darkness of her past.

He pulled her closer, his hands gliding down to settle in the small of her back. His tongue brushed out, parted her lips and thrust inside. She accepted him eagerly, her tongue gliding against his as liquid heat built inside her. She wanted to drown in him, in his body, in his scent.

She shifted her legs to either side of his and climbed onto his lap, wrapped her hands behind his neck. He gripped her hips, and his thumbs brushed the exposed skin at the top of her jeans, sending flickers of heat through her.

He pulled back long enough to say, "Siren, if you don't want to—"

"I want." Judging by the glazed look in his eyes and the way his thumbs still brushed her hipbones, he did too. She kissed him again, slipped her hands beneath his shirt and trailed her fingernails up his back. She rained kisses along his jaw, up to his neck. When she reached his ear she whispered, "I want you very, very badly," and nipped his earlobe.

He took a short, sharp breath and she leaned back, tugged at the hem of his shirt. "You're wearing too many clothes."

"I could say the same thing about you."

"You first."

He pulled his shirt off in one single, fluid motion.

She ran her hands over the flat planes of his stomach, the feel of smooth skin over hard muscle heightening the delicious ache building between her legs. This was…it hit her suddenly that she hadn't done this in years. Oh, she'd had sex plenty of times, but this wasn't a quick, impersonal tryst, wasn't a one-and-done where she'd never see him again.

This *mattered*. She stared unblinking at the wall of his chest, frozen.

"Hey." His hands cupped her face, drew her gaze up to his. "Where'd you go?"

"Nowhere."

He made a noise that clearly said, *Bullshit.*

"What if I screw it all up?"

He grinned at her. "It's sex. Screwing is the entire point."

"You know what I mean."

"You're giving me too much credit. Ten percent of me is restraining the other ninety from ripping your clothes off. I'm incapable of deductive reasoning right now."

His words cut through her spiral of depressive thoughts and reminded her that she would rather be doing other things than talking.

"It's just been a while." A while since she'd bothered to have sex at all. Far, far longer since she'd been stupid enough to care about the other person. And she cared about Jace. Too much.

"Can I tell you a secret?" His thumbs stroked across her cheekbones, and when she nodded, he said, "It has been for me too."

The way he said it, the way he looked at her, told her that he understood what she'd really been trying to say. That he hadn't just told her something to make her feel better, but the truth. And that was all she needed.

She drew back and pulled off her shirt, unclasped her bra, and tossed it aside.

His eyes drank her in, hot and full of need, but he didn't pull her closer, didn't move.

"For clarity's sake, are we still talking, or—"

She settled her hands on his shoulders and ground against him in answer. The ache between her legs met the hard length of his erection where it strained against his jeans. He groaned. His hands gripped her hips and he pulled her harder against him.

His mouth closed over her breast. He licked and teased until her nipple was hard in his mouth and a tug of fierce need shot straight through her core. He came up for air, his hands trailing down her stomach to the waistband of her jeans.

"These need to go."

"Yes, please."

He stripped them off and then pressed her gently onto the mattress, kissed his way down her neck, down her stomach to the insides of her thighs and then, finally, finally, to the aching center of her need. He ran his tongue around her clit in a slow, lazy circle before he took it fully in his mouth, sucking and rolling the center of her pleasure ever-so-gently between his teeth.

She gasped and arched against him.

He made a pleased rumble in his throat and worked her harder, faster, until she felt that delicious pressure building inside her. She almost lost herself in it, but this wasn't how she wanted it the first time, and she reached down and drew him up to her.

He quirked an eyebrow at her.

She could barely get the words out, her voice a hoarse whisper. "I want you inside me when I come."

The look of pure male pleasure that lit his eyes almost drove her over the edge right then.

She fumbled for the button of his jeans and growled with impatience while he slipped off the bed to pull them off. Then he was back, the hard length of him free, and she couldn't resist the urge to reach out, to run her hand over the velvet softness of his skin.

She wanted him inside her, now.

She realized, then, that she'd forgotten one very important thing, and she froze. He caught her eyes and must have understood the frustration in them because he leaned over to open the drawer on the nightstand and pull out a condom.

At that moment, she was almost willing to believe there were benevolent gods.

She helped him roll it on, her fingers glorying in the feel of him. He settled between her legs and his shaft nudged her entrance, teasing her again. She was torn by the twin desires to rub herself along his length and to simply pull him into her. She went with the latter, wincing a little because she was tight, and he was, well, *not* small.

He stilled and waited for her to adjust, his mouth pressing kisses down her neck, along her collarbone, until she relaxed, her body grown accustomed to his presence inside her. She arched her hips against him and took him deeper. His mouth returned to hers and he kissed her as thrust inside her fully.

He pulled out, drove back in. She rocked up to meet him, matching his pace, grinding her center against the deep v of his abdominal muscles. It was good, but it wasn't the steady pressure she needed to come, no matter how amazing he felt inside her. She wanted to put her hand between her legs but some guys could be weird about that, as if they took it personally that their cock wasn't magically enough to get a woman off.

She swore he must be able to read her mind because he drew her fingers to his mouth, sucked on them, and then guided her hand to her center.

"Do you want to show me what you like?"

Fuck, yes, she did. It was beyond hot the way he leaned back, watching her, watching *them*, as she built her climax while he moved in and out of her in slow, lazy thrusts. As her pleasure grew, she moved her hips faster, demanding he increase the pace. He obliged, seating himself to the hilt with each rock of his hips until the world came apart and she shattered around him.

She clutched him to her as he gave two hard, final thrusts and emptied himself into her, the pulsing release of his cock echoing against the aftershocks of her own pleasure. He collapsed on top of her, and the feel of his weight against her, the warmth of him, made her want to do it all over again. She drank in the scent of his hair, his skin, ran her fingers along his back, exploring leisurely.

"If you keep doing that," he murmured in her ear, "we're going to be right back where we started."

"Complaining?"

"Definitely not." He rolled to his side, slipping out of her, and pulled her with him so they lay face to face. There was something terribly intense in his gaze, as if words hovered on the tip of his tongue and he was tortured by the thought of saying them. It terrified her, that look, so she ran from it, tucking her head into the crook of his neck and shoulder.

When he pulled her snug against him and rested his chin on top of her head, it was the happiest she had ever felt.

TWENTY-NINE

S pending the rest of the day lazing about in Jace's bedroom, however much Siren might have liked doing just that, was not to be. Jace's phone went off, and for a moment she thought it was ringing before she realized it was his alarm.

"Why do you have an alarm set for," she glanced at the clock, "four o'clock in the afternoon?"

"I have no idea. Oh." He turned the phone screen to her so she could see the alarm memo: *Meet Meredith at 5.*

Meredith had finally taken Siren's advice and called Jace a few days ago. Siren hadn't exactly forgotten they were going to talk, but she had forgotten it was today.

"You picked the worst day for that."

"If I'd known a beautiful woman was going to seduce me, I would have picked a different day."

"Mmm-hmm."

"Hey." He tilted her chin up. "You know you have nothing to be worried about, right?"

She sighed, propping herself up on her elbow. "I know. I *am* the one that told the two of you to talk to each other, remember?"

Now that it was actually going to happen, however, she was convinced she was ten kinds of stupid for orchestrating it. It was one thing to be logically certain that Jace didn't want Meredith. It was a completely different thing to send the man she'd just made love to off to talk to his gorgeous, impeccably dressed, wealthy ex-girlfriend.

"What are you thinking?"

She groaned and fell back on the bed. "That I'm an idiot."

"Hey, no girlfriend of mine is an idiot. Come on, get dressed. I'll take you downstairs and make you coffee."

Mmm, coffee. Possibly the only thing that could get her out of bed right now, and they did have that fancy espresso machine downstairs that Jace wasn't half-bad with. She could do it herself, but there was just something nice about having someone else make coffee for her. She was dressed and halfway across the room when his words sank in.

Jace walked over and put a hand to her forehead. "Are you okay?"

"Huh? Why wouldn't I be okay?"

"You just froze in the middle of the room and smiled like the sky split open and started raining gold."

"I'm quite certain I don't know what you mean." To prove it, she resumed her walk to the door, leaving Jace standing in the middle of the room. If her walk was a little bouncier than usual because she was battling the urge to skip, well, that was her business.

"It's because I said the 'g' word, isn't it?" he called after her.

She just laughed and called back, "Race you downstairs."

Jace caught Siren around the waist as she reached the kitchen island.

"Heavens, woman, do you ever stop running?"

"Rarely. You," she stabbed a finger at his chest, "promised me coffee."

He gave her a mock bow. "As you command."

Sitting on her favorite stool at the kitchen island a few

minutes later, sipping her latte while flipping through the newspaper and watching Jace open his mail, she realized she could see herself doing this for the rest of her life.

The thought stopped her cold. As much as she had longed for stability, for normality, there had been a part of her that had always feared if she ever got the chance at it, she would find she didn't like it, had worried that she had been running for so long that she no longer knew how to be still.

"What are you thinking about?" Jace looked up from the stack of papers and assorted other odds and ends he'd pulled out of a small shipping box.

"Nothing," she replied automatically. Her gaze caught on a paperback he had extracted from the envelope and set on the island in front of him. When she made out the title, she leapt out of the chair and grabbed it.

"How did you get this? This isn't due out for another six months." It was the next book in the Blood and Power series by JC Morden, and she had been pining for its release ever since rereading the last book that came out. She caught the words Advanced Reader Copy stamped across the bottom of the cover, along with the official release date.

"I—" Jace didn't manage another word because Siren forged ahead with the conversation.

"You know what? I don't even care. Tell me I can have it."

"You…like that series?" he asked hesitantly.

She pulled the book protectively to her chest. "It's my favorite author, so don't you dare say anything bad about it. So can I have it?"

He gave her a strange look she couldn't identify, but finally said, "If that will make you happy?"

"Great." She scooped up her latte and kissed him on the cheek. "I will be on the porch with this. Have a nice chat with Meredith." She was out of the room before he could say anything else.

~

AN HOUR and a hundred pages later, the screen door opened and Siren nearly growled at Valkyrie to *go away* so she could be alone with her book before her senses returned and she remembered she was living in Valkyrie's house. She managed, through sheer dint of will, to drag her eyes away from her novel and smile politely at the other woman.

Whatever Valkyrie had been about to say died on her lips as she caught sight of the book in Siren's hand, a frown curving the corners of her mouth.

"Is Jace making you read that drivel?"

At the word "drivel" Siren's hackles went up. "Why would Jace make me read anything? And this *drivel* saved my life. These books are the only reason I learned any control over my power at all." The only reason she had sometimes been able to drive it back into its cage when its use would have gotten her in trouble.

Valkyrie gave her a considering look. "You read these and learned to control your power based on what the characters did?"

"Yes."

A small smile tugged at the corners of Valkyrie's lips.

"What? Is that funny to you?" Siren couldn't help snapping. She had found *Blood and Power* at a particularly low point in her life on the run, and the books had made her feel more human, less *other*. If it had always seemed a little too fortuitous to Siren that the methods for control the characters used worked so well for her in real life, well, now it occurred to her that the books had probably been written by someone with Aspect.

Valkyrie's smile faded. "No. No, in fact, I find it very impressive that you managed to cull out and apply the basic principles of Aspect control from what you read in a fiction novel. What is funny, is that it seems you owe my brother your life. He wrote those."

It took a full ten seconds for Siren's brain to form actual thoughts, and another ten before she managed to speak. "Jace?" she squeaked. "*Jace* wrote these?"

Valkyrie nodded, tapped her fingers to where "JC Morden" was stamped on the cover. "Jace Christopher. Morden was our mother's maiden name." Valkyrie looked Siren over, as if searching for some minute expression she was expecting to find. "You really didn't know they were his?"

Siren shook her head. Thinking of how she'd demanded the book from him and then threatened him should he disparage it filled her with mortification. Suddenly his comment about freelancing and all those hours typing away at his laptop for "work" made sense.

"I don't think I'd have managed to speak to him, if I knew." Gods, this was embarrassing. Best to stop thinking about it. Definitely best to stop *talking* about it. "Did you, uh, need anything else?"

"I just came to tell you I'm heading out for a few hours. You know the drill?"

Siren counted off on her fingers. "No leaving the estate, no using Aspect, and no touching the shiny weapons." Valkyrie guarded her weapons trove like a dragon guarded its hoard, and she was terrified of anyone leaving so much as a smudged fingerprint on her precious implements of death.

"The Council has two people stationed at the gate and two at the front door." After the attack outside of Target, they'd grudgingly agreed to supply security if neither Jace nor Valkyrie could be home with her. "I won't exactly be available, so if you need anything—"

"Call Jace or Random," Siren finished. Siren had only been left entirely alone twice, but twice was enough for Valkyrie to drill the laws of Siren's new existence into her brain. Every time Valkyrie went out, she was "not exactly available," and it made Siren wonder just what the woman got up to.

Siren suspected it had something to do with Valkyrie's and

Jace's search for their father, only Jace said he'd found exactly nothing on Elijah Winters's disappearance since he'd gotten here. Which made Siren further suspect that, whatever it was, Valkyrie didn't want to tell Jace about it for some reason.

Not my business, she reminded herself. "Have a nice time."

Valkyrie grunted something that could have been considered a reply and left, leaving Siren alone with a softly snoring Percy. Honestly, the dog spent half its life asleep.

Siren stared at the book in dismay. How was she going to *look* at Jace when he got back? Much less speak? Much less all the other fun things they'd just started doing together?

She sighed and, because books always made her feel better when real life was difficult, plopped back into her patio chair and started reading again. Perhaps she would just pummel Jace when he got back, and then everything could go back to normal.

CHAPTER

THIRTY

Siren dropped the paperback onto the kitchen counter along with Charles's book and turned her attention to the espresso machine. Despite her noble intentions, focusing on the novel to the exclusion of its author had proved fruitless, and she'd given up the pretense after about fifteen minutes. She'd tried to move on to Charles's book after, but she couldn't focus on it, either.

Percy gently butted his head against her leg, then sat down and gazed adoringly up at her, his chocolate-brown eyes filled with puppy hope. Siren reached for the bag of dog bones on the counter, retrieved one and held it out to him. He took the bone daintily, like a lady accepting a cup of tea, walked three paces away, turned in a circle and laid down, bone held carefully between his paws, and proceeded to gnaw on it with delicate vigor.

Siren shook her head and returned her attention to the espresso machine, wishing her own mood were as easily improved as Percy's. When the doorbell rang, it jolted her enough she sloshed half her newly made latte out of the cup, scalding the back of her hand. She set the cup down then grabbed a towel to dry her hands.

Maybe it was the Council's security? Had to be, because the callbox for the gate had never rung through to the house. Only they'd never approached her the other times she'd been alone here, just lurked outside, silently doing their jobs.

She was thinking of an exit strategy even before the doorbell rang a second time, more insistently, a double-push of the button interrupting the bell tone, making it start all over again. Panic teased at her spine, cold tendrils of it prodding and pushing.

Running on foot was stupid. The estate was remote. No one would hear her screaming for help, and she would be caught before she ran very far. She put her chances at successfully hiding in the house up there with running. If she didn't give herself away, Percy no doubt would.

Percy. She needed to get *him* out too, somewhere far away, somewhere safe. Maybe she was being paranoid. But in her bones, she didn't believe it, and safer was better. If she was wrong, if she left and no one followed her, she could always come back.

Her gaze snagged on the key hooks on the far wall. Jace's and Valkyrie's keys were gone, but another pair remained. Another car in the garage? Their father's, perhaps. She hadn't driven in years, had barely driven at all even then, but it wasn't that hard, right? Put the car in drive, push the gas pedal. She crept forward, feet placed gently to avoid sound, and silently pulled the keys from the hook.

She walked backward, her gaze trained on the kitchen entrance, past which lay the foyer and the front door. She motioned for Percy and he came, the click of his claws on the tile sounding far too loud. She told herself to calm down. All she had to do was make it down the short back hallway off the kitchen, through the door into the garage.

Garage. Car. Safety.

The explosion shook the house like an earthquake and sent her sprawling. The sound of buzzing flies filled her ears, followed by a series of low, keening cries.

Carrion hounds.

The gray-eyed man appeared in the doorway like some macabre apparition straight out of her nightmares, splintered wood dusting his long coat. Four hounds flanked him, their ribs exposed, bits of flesh sticking to the white hulls, a putrid stench emanating from their slavering mouths.

It took less than a breath to coax her Aspect from its cage. The sense of power filling her returned some measure of her calm, and she regained her feet. The hounds and the man stood unwavering, unmoving. She stood there, staring at him, her limbs trembling, and gauged her options. If she ran, the hounds would chase her, and the memory of teeth and claws tearing into Thomas froze her feet to the floor. If she attacked first, she might throw the man off guard. She didn't know how to replicate the explosions of power that had killed the first carrion hounds she'd seen and that had torn the harpies to bits, but she could concentrate her power, send it out in a burst that might have a similar effect.

The gray-eyed man did not speak, did not move, his silent, stationary presence more frightening than any threats he might have uttered. Her eyes locked with his. Siren took a careful, deliberate step back. The gray-eyed man gave a silent, disappointed shake of his head that made her freeze. His Aspect rose around him. Where Jace's and Valkyrie's Aspects always felt warm to Siren, his felt cold and greasy, shimmering sickly in the air like the sheen of oil on water.

A terrible grin split his face, his eyes utterly inhuman as he narrowed his lips and gave one high, piercing whistle. The doorway behind him filled with hounds. They spilled into the kitchen, packed so tightly against each other she couldn't see where one hound ended and another began.

Copper-spiked adrenaline spilled down her throat, along with the eye-watering stench of so many hounds packed into one space. Chunks of flesh dropped to the floor as hound bumped into hound, the raw scrape of bone against bone grating on her ears.

She couldn't fight them all. The glint of hunger and anticipation in the man's eyes told her that after hunting her for so long, after losing her so many times, he was waiting for her to move first, for the game to begin, certain that this time he would win.

Fuck that.

Primal rage sparked inside her. She would not end here, not after everything. She couldn't beat him *and* all the hounds, but if she was lucky, she could outsmart him. She called her Aspect, concentrating a high volume of it into a small ball, like building up pressure inside a tank. When the pressure built high enough, the tank would burst, releasing its contents.

The gray-eyed man's smile grew wider, hungrier.

Think you know what I'm doing, don't you, you bastard?

While his attention was on the flashy display she made of building her power, Siren sent unnoticed tendrils of Aspect through the kitchen's second doorway at her back, forming simulacrums of her and Percy in the hallway beyond. She built as many as she could before the ball of Aspect in her hands shattered its containment, a shockwave of power punching in an arc across the room.

The front four lines of hounds exploded and the gray-eyed man, a shield of Aspect pulled in front of him at the last moment, dropped to his knees, laughing. He'd let her do it, let her hit him, so utterly convinced she had no hope of escaping.

Siren swiped Charles's book off the kitchen counter, grabbed Percy's collar, and ran. She heard the pursuit of man and hounds, sent the simulacrums running in random directions through the house, had the satisfaction of hearing the hounds split their pursuit.

She hit the door to the garage, fumbled for the deadbolt, and flicked it open. Percy growled and sent up a torrent of barks as a hound's teeth sank into her ankle. A hot spike of pain flared as the hound broke through her old scars. She hit the ground, twisted to face the hound, and jabbed the car key into its eye.

The hound growled, but the grip of its jaws didn't lessen. Percy lunged, his mouth snapping around the hound's neck. The hound dropped her, twisted and lunged at Percy, but her dog's lock on its neck didn't give. Percy clamped down and shook the creature back and forth in his mouth as if it were a chew toy. The neck gave with a sickening crunch and the hound slumped, lifeless. Percy didn't let go. Caught in the throes of battle lust, he growled and shook the hound again.

"Percy, let's go, boy."

He ignored her, even when she threw open the door to the garage. She was afraid to touch him, to get between him and the fight. A scuffling noise skittered down the hall. The gray-eyed man turned the corner, a cadre of hounds at his heels. He made a clicking noise in his throat and the hounds surged past him.

She grabbed Percy's collar. He dropped the hound, and she dragged him through the door. It slammed shut and she threw the dead bolt home just as the hounds rammed into it.

The only vehicle in the garage was a shiny black SUV. Siren ran for the driver's side door. Her bitten ankle landed with a shock of pain. It gave and sent her sprawling. She regained her feet, conscious of the sound of the deadbolt sliding open behind her, and limped to the car door, praying to gods she didn't believe in that the keys she had went to this vehicle. She hit the unlock button and was rewarded by the sound of the lock shifting, vehicle lights blinking in accordance.

She pulled the door open and motioned for Percy. He jumped in, and she shoved him over to the passenger side, hauling herself into the driver's seat. She slammed the door shut just as the hounds burst into the garage.

Siren fumbled with the key, hands shaking, got it in the ignition on the third try and twisted. The SUV roared to life. Gray eyes locked with hers in the rearview mirror. She didn't stop to think. She threw the gear shift in reverse and slammed on the gas pedal. The SUV careened into the gray-eyed man. She hit the brakes as the SUV connected with the wall a fraction of a second later.

She hit buttons in the car at random, until the garage door started sliding up. In the rearview the gray-eyed man, pinned between the car and the wall, still moved. Red trickled out the sides of his mouth, but despite the blood, he didn't look fatally injured like he should. He looked furious. His hounds brayed and barked, scratching at the car with an intensity and focus that made her think maybe they *could* claw through solid metal.

Then the garage door opened and she threw the SUV in drive, slamming the gas pedal again. She winced at the pain that spiked through her ruined ankle, but it didn't matter because the vehicle shot out of the garage and into sunlight. She headed for the long drive that led to the main road when a foreign car in the circular driveway caught her attention, a tan Lincoln town car.

The gray-eyed man's, it had to be, because she'd never seen it and it wasn't the standard issue black of the Council's security. She hit the brakes, calling up Aspect, fear and need begging it to do what she wanted, what she needed, even if she didn't know how to ask. Aspect answered, flooded out of her in a torrent that made it difficult to breathe. The car exploded. The windows shattered. The metal melted and twisted. Gasoline leaked from the tank, and she *felt* her Aspect draw toward the fumes and ignite them. Plumes of smoke billowed up.

Good enough.

It would have to be good enough, because a glance in the rearview showed the gray-eyed man stumbling from the garage in far, far better condition than he ought to have been after being hit with a vehicle. Carrion hounds abandoned the house like rats fleeing a rising flood, tearing down the path after her.

She clicked her seatbelt into place and slammed the gas, taking the winding road as fast as she dared, her inexperience at driving making her overcompensate the turns, adrenaline turning her limbs to fluttery, trembling extensions.

She had a moment to worry about the gate, about having to stop the vehicle to wait for it to open, but then she rounded the final bend in the road and saw the gate on its side, the wrought-iron crumpled and bent, the entire mass flung aside as if a giant had grasped it in both hands and torn it free. The Council's two guards sprawled motionless amongst the wreckage.

She hit the main road, tires squealing on asphalt, and glanced in the rearview to see every hound stop dead at the property line. She didn't have time to wonder why, just to be grateful. She shoved the gas pedal to the floor and didn't let up.

CHAPTER

THIRTY-ONE

S iren ran a dozen red lights, passed more cars than she could count, and nearly crashed into oncoming traffic five or six times before her flight response cooled enough for her to slow the car down to the speed limit. Her ankle throbbed and the way it was swelling she feared if she stopped driving, she would never get it to bend enough to press the gas pedal again.

Fifty miles and two towns later, she finally pulled off into a small park after she nearly sideswiped a minivan. She parked the SUV and stumbled out, fell to all fours, and wretched on the harsh asphalt.

Trembling, she pushed herself up to lean back against the SUV. Percy clambered out of the still-open driver's side door, whining and pushing his body up against her. She wrapped her arms around him and scratched behind his ear, the act of comforting him doing more to comfort her. She didn't realize she was crying until he licked at her face and his big paws scrabbled to pull himself into her lap.

"We can't go back, buddy."

He tilted his big head as if to ask, *Why not?*

"Too dangerous."

Jace had said he understood the danger she'd put him in, but he didn't. He *couldn't*. There had to have been hundreds of hounds at the estate. Thank goodness Jace hadn't been there. She could have gotten him *killed*. Just like she'd gotten Thomas killed. At least back then she hadn't realized she was putting Thomas in any danger.

She didn't have that excuse now.

She'd known what was after her when she'd gotten involved with Jace, *known* the gray-eyed man would never stop coming after her. She'd told Jace what she could, but it wasn't the same as experiencing it, as feeling that awful hunger that saturated the air whenever the gray-eyed man was near. Jace couldn't consent to a danger he couldn't fully understand, and she should never have let him do it, should never have let him tell her it would be okay, that he could handle it. It wasn't his problem.

She'd just destroyed part of his house, stolen his dad's car, and no doubt gotten him in trouble with the Council. If she went back, things would only get worse. The gray-eyed man would come for her again, and she had just proved she didn't know enough about her own power to defeat him.

Something square and hard dug into her, and she felt in her back pocket, pulled out the book Charles had given her. She had only peeked at it, at the things she could do, because she'd been afraid. Afraid of her Aspect, because the Council had been afraid. Because even Jace hadn't known what she would be capable of if she ever fully broke the cage inside her. Because Anne and Mark had wanted to use her.

But being afraid of her power hadn't helped her, and running for the rest of her life wouldn't help, either. She couldn't go back to Jace *now*, wouldn't be able to live with herself if something happened to him. But if she was as powerful as everyone seemed to think she could be, and if Charles's book held the answers to her Aspect, maybe *she* could put an end to this.

"That's what we'll do, boy," she told Percy. "We'll read, and we'll practice, and when we're ready, we'll hunt him like he's hunted us and when it's done, when he's *gone,* we'll go home."

To Seclusion. To Jace.

She wiped her eyes and pulled herself up, ushering Percy back into the car. Calmer now that she had a plan, a purpose, she turned the ignition with a steady hand, looking over at Percy as she pulled the car back onto the road.

"Are you ready to kick some ass, boy?"

He gave a short, excited yip.

"Good. Because I want to go home. Soon."

THIRTY-TWO

Jace read the note a second time, then crumpled it into a ball and threw it at the trash can. It missed and landed on a tile still stained with carrion hound blood.

Three lines. Siren had been missing for a week, and he got *three lines*.

He'd felt it the second the estate's wards shattered, had broken every traffic law on the books getting back to the house, but he'd been too late. He'd found a half-melted Lincoln town car in the drive, the front doors and half the front wall had been obliterated, and the bodies of carrion hounds had littered the kitchen and the garage.

Siren and Percy were gone, and so was whoever had come after them.

He'd searched every corner of the city for her in the last week, not knowing if she'd been killed or captured, and she'd sent him three goddamn lines.

I'm safe.
Percy's with me.
I'll find you when it's over.

Valkyrie walked into the kitchen, stopped cold at the look on Jace's face.

"Is she—"

"She's fine." Jace gestured at the crumpled piece of paper on the floor. "Apparently."

Valkyrie retrieved the paper and smoothed it out.

"Was there—"

"No return address. No information. No idea what actually happened." He stalked to the refrigerator and pulled out a beer. He didn't care that it was barely one o'clock in the afternoon. "It's postmarked from somewhere in Ohio, but I'm sure she's long gone from there by now."

He couldn't track her through her cell phone because she'd left it at the house. He couldn't track his dad's SUV because it was his dad's SUV. The man took paranoia to new heights. The thing had enough attention-diverting, anti-scrying, look-the-other-way charms on it to befuddle every cop and private investigator in the continental US.

He'd hired a private investigator anyway. Two, actually, for all the good it was doing.

He popped the cap off the beer and drained a third of it in one long pull. "What the hell does that even mean, *when it's over?* What does she think she's going to do?"

Valkyrie winced. "About that. I finally got in touch with Charles. It would seem he was in possession of a copy of *Life Aspect: Its Histories and Methods.* He loaned it to Siren. I've searched her rooms and the library, but I didn't find it, so I'm assuming she took it with her."

And she hadn't told him about it. Had she thought she couldn't trust him? Did she *still* think she couldn't trust him?

"I'm glad she has a guide to her particular abilities." There. That was a nice, neutral thing to say. "What does it have to do with the cryptic meaning of her message?"

Valkyrie shrugged. "If you chase an animal long enough, then corner it, it will eventually bite back."

"I thought biting back was what she did to the driveway," he answered drily. He set the beer on the counter, its appeal lost. "You really think she's going after him? Actively?"

"She's been running for years. She'd have no reason to tell you she'll come back when it's 'over' if she isn't actively planning for there to *be* an 'over'."

"If she wanted to go after him, why didn't she come to me? I would have helped her."

"You would have told her to stay away from him."

"Obviously, because that makes sense. But when she inevitably insisted, I would have helped her. She wouldn't be on her own."

"She's used to being on her own," Valkyrie said, gently. "Whatever happened here scared the hell out of her. When she's scared, she runs. She's used to running, and she's not used to relying on people. A lifetime of that doesn't go away because one man tells you that you can trust him."

Jace fought back a smile. "I didn't think you liked her, sister."

"Oh, I liked her just fine. I only worried she'd break your heart."

A little late there.

"You think I should stop looking for her, then?" He wouldn't—couldn't—even if she told him he should.

Valkyrie snorted. "Goddess, no. She's going after the man who probably tortured our mother and has who knows how many people in the upper echelons of Aspect Society backing him. The woman needs all the help she can get. All I am telling you to do is not beat yourself up about this mess thinking it's your fault. And maybe go easy on her when you do find her."

Random strode into the room, hair sticking out even more than usual, decked out in a full suit with briefcase in hand. "The Council is in a gods-damned uproar. I swear, if I weren't Aunt Ella's favorite nephew, I'd be dead."

"You're her only nephew," Valkyrie pointed out.

"Doesn't automatically make me her favorite."

"I think, by default, it does."

"What did the Council say?" Jace asked.

"Aside from wondering why you, the person who should be most interested in what happened, did not feel compelled to show up to a hearing about it?"

"Yeah, aside from that." Earlier today, he'd thought sitting in a room with the Council arguing about what had or hadn't happened was a waste of his time, time he could be spending looking for Siren. Especially when Random could handle them far better than he could. Now that he'd gotten her note, he realized he might as well have gone, because he'd been looking for her in all the wrong places. "So what'd they say?"

Random all but threw up his hands in exasperation. "You will be pleased to know that while Julian and Kara argued strongly for the belief that Siren was somehow the cause of everything that went wrong, Theo and Ella reasonably pointed out that the wards to your estate had clearly been broken from the outside.

"Therefore, I argued that the most reasonable explanation for Ms. Savage's disappearance is that she was kidnapped. Once they came around, they decided to turn their attention to what they should have been doing all along: tracking the owner of the melted hunk of car towed off your property. They should turn something up soon."

Jace was quiet a minute. "She hasn't been kidnapped."

"Beg your pardon?"

Jace nodded at Siren's note.

Random walked over and scanned it. "When did you get this?"

"Fifteen minutes ago. It came with the mail."

"You can't show the Council."

"I know."

"If they find out she left voluntarily, no matter the circumstances, she'll be in breach of her probationary entry into Aspect Society."

"I know."

"They could hold her indefinitely without trial or approval from all Council members, and Julian and Kara would do it just to get their hands on Life Aspect."

"I'm not an idiot, Random, *I know that.*"

"I'm just making sure."

"I don't need you to make sure. I don't need you to tell me she's in danger or that we need to find her. *I'm* the one who's in love with her." He found himself shouting the last part, unreasonably incensed that Random should feel *he* needed reminding that Siren should be protected. He didn't need reminding. He was the one who'd promised to protect her and, as he'd just said, *he* was the one who was…

In love with her?

Valkyrie and Random stared at him.

Shit.

"I need a minute." *Or two or three thousand of them,* he thought as he walked outside and down to the lake, letting the water speak to his Aspect and calm him.

He was in love with Siren. Given a moment of self-reflection, it shouldn't have come as a surprise. What was more surprising, more frustrating, was that he hadn't figured it out while she was here. And now she was gone.

A niggling doubt told him he had no idea how she felt about him. Maybe she'd just sent that note so he wouldn't look for her. There was nothing personal in it, nothing to make him think she really wanted to come back. They had been thrown together by circumstance, two people who were attracted to each other, and things had taken their natural course. It didn't mean he *meant* anything to her.

He drew out his phone and dialed Meredith. Ironic, that Siren had convinced him to patch things up with her, and Meredith was the one person who might be able to find Siren when she didn't want to be found.

"Yes?"

"If I tell you something, can I trust you not to go to the Council with it?"

A pause, then, "Yes."

He explained. "I need you to find her."

Siren might think she could handle this on her own—and maybe she could—but he wasn't going to let her face her demons alone. He would find her, he would help her, and if she wanted him to leave once he had, then he would leave. But she owed it to him to tell him to his face.

"The Council has already asked me to find her, Jace," Meredith said gently. "I can't. I Track a person's Aspect, and the containment around hers makes it impossible to locate. She would have to be actively using it at the exact time I'm trying to Track her for it to be successful."

"I know. But that's if you're searching specifically for her. What if you aren't? What if, instead of trying to lock onto her, you're instead searching specific locations for her absence?"

"That...*could* work. But, Jace, there are a great many places in the country where a person might not be, let alone in the world. And if she's on the move, it will make things more difficult. This could take weeks." The tone of her voice plainly said she more likely thought it would take months. "We might not find her."

"I have to try."

She sighed. "I'm going to regret this. Buy me coffee and we'll start looking."

CHAPTER

THIRTY-THREE

Six Months Later...

"This is a bad idea." Siren tipped her sunglasses down and looked over at the occupant of the SUV's passenger seat.

Percy, nestled into the dog bed that had become a near-permanent feature of the passenger seat, gave three short, decisive barks.

"Well, if you think it's *that* bad of an idea, why aren't you stopping me?"

The dog dropped his head between his paws and looked more miserable than she'd realized it was possible for a dog to look.

"You miss him, too, huh?"

Whine.

"Well, we can't sit in the car all night."

She'd been debating doing precisely that, had been sitting in the car for the last fifteen minutes, engine idling, trying to talk herself into or out of this idea. And it *was* a terrible idea. Still, looking around the SUV, she thought spending some time in an actual apartment might be good. Almost every side door was full of fast-food wrappers and the other collected trash of road-trip life. Her sleeping bag and pillow were laid out on the back seat, and the cargo area was taken up by Percy's assorted paraphernalia and two duffel bags, one bursting with clothes that needed the Laundromat and the other a nearly empty clean-clothes bag.

The SUV had been a godsend. She'd been terrified of being tracked by it at first, until she'd learned the nature of the Aspect stitched into every inch of the car and realized no one was ever finding it. After that, her freedom to run, and run far, had been exponentially increased. She could sleep in it without fear of being found, and all she had to do to get to a new state was put gas in the tank.

She'd found a surprising amount of money dumped without care in the glove box, enough to keep her going for a while, and she'd worked odd jobs to supplement it. Life on the run was distinctly cushier this time around. The car gave her stability, and Percy staved off the loneliness she'd done her best to deny all those years, but even he couldn't do anything about the festering wound in her chest that broke open any time she thought about Jace.

And she thought about him all the time. Whenever she drank coffee, she saw his smile as he made her a latte. When she walked Percy, she couldn't stop the sense that something was missing, until she realized she was missing Jace, his hand tucked into hers. Any time she walked past a bookstore, it sent a pang of longing through her.

It was a book that had brought her to this location. She'd spent the last two months in Seattle, working on her Aspect and taking self-defense classes. Then earlier today, she'd walked past a bookshop and had seen it on display and couldn't help herself from buying it. Having his book was the closest she could get to having Jace. She'd been prepared to drown in self-pity for the rest of the day after buying it.

She hadn't been prepared for the dedication page, three short lines that destroyed her soul.

For Siren. I miss you. Come home.

For the most part she'd tried not to imagine what he was doing, what he was feeling. If he still thought about her. If he was angry with her. If he'd just decided she wasn't worth his time and had moved on. Maybe moved on with Meredith. If he did think about her, would he still want her if—*when,* she corrected herself—this was over and she came back? How would she even go back?

He had every right to be angry with her. But when he'd had the chance to reach her in the only way he knew how, he'd just asked her to come home.

Home.

I want to. I'm trying.

After reading the dedication, she'd flipped to the back and read the only line in the author bio: JC Morden lives in Portland, Oregon. With those few words, a phenomenally bad idea had been born and cemented when, on a hunch, she opened the SUV's GPS and found a Portland address in the history. She knew Jace's father hadn't spoken to him since Jace had left home, but his father had, it seemed, checked up on him. She hadn't thought. She'd just activated the GPS to take her to Portland and had driven in as the sun set.

Now, she sat in the private driveway of a red brick town-house, trying to convince herself to either go inside or leave.

Going inside was stupid. She had no evidence to back her belief that Jace was still in Seclusion, so for all she knew, he was in there right now. Even if he was still in Seclusion, he did *live here.* Odds were he came back periodically to check on the place. Or maybe he had a friend or a neighbor checking on it who would report a strange car outside with a strange woman inside.

She should drive away, pretend she'd never found the place.

She turned the SUV off, grabbed her bag and Percy's leash, and walked to the front door. No one was around, but she walked confidently anyway, like she belonged here, like this was her daily routine. At the door, she pretended to look for something in her bag while her Aspect felt past to the rooms within, looking for any sign of life. Nothing, not even a ward on the door, which she found odd.

She had proved to be a terrible locksmith by conventional means in the past, but her recent studies showed Aspect could be adapted to a number of useful, if banned-by-Council-law things, and a quick nudge of her power had the door swinging inward. Percy trotted in eagerly ahead of her, and she followed, shutting the door behind her and feeling for the light switch.

The kitchen and living room were sparsely decorated but comfortable, and the townhouse just *felt* like Jace, from the bookshelves flanking the fireplace to the antiquated landline phone mounted on the wall next to the fridge, to the espresso machine sitting on the granite counter top. Two items were tacked to the fridge: a picture of Jace, Random, and Valkyrie, and a menu for a local Thai restaurant.

Siren's stomach rumbled, reminding her she hadn't eaten anything since a granola bar that morning, and she figured, *Why the hell not?* She opened the menu, found the vegetarian Pad Thai and the eggrolls circled, and smiled. It looked like she had her order picked out for her. She called it in, got Percy's travel bowl and food out of her bag, and set out his dinner. While he was eating, she opened the garage door, climbed into the SUV and pulled it into the garage. It might be immune to most attention, but since she had a garage to hide it in, she figured she might as well take advantage.

She prowled the downstairs while waiting for the takeout to arrive, unwilling to admit to herself that she was avoiding going upstairs where the bedroom was. She perused his bookshelves— he had a real thing for space operas and war history—sat on his couch, even tested out the weight bench in the corner. By the time the doorbell rang, Percy, who had settled onto the loveseat, watched her with a long-suffering air and the look of a dog who believes his human has lost the few shreds of sanity she had previously been possessed of.

Siren paid for the takeout and found her appetite had disappeared again somewhere between placing the order and its arrival. She didn't want to be in Jace's house, eating Jace's normal takeout order, looking through Jace's book collection. She wanted Jace. She wanted his arms around her, wanted to hear his voice, wanted to see him smile.

She gave up on eating and put the food in the refrigerator. She found a door that let out onto a patio and a small backyard not much larger than a walk-in closet, and took Percy outside to do his business. She stayed outside for twenty minutes or so, letting Percy roll in the grass and run around sniffing the new terrain, as dogs were wont to do.

Tomorrow, she decided. She would start looking for the gray-eyed man tomorrow. She had finished reading the book Charles gave her last night, was as prepared as she was going to get for this hunt, and she wanted it over.

She would need to send Percy off. If something happened to her, he couldn't be left on his own. For just this eventuality she had looked into services that moved pets, had found one that seemed to take the welfare of the animals they transported seriously. She would send Percy home to Jace and Valkyrie, and she would end this.

Feeling lighter now the decision had been made, she took Percy upstairs. She hadn't slept well in weeks, and making the decision to move forward seemed to have given exhaustion permission to move in. She shrugged out of her clothes, wandered over to Jace's closet. Mostly a collection of jeans and t-shirts, a couple of dress pants. She pulled a long-sleeved flannel shirt off a hanger and wrapped herself in it before flopping onto the bed.

She reached over to flick the bedside lamp off, paused when

her fingers tangled in something as she did. She tugged the item free. It was a necklace made of thick black cord, the pendant carved of dark wood worn smooth. It took her a moment to recognize it as the Aspect symbol for water.

Unable to stop herself, she slipped it over her neck. The pendant nestled against her chest, warm and comforting, as if it had rested there a thousand times, and it made her smile. At least she would have something of him to take with her.

She turned out the light and rolled onto her side. The pillow still smelled faintly of Jace. She inhaled deeply, closed her eyes, and allowed herself the silly fantasy that he was here. Percy jumped up on the bed and curled up against her back. She hugged Jace's shirt tight to herself and fell asleep.

CHAPTER

THIRTY-FOUR

J ace was running on caffeine and pure determination by the time he picked up his rental car at the Portland airport.

When he'd felt the latent alert spell go off on his Portland townhouse last night, he almost hadn't believed it. He'd made a trip up and deactivated the primary wards shortly after Siren had disappeared, thinking that whoever was after her might use her connection to him to search for her. He'd left only an alert that would tell him if anyone entered the house, but wouldn't prevent them from entering or otherwise let them know they'd been detected.

After a couple months had gone by with nothing, he'd all but forgotten about it, given up on the hope that it would lead him anywhere. But now, six months later, someone had come looking. He told himself this was good news. If someone was still looking, it meant they hadn't found Siren. It meant Siren hadn't found *them*. That she was safe.

He didn't harbor any illusions that whoever had broken in was still in the townhouse. He'd jumped on the first flight he could get, but it had still taken him over nine hours to get here. The townhouse had been broken into around eight last night, and it was already past seven the next morning. Chances were, they wouldn't still be there, but they would have left clues, clues that he could track.

Well, that Meredith could track.

"Thanks for coming."

Meredith pressed ice-blue fingernails to her eyelids. "That is the seventh time you have thanked me for coming. It's overkill."

"Merely expressing my gratitude."

"You can express your gratitude by pulling into that coffee shop," she pointed ahead on the right, "and getting me a triple on ice."

Jace pulled the car into the drive-through.

"Besides, it beats the hell out of searching the world for where Siren isn't. *Again.* I think I've performed more tracking spells than any Tracker in Aspect history. I deserve an honorary medal of some sort."

"I'll look into honorary medals. You have to admit, though, it did work. We found her four times." Jace gave his order to the barista at the window and handed her a twenty.

"We found her," Meredith agreed, "and every time she was gone before we could get there. Couldn't you have fallen in love with someone a little more stationary?"

"It makes life interesting?" Jace offered.

"More like a pain in the ass."

"But you have coffee now." Jace handed her the triple espresso on ice, took a drink of his own hot Americano. He didn't know how people managed to drink iced coffee. Siren, very sensibly in his opinion, liked hers hot. "I wish Random or Val would have come."

Meredith laughed. "Valkyrie is too obsessed with finding someone who doesn't want to be found. You two have that in common, albeit you're chasing different people. And Random is too busy moping over Valkyrie and hoping one day she'll wake up and notice he's there to leave her side for one precious minute."

"Did everyone besides me know he had it bad for her?"

"Everyone besides you and her. You Winters siblings share a singular lack of ability to recognize when someone is interested in you."

"I'm not *that* bad at relationships."

"You are great at relationships. You are terrible at recognizing someone wants to be in a relationship with you. And before you go and say you did just fine with Siren, I maintain it doesn't count because you were interested in her first so you were already on the lookout for signs of reciprocation."

"Signs of reciprocation?" Jace repeated. "With phrases like that, you should write a dating book. I know a great agent."

"You know, I would," Meredith said with dramatic languor, "but I spend all my time these days doing pro-bono tracking jobs for all of my friends." Her expression soured. "I think the only reason Val hasn't murdered me is because I tried to track your father for her."

Jace winced. "She's a very protective older sister. And since I can't explain to her why we're suddenly on good terms again—"

"No, you can't."

"I can't," Jace agreed, turning into the drive for his townhouse, "but you could." The argument was one they'd had several times before, and he didn't expect a different outcome this time.

"Telling you what happened was difficult enough. It's my business, and I don't have any interest in talking to anyone else about it." She unbuckled her seatbelt as the car slid to a stop. "Now, let's go inside and see if I can't track something interesting for a change."

The first odd thing Jace noticed as they stepped inside was that the house smelled of Thai food. The second was that nothing looked disturbed. The third was the collapsible pet travel bowl of water on the floor.

Someone had broken into his house, ordered Thai food and… brought a pet?

Meredith looked as confused as he did, even before the giant dog bounded down the stairs and barreled straight into Jace, pawing at him in excitement.

"Percy?"

Meredith looked from hound to Jace. "You…know this dog?"

"Yeah, he's—" He broke off, looked up the stairs. Couldn't be.

Jace ascended the stairs slowly, quietly, Percy following calmly at his side, Meredith behind him. In the door to his bedroom, he froze.

Siren was in his shirt, in his bed, asleep.

"Looks like your girl found you," Meredith whispered. "I'll just take the car. Call me whenever you…sort this out."

THIRTY-FIVE

J ace didn't know how long he stood in the doorway staring at her, afraid to move, afraid to breathe. Afraid that if he blinked the spell would break and she wouldn't be there.

She moaned and twisted, as if in the grip of unpleasant dreams, and he was across the room in a breath, slipping under the covers beside her. The need to comfort her was instinctual, irrepressible. She sighed and snuggled into him. She was not wearing anything other than his shirt, and the soft warmth of her pressed against him made his throat tighten.

"Jace." His name on her lips was barely more than an exhale.

He let his forehead rest against hers, let his arms wrap around her, and pulled her closer.

Then she kissed him, hot and hungry, her tongue eager against his, as if she'd been waiting to kiss him the entire time she'd been gone. He lost himself in her mouth, in the taste of her, before he remembered he was angry at her, that she'd just *left*.

He gently pushed her back.

"Siren." He couldn't stop her name from being a caress, couldn't put any of the anger he knew he should be feeling into his words.

Gods, he'd missed her.

"You can't just kiss me and expect it to fix everything."

"Mmm. It's a dream, I can do whatever I want. But we don't have to kiss." She tangled her legs in his and buried her face in the crook of his neck.

Dreaming. She thinks she's dreaming. Of me. That was…sweet?

No, he reprimanded himself, *not sweet*. It was her own fault if she missed him, because she was the one who had left. He had to keep that thought first and foremost in his mind. Though if her lips didn't stop trailing down his neck, he wasn't going to be capable of any thoughts, much less be able to keep track of which ones he was supposed to be thinking.

"You're not dreaming."

"That's what Dream-Jace always says."

"Open your eyes."

"Nope. When I open them, you disappear. And I miss you."

"I miss you too." His hand brushed her cheek, and she opened her eyes. Opened them, and froze.

"Jace?"

"Hey, baby."

"What are you doing here?"

He arched an eyebrow. "I do live here, technically. The question is what are you doing here? In my house, in my bed, wearing my clothes?"

She reddened. "It was comfortable."

"The shirt, or the bed?" Damn it, he was flirting again when he was supposed to be mad.

"Both. Are you mad?"

"Of course I'm mad. I thought you were dead or kidnapped, and then I got a cryptic message that amounts to you leaving me, and then I spent the next six months looking for you. Actually, put in that light, mad doesn't begin to cover it."

Mad or not, now that she was awake, he couldn't resist running his hand down her side, feeling goosebumps crop up on her soft skin.

"I wasn't leaving you. I was keeping you safe. And I can't think when you do that."

"Tough luck. You're in my bed." His hand slid beneath soft flannel, caressed the curve of her hip. "Did you ever consider that keeping me safe wasn't your decision to make?"

"No. I've seen what's after me, you haven't. And I was coming back when I finished this." She traced the flat line of his stomach along the top of his jeans. At the look he gave her, she said, "What? If you get to be distracting, so do I."

"Fine. And your point's irrelevant. How do you think I would have felt if you died? If you didn't come back, if I never heard from you again, was I supposed to spend the rest of my life wondering what happened to you?"

"I didn't think about it that way."

"Obviously," he said, unable to keep the bite of sarcasm out of his words.

"I didn't plan on dying."

"People rarely do." He skimmed his fingers up her side to the outer swell of her breast. She inhaled sharply and made a soft noise in the back of her throat that had his blood rushing south.

"I'm sorry," she ground out.

"You think?"

Her fingers danced across his back, nails dragging lightly against his skin. "Are you leaving?"

"I chased you across the country. I spent the last few months driving my friends and family crazy looking for you. No, I am not fucking leaving."

His thumb glided across her nipple, and she arched against him.

"Are you still mad?" Her fingers went back to the waistband of his jeans and slipped inside, grazing lightly against him.

"Like I said, mad doesn't begin to cover it. I've been worried sick, I've been pissed, I've been depressed, and I love you so much I can't fucking see straight."

She stilled, looking him in the eyes. "You love me?"

"I love you."

She kissed him again, took his mouth with a ferocity that drove every last thought from his mind. She pushed him onto his back and tore at his pants. Hands fumbled and shirt and jeans went flying. She straddled him and sank onto his cock, her eyes rolling closed as a moan escaped her, and he couldn't remember what the hell he'd been mad about in the first place.

THIRTY-SIX

"You look exhausted. You should go to sleep."

"If I go to sleep, are you going to run away again?"

Siren bit her lip. "I haven't decided."

"Then I'm not going to sleep." Jace rolled out of bed and pulled his jeans on. "And we haven't fixed anything."

Siren fumbled for her own clothes as Jace pulled on his shirt and headed for the stairs.

"Where are you going?" She already knew. Leaving. He was leaving, and why not? She hadn't given him any reason to stay.

"To make coffee. I'm tired, and I suspect I have a headache-inducing argument ahead of me."

Relief poured through her. *Not* leaving, then.

Percy followed Jace, shooting a look over his doggy shoulder that clearly said, "Sorry."

"Traitor," she muttered and, not having any idea how to fix the mess she'd made of things but needing to try, she followed them both downstairs.

They didn't speak the entire time the coffee brewed. Siren even repressed her need to comment on the fact that the coffee in his cupboard was at least six months old and, therefore, probably wouldn't taste very good. Somehow, she didn't think the observation was one he would appreciate at the moment. Instead, she gave Percy his breakfast, opened the sliding glass door to the patio, and let him run around like a maniac in the small backyard enclosure.

When she came back inside, Jace filled two coffee mugs, slid one across the counter to her, and seated himself on a barstool. He gave her his full, undivided, and very pointed attention.

She wrapped her hands around the mug and organized her thoughts.

"You asked me how you were supposed to feel if I died," she said finally. "But how was I supposed to feel if I stayed, and *you* died? I already watched one person I cared about die in front of me. At least that time, I didn't know what was coming. This time I do. This time, if something happens to you, that's on me."

"You aren't responsible for what other people choose to do."

"No, but I am responsible for what *I* do. And if you weren't with me, if you'd never met me, you wouldn't be in any danger right now."

"That may be true," Jace assented, "but I'm not unaware of it, and I wouldn't change anything. I don't want to be safe. I want to be with you." He grinned at her. "Am I cliché if I say I want you even if it kills me?"

Siren didn't laugh. "And what if *I* kill you?"

He didn't answer at first, studying her. "You're serious?"

"I've learned a lot about my Aspect since I left. How to use it, manipulate it. I've learned just how much of it I'm carrying inside me. I've *felt* it and it…" She swallowed. "No one's meant to carry that much power. If it weren't for the barrier inside me, I'd be dead."

"You can't be certain—"

"I *can*," she said gently. "I'm Life, remember? I can tell you what anyone's limits are, so I damn well know my own. It doesn't happen every time, but sometimes when I use Aspect, it breaks a chunk of that barrier away. The more that falls away, the harder it is for me to control what's inside. When the entire barrier goes, it's over. Valkyrie had it right. I'm a ticking time bomb, Jace, and when I go off, the only question is going to be who's in the fallout zone."

"You're saying it's going to kill you?"

"If I can hold on to it, keep it inside me? Yes, it will kill me. Like I said, no one's meant to carry that much power."

"And if you don't hold on to it?"

"It will kill everyone around me."

"For how far?"

"I'm not sure. I tried applying some Aspect amplification models to get an idea."

Jace perked up. "Vertigen's Primary Theorems?"

She nodded.

"Her work was really overlooked, if you ask me. Did you find them in Advanced Aspect Mathematics or Manipulation Theory?" A hint of the usual Jace was back in his face, the Jace who geeked out over Aspect theorems, and she was happy to see he was still there, even if it wouldn't last.

"Neither. I went to the primary source."

"You found a copy of Morah Vertigen's *On Aspect*? Where? I've been looking for years, and every available copy is out of my price range."

"Fifty cents at a garage sale in Baton Rouge?" she offered.

"Fifty—" Jace swallowed, a look of pure horror on his face. "Fifty *cents*? At a garage sale?"

"Well, there's a Wild Magic coven in that area, and this lady was selling off a bunch of things after her grandfather passed away. Wasn't big into 'technical jargon,' as she put it."

"Do you still have it?"

Siren hid a smile. "It's in the car."

He looked like he wanted to jump up and run for the car. Then the light in his eyes dimmed, his shoulders slumped, and she knew the brief distraction was over. He rubbed at the back of his neck. "What did you conclude using the theorems?"

"If I have even half as much Aspect in me as I think I do?" She shrugged. "I could probably annihilate a small town."

He looked at her sharply, but she wasn't joking. She watched the color drain from his face. It hurt to see, but it was good. It meant he was taking her seriously.

"By annihilate you mean…"

"Kill everything. People. Plants. Animals. Anything living."

"But you *are* Life Aspect."

"Unconstrained Life Aspect without direction accelerates life. The uncontrolled acceleration of life is death."

She saw the gears turning in his mind, loved him for trying to find a solution even though she knew one didn't exist. She'd run through every scenario she could think of and hadn't found a single answer.

"What if you try to burn through your Aspect? Get the volume down to manageable levels?"

"I'd only accelerate the barrier's deterioration."

"Then we build another barrier."

"My body won't accept it. You heard Theo. I bonded with this one because I was so young when it was put in. That won't happen again."

"Nullifying spells."

"A nullifying spell has to be created with the same amount of Aspect it's meant to contain, and they start degrading after a few days. Even if you could keep me in one twenty-four-seven, it would lose efficacy while you wait for me to explode, and you couldn't build one strong enough to contain me in the first place."

Jace frowned. "How did you learn so much about Aspect?"

"I've read a lot more than *On Aspect* in the last six months." Once she'd known what types of books to look for, finding them had been surprisingly easy.

"So we can't get rid of it, we can't cage it, and we can't nullify it. What do we do?"

Siren shrugged. "Put me on a boat in the middle of the ocean and pray for the whales' forgiveness?"

"I'm not joking."

"You're right, cost of life is still too high. If your sister's rich enough to put me on a rocket into space, that's probably the safer option."

"Still not joking."

"Of course, who knows how Aspect travels in space, so if I destroy other intelligent life in the universe, I could unwittingly set off an intergalactic war."

"*Siren.*"

"What? What do you want me to say? Either I manage to contain this and I die, or I don't and I kill who knows how many other people."

"You had to have had some kind of plan or you wouldn't be sitting smack in the middle of a densely populated city."

Siren snapped her fingers. "You're right. I *did* have a plan. It involved you being safely on the other side of the country while I hunted down the people who did this to me, lured them to an unpopulated area, and hopefully got enough Aspect out of me to kill them before I imploded."

"Terribly sorry for ruining your plan because I happen to *not want you dead.*"

At some point both Jace and Siren had risen from their seats and stood facing each, barely a hairsbreadth between them. Siren was gripped by the desire to shake sense into him and the equally strong yet opposing desire to rip his clothes off again.

Jace's phone rang. He ignored it, maintaining an alpha stare Siren refused to back down from. His pocket continued to ring.

Siren crossed her arms. "Are you going to answer that?"

"Wasn't planning on it."

The ringing cut off, started back as the caller tried again.

Siren arched an eyebrow.

Jace pulled the phone from his pocket and answered without ever breaking eye contact. "Yeah?"

"It's been over three hours. Is everything okay?" a woman's voice asked.

Siren couldn't hear it well enough to place it, only well enough to know it wasn't Valkyrie's.

"Who the fuck is that?"

Jace ignored her. "Everything's fine. I'll call you when I get this sorted out." He hung up. "That was Meredith."

"You came here with *Meredith*?"

"Yes, because I thought whoever was after you broke into this place, and I might need a Tracker. Instead, I found you."

She threw his words back at him. "Terribly sorry to disappoint."

"Disappointed? No. Infuriated? Yes."

"If you're so pissed off, why are you still here?"

"Which part of *I love you* did you not understand earlier?"

"The part where you're pissed off, but you're still here."

"That's what love is."

"Being pissed off and still being around?"

"Yes. You get pissed off and then you work through it. So I'm pissed that you ran off, but I'm staying, because no matter what happens, I want to face it with you."

"A sweet sentiment," a voice said from the doorway. "I believe the last boy who died for her shared it. She does seem to have that effect on men, does she not?"

Siren couldn't breathe. How could she not have felt him, not have noticed his approach? The gray-eyed man stood in the doorway, and no prickles had lit her skin, no hunger had saturated the air, no buzzing of flies had filled her ears. Something about the words he'd spoken, his voice, was off, too. It wasn't until she realized that his lips hadn't moved, that the voice had sounded more female than male, that it dawned on her he *wasn't* speaking. Someone else was speaking through him.

She moved instinctively in front of Jace.

"Noble," the woman's voice said through him, the gray-eyed man's lips curving into a smile. "But it won't do any good."

Creatures poured into the room, not carrion hounds this time but something new, all manner and size of serpent-like creatures slithering forward, turning the floor into a churning mass of reptilian bodies.

Jace pulled a shield around them even as her own Aspect surfaced. She was Life, and that was what she reached for, her Aspect seeking out dozens of reptilian heartbeats. It wrapped around them and squeezed. The first wave of serpents dropped, their deaths echoing through her with a wave of sadness. Whatever they were, it wasn't their fault they'd been brought here.

But that wouldn't stop them from killing her. From killing Jace. The dozens she'd killed barely made a dent in the hordes, their bodies buried beneath the ones that followed, new monsters slithering and crawling over their fallen brethren.

Siren stretched the net of her Aspect farther, finding more heartbeats to wrap her power around, twice as many deaths reverberating through her as she clenched her fist and the heartbeats stopped.

The barrier inside her shuddered, hairline fractures spider-webbing across its surface, another chunk of it falling away. Aspect surged out of the new opening and reveled in its freedom, filled her veins and demanded release. It felt Jace behind her and recognized him, not as she did, but as just another heartbeat among the many.

Her power lashed out and wrapped itself around him.

Horror slammed through her and she *pulled* at her Aspect. It answered reluctantly. She peeled it off him like prying loose glue that had almost set.

In the absence of her own attacks, the creatures pounded at the shield Jace held around them. Power flooded out of him, the non-combat nature of his Aspect forcing him to pour more and more into the shield to hold it together. At the rate he was going, he'd burn out soon.

She didn't dare unleash her Aspect on the scale she'd done before, couldn't risk that in the reach for dozens, hundreds, of heartbeats, she wouldn't stop the wrong one. But she could find *one* heartbeat, specifically, and end this.

Siren turned her focus on the gray-eyed man and slipped her Aspect's leash. It lunged for him, engulfed him, and Siren felt… nothing. No heartbeat. No vitality. Nothing to suggest a living person.

What the hell?

A smile split the man's face and the woman's voice taunted, "You didn't really think you were the only one with Life Aspect, did you?"

A simulacrum. He was a simulacrum. That was why she hadn't felt him approach, hadn't heard the telltale signs that always warned her of his presence. Because he wasn't really here. And if he wasn't here, she couldn't stop him.

Dark Aspect punched the air around the man's illusion and spectral harpies blossomed above, dozens of them, all crowded into the small space. They dove at Jace's shield, one after another, dying as they hit it but thinning the shield with their deaths.

Jace dropped to his knees. Sweat ran in rivulets down his face. His skin blanched, and his breath came in harsh, ragged gasps. The ward would give, or he would.

She had to find the gray-eyed man and end this. She didn't know if he was the Life Aspect user, or if it was the woman who spoke through him, but one of them had to be nearby in order to hold the simulacrum in place.

The creatures. To control them, they had to be linked to the man. She could follow that link.

Siren closed her eyes, spread her Aspect out through the creatures surrounding them, looking for a commonality among them.

There. A slender, invisible thread clung to each creature. She picked one and followed it, her Aspect sliding past the simulacrum and out the door, traveling until she felt him. He was close, maybe a block away.

Hundreds of threads fed into him, forming a thick, ropy vine, each thread alive with the heartbeat of a serpent, a harpy. So many lives, each one tethered to him. If she severed them, all at once, could he handle the backlash?

One very important, very precious, heartbeat thumped behind her, and she knew it didn't matter. She couldn't risk it, couldn't risk *him.*

A plan formed in her mind. It would never work if the gray-eyed man was actually in the room, but he wasn't. He couldn't *feel* her and Jace with his Aspect, he could only watch them through the eyes of his creatures.

"Jace, you have to let the shield go."

Predictably, he looked at her like she was insane.

"You're spending too much power. It'll kill you." She didn't have to work to bring panic into her voice.

"If I let it go, we're dead."

"Jace." She brought her voice to a hysterical pitch. "*Please,* you can't—" Her Aspect struck, commanding him to *sleep.* Jace dropped. Her Aspect suppressed his breath to shallow sips. If she didn't *know* he was alive…

She let out a sob and lunged for Jace even as the shield crumpled around them and the creatures poured in. Serpentine bodies wrapped around her, buoyed her up and carried her out to the place where the gray-eyed man waited.

"You killed him," she screamed and fought the hold of the serpents twined around her, their scaled bodies pressed sickeningly against her skin. "You bastard, you *killed him.*"

Away from Jace, she drew her Aspect to her in a torrent and unleashed it. It collided with the gray-eyed man's, and for one ludicrous moment, she thought she might even kill him. Then he laughed. His Aspect slipped around hers, hit her skin like frostbite. Pain blossomed inside her skull, filtered down through her veins, her nerves, her muscles, melding to her until she *was* pain, and pain was her.

Her last thought as her vision blurred and darkness chased out her agony was a bittersweet one.

I love you, too, Jace. I never got to tell you.

And now, she never would.

THIRTY-SEVEN

S iren knew someone watched her even before she opened her eyes. She *felt* it, the weight of a gaze heavy upon her. She lay on a thin mattress that felt more like a cot than a bed, and the air tasted stale, as if the area didn't get good ventilation, and it was cold.

She opened her eyes. She was in a small cell, the walls at her back and side cement-block. The other two were prison bars. In the cell across the aisle from her, a girl lay asleep on her own cot, snow-white hair a delicate contrast to her dark skin. Even in sleep, she looked exhausted, her fingers twitching in the grip of unpleasant dreams.

Siren pushed herself up, arms and fingers leaden with cold, traced the feeling of being watched to the cell next to her. A man with acerbic blue eyes watched her. His black hair had grown long to brush the tops of his shoulders, and she put him at late fifties, maybe, though it was difficult to tell.

She had no trouble placing him—she'd dreamed about eyes that exact shade of blue for the last six months, though the pair in front of her lacked the warmth of the ones she knew so well.

"Elijah Winters."

His gaze narrowed. "I don't know you."

"No. I know" —*your son*, she almost said, before she thought better of it and finished— "your daughter."

"Oh?" He settled back against the stone wall of his cell. He looked oddly at ease for a man imprisoned, supremely unconcerned with his captivity. "And how is my Valkyrie?" He asked after her like he might ask how his estate's gardens had fared in his absence.

"She's fine. Good." Siren found herself biting off the words because his manner put her hackles up.

"Unfortunately, she can't say the same thing about your son," said a voice from the end of the aisle between cells. A woman emerged, the gray-eyed man following in her wake. "After all, he did die trying to save her." The woman's voice slurred and lisped, as if she didn't have full control over her speech. It was the same voice that had spoken for the gray-eyed man's simulacrum in Jace's townhouse. There was something familiar about it, but the woman stood just far enough away, her face covered in shadow, and Siren couldn't place it.

Hearing the proclamation of Jace's death hit her with sickening intensity. She didn't know if the woman said he was dead because they had fallen for her ruse, or if they had gone back to the townhouse and finished the job. She waited for Elijah Winters to round on her, to demand to know if it was true.

Instead, he shrugged. "I don't have a son."

Siren gaped at him. Yes, he'd disowned Jace, but *that* was his response to hearing that his son was dead? To just claim he didn't have one?

Down the aisle, the woman moved forward. She leaned heavily on the gray-eyed man, her gait slow and shuffling as she hitched and dragged, her approach more like that of an ambling monster than a woman. She stepped into the fluorescent light in front of the cell, and Siren gasped.

"Not quite as I used to be, am I?" The left side of the woman's face curved up in a macabre smile, half of it paralyzed and immobile. The entire right side of her body sagged, the skin wrinkled and desiccated, her right eye clouded over and sightless. She reminded Siren of nothing so much as the description of the Norse goddess Hel, born half-dead, half-alive.

"Anne," she whispered, the name a hoarse scratch in the back of her throat.

"Do you like what you've made of me?" Siren's foster mother gestured grandly at her withered half.

Siren swallowed her revulsion, her fear. "I'd like you better if you were dead like I'd intended." Now that Siren could feel her own power, she felt Anne's, too, and understood why the woman *hadn't* died that night alongside Mark.

You didn't think you were the only one with Life Aspect, did you?

Anne *tsked* again. "Is that anyway to talk to your mother?"

"You were never my mother. Mara Savage was my mother."

"I raised you, didn't I? Quieted all of your annoying little cries—you were such a tiresome baby, always needing attention. I watched you grow up. If that isn't the definition of a mother, what is?"

"You only did that so I would have something to lose." Her voice grew thick. "You killed Thomas for what? So I'd break this containment? What do you even want me for?"

Anne's gaze flicked to Elijah, so briefly Siren almost missed it. "That isn't for me to divulge."

Whatever it was, she clearly didn't want to say in front of Elijah, though what she thought he would do with the information when trapped in a cell, Siren didn't know.

"Then who can?"

"James wanted to kill you, you know?" Anne said, rather than answer. "You *did* almost kill me, and he took it personally."

The gray-eyed man—James— put a hand on Anne's shoulder. Siren read genuine affection between them, and it made her sick. It seemed wrong somehow that people who could kill without remorse could share emotions like affection.

"I was catatonic for months. Life Aspect has its limits, you know? People who haven't seen it in decades imagine it as some cure-all for disease and death. They envision an end to cancer and chronic health problems. But we are like any other Aspecter. We create a finite amount of power each day. If you fed it into a cancerous individual day in and day out, then yes, you could cure that person's cancer. But the world's? No. It's taken me six years to reach this lovely state you see before you now."

"What's your point?"

"My *point*," Anne snarled, "is you should be grateful I didn't let James kill you like he wanted."

"Why bother?" But even as she asked, she looked at Anne's half-dead body and knew. "You think I'll *fix* you? After everything you did to me, everything you've *taken*, you think *I'm* going to help you?"

"Oh, you are. Whether you want to or not, you *are* going to fix me." Anne's Aspect snaked out, wrapped around Siren, stroked against the containment inside her body. "So much power. It strengthens as it sits, you know? It's why we're compelled to use it. You have twenty years of it, yes, but not only that. Twenty years of it compounding over and over and over again.

"I'm going to drain you dry. And when I'm whole again, I'm going to do marvelous things."

Siren's heart thudded against her ribcage. Was that really something they could do? *Take* her power? She was dangerous enough with it, but if *Anne* had it? Anne, and James, and whoever the man was who had engineered Siren's containment in the first place?

"I'll never that happen."

"You won't be able to think clearly enough to stop it."

Anne raised her left hand and twisted it into a fist. Pain, as if a grenade had detonated in the center of her chest and traveled outward, punched through Siren. It hit the frail shell of her body and rebounded. The agony, unable to dissipate, circulated inside her. Each time it hit a surface off which to bounce it amplified, until her body was nothing more than an echo chamber for pain.

THIRTY-EIGHT

Time passed for Siren in an abstract way, extending to her only the knowledge that time *had* passed, because that was what time did. How much or how little was a level of awareness she no longer possessed.

Pain melded to her body, suffused itself into her being and refused to leave. It had settled into a steady rhythm that coursed through her anew with each beat of her heart and stole her ability to think.

Her moments of lucidity were few, but she learned what she could when they came. She had not been moved. She had not been tied up. Neither fact mattered overmuch because it took all her concentration to keep breathing despite how the rise and fall of her chest sent crackles of pain radiating through her body. Her eyes were grainy and dry, and closing them hurt, a sign they had been open too long without blinking.

Raising herself to a sitting position took several falls in and out of consciousness, and in terms of minutes or hours or days, she had no idea how long it took her to accomplish the feat. She was aware on occasion of a voice talking to her.

When she came fully back from unconsciousness, her head was fuzzy and she didn't know where she was. *Who* she was.

Little details trickled in. Her back propped against the corner formed by two cold cement walls. The hard cot beneath her. Pain.

Siren. She was Siren, and she was trapped.

"You awake?"

It took her a minute to place the voice, but it came to her: Elijah. Jace's father.

Jace. Was he alive?

"He is," an angelic voice said, the one she remembered had spoken to her frequently while she drifted.

Siren turned, slivers of pain slicing through her neck at the movement. The girl was older than she'd first thought, maybe twelve. She had wide, haunted, chocolate-brown eyes that held a faraway glaze, suggesting she might slip away at any moment.

"I didn't think I asked that out loud."

"Oh, you didn't." The girl beamed. "But you were *going* to ask at some point, so I already knew that look on your face just now meant you were thinking about it."

Siren frowned. Even that small movement sent flickers of pain across her skin, but she was getting better accustomed to the small pains, better able to withstand them.

"So let me get this straight. You knew what I was *going* to ask and you—"

"Don't ask her any questions," Elijah snapped, cutting Siren off before she *could* ask the question. Even with his intervention, the girl's eyes had momentarily shuttered over, and it struck Siren where she'd seen the look before.

"You're related to Charles." She wondered if the girl's eyes would one day give way entirely to white mist, as his seemed to have done.

"I *am.*" The girl smiled, and Siren wondered how she could sound so genuinely happy in a place like this, as if Siren putting the connection together was the most exciting thing that had happened to her in a long time.

Then again, maybe it was.

"I'm his granddaughter. Lucille. But Charles raised me. My Mom got lost in the Sideways Place, and Dad was never around, so Charles is all I have. He promised *I* wouldn't get lost in the Sideways Place, that he could teach me to always come back, like he does." She bit her lip, some invisible weight slipping onto her shoulders. "I *try* to do what he taught me, but it's hard. They ask so many questions here. Sometimes they ask so many that I start seeing the questions they're going to ask, the questions other people are going to ask, and I answer those, too."

Like you did with me. If she's right, if she really knew what I wanted to ask, then...

Jace was alive.

She remembered the deal she'd made with Charles for the book he'd lent her.

She knew, now, what service he would have asked of her and she was sad that she would never get to perform it for him. That she would never help him find his granddaughter.

"Charles is looking for you," she said, hoping that would offer Lucille some comfort. "I think he thought I'd be able to help. I'm sorry that I won't."

Lucille looked bewildered. "But you already have." She frowned, bit her lip again, a trickle of blood running down her chin. "Or you will. Maybe. I think, I don't—" Her eyes glazed over, and she cut off. She brought her arms in front of her face and her fingers curled into her hair, pulling at the strands until Siren was afraid she would rip them out.

She reached out on instinct, fought past the pain to brush a tendril of Aspect against the girl. "Sleep now."

The girl let out a long sigh and stumbled to the cot, her eyelids shuttering closed.

In the cell next to Siren, Elijah crossed to his own cot and settled onto it. "She isn't lucid very often these days."

"Do you care?"

He shrugged. "I suppose not. Is Jace truly dead?"

Not, *Is my* son *dead?* Just a cold, dispassionate inquiry. Either

Elijah Winters was far more of a bastard than even Jace had indicated, or something wasn't right here.

"Yes, he's dead." And even though she knew it wasn't true, saying the words sent a twist of hurt through her. "I understand why they're keeping Lucille, but why are they keeping you here?"

From what Valkyrie had told her about why Elijah had been hunting Anne and James, Siren would have thought they would kill Elijah and be done with the problem, not lock him up in a cell and do...what? He wasn't beaten blue and bloody, but then Siren's current condition was a testament to the truth that pain didn't have to leave visible scars to be felt. Even so, he didn't look malnourished, either.

He didn't, she realized, look like a prisoner at all.

"I honestly don't know."

And that, Siren thought, *can't possibly be right*. Elijah Winters had been hunting these people since he rescued his wife, and he *didn't know* why they were keeping him alive?

She nodded, outwardly accepting his answer. She tried reaching for her Aspect again, but the pain this time was swift and strong, sending her vision swimming with black dots.

"I wouldn't bother. The more you use it, the more painful it will get."

"What did they do to me?" she asked, though she was beginning to wonder if the more accurate question was, *What did* you *do to me?*

"Tied a pain spell to the nature of your Aspect."

And the nature of her Aspect was life. "So it hurts to live?"

A smile ghosted across his face. "You catch on quick."

Not quick enough.

"I do. So why don't we quit playing games? You're not Jace's father."

"Too true." The image of Elijah Winters faded, replaced by a younger, thinner man with wavy brown hair. Siren had no trouble placing him at all.

"The scribe from my Council hearing. But I'm guessing that's not your real appearance, either."

"What is reality? One face is as good as any other."

"What should I call you then?"

"This face went by the name Gary. It's boring as sin, but it'll do. Oh, don't look so disappointed. You didn't think I'd tell you my real name, did you? "

No, she supposed that would have been asking too much.

"Even if I told you, it wouldn't do you any good. I've been doing this for decades and I've never come close to being caught."

"Elijah took down your operation once. When he rescued Jace's mother."

The man snorted. "He took down a fraction of my work. Evelyn and you were around the beginning of my career. And while *you* are certainly my most powerful success in terms of raw Aspect, and I do have a very important use for you, you certainly aren't the most interesting thing I've ever created."

"I'm not a thing."

"Semantics are so very tiresome, wouldn't you agree?"

She wouldn't. "Do you even *have* Elijah?"

His lips twisted into a smile, as if her question—or his answer—amused him in some particular way. "As it so happens, I do. Though I don't bring him out much these days."

"And what are you hoping to get out of me? Why the charade?"

He shrugged. "Just a bit of fun. A couple days from now, you won't even remember your own name, and after that, well..." He grinned at her. "Do you want to know what the problem with the Council is?"

"No."

"They have no vision," he went on, as if she'd said *yes*. "They've chained themselves to the antiquated methods the original Aspecters used to control power and society, and they view any deviation, any *progress*, as a sign of social abnormality."

Gee, I wonder why.

"The Wild Magic Alliance is worse. They don't cling to foolish ideals but they're lazy and incompetent, blathering on about the natural order of things. They can't build anything because they'd have to get along with each other to accomplish anything of note.

"Neither of them could have created that barrier inside you. They couldn't even have conceived of it. You wouldn't believe how many designs I had to go through to find one that could contain the power you hold *and* that would eventually break down if triggered in the right manner."

"Am I supposed to congratulate you?"

"It wouldn't be unwarranted. You're the culmination of years of research. You're one of a kind. It's a shame stolen Aspect can only be used by another with the same affinity. I had to dredge the backwaters of the Wild Alliance to find Anne once I discovered what you were, and then she wouldn't come without that *thing* she calls a husband. He barely has the intellect of an insect.

"But you're going to be worth it." He stalked to the bars that separated them and they disappeared. Disappeared, because they had never been there. Because they'd only been illusion this entire time. He gripped her jaw in his hand, his power slicking over her in an oily caress.

"With you, I'm finally going to destroy the Council. And once they're gone, I'll put on a new face and fill that void. I'll finally make Aspect Society into something *useful*." He stroked his hand across her face. "I hope you survive the harvest. There's still so much I could do with you." He pressed his lips to her forehead. Pain radiated from his touch, blossomed inside her skull. Her vision exploded into a blast of white light before it all went dark.

～

SHE WOKE because someone kept saying a word over and over, frantically, as if it were important. *Siren. Siren. Siren.*

She blinked, barely registering the little crackles of electric pain the action caused. Other pains had become too great for the little ones to matter.

"Siren, you have to wake up."

Siren. Was *she* Siren? The girl staring at her, begging her to wake up, certainly seemed to think so. She didn't recognize the girl, but then, she didn't recognize anything.

"Yes?" she asked hesitantly, mostly to make the girl stop shouting. Each syllable was an explosion inside her head. Even her own speech hurt her ears, slurred and barely audible though it was.

The girl pressed close to a row of bars. "You need to hold on."

Siren's eyelids fluttered shut. They were heavy, eyelids, and keeping them open took effort. "Hold on to what?" she managed.

"Who you are. Who Jace is. It doesn't work out if you don't remember."

Jace. It was a nice name. It probably belonged to a nice person.

The name faded as she drifted back under the heavy veil of sleep. She didn't understand why the girl thought it was so important she remember a name, but she'd sounded so earnest, so desperate, that Siren would try.

But the next time she surfaced, she'd forgotten her name again, her entire world narrowed to a constant thrumming beat of pain, and the feeling of walls inside her slowly disintegrating. She wasn't certain what the walls were, but she knew that the power on the other side of them, power that danced in kaleidoscopes of colors, was hers. It called to her, wanting her to join their dance, *become* them. To lose herself in power.

She tried, but she never could reach it, the pain from each attempt taking her under into a state that was not quite unconsciousness, but wasn't wakefulness, either. When she hovered in that in-between place, a part of her remembered that something was terribly wrong, that there was a danger in the power that called to her, and in those times she longed to sleep fully and never wake.

But sleep, too, eluded her. Each time she came close to it a sound like a gong being struck sent shockwaves through her, jolting her back to wakefulness and setting her teeth on edge.

When was the last time she'd actually slept? A faraway, rational side of her whispered that the sleep deprivation was intentional, that it put her in an increasingly fragile state of mind, and she should fight its effects. But the part of her that remembered the importance of keeping her sanity drifted further away with each ring of that accursed gong, until she woke to it each time like a snarling animal, yipping and biting at the pain and not understanding why the more she struggled, the worse the pain became.

CHAPTER

THIRTY-NINE

Jace prowled among the shelves in the library, testy and sullen, feeling every bit like a wounded animal hiding in his territory.

She'd *knocked him out*. Once again she hadn't trusted him, and once again she was gone, and he was stuck here trying to find her. There'd been no trace of her in Portland, and he wasn't having any more luck in Seclusion. He hadn't slept much in the last two days, and his mood was so foul that even Percy, who insisted on hovering in his general vicinity, didn't want to come *close* to him.

"For goddess' sake, Jace, this has to stop."

He stopped pacing, saw Valkyrie in the doorway.

"*Look* at yourself."

He didn't know what the devil she was going on about, but it was better to just do what she asked when she was in one of these moods. He looked down. He wore a pair of gray sweats and a white t-shirt. Perfectly respectable around-the-house wear. If he'd been in the sweats since he'd gotten home, what business was it of hers? He could walk around the damn house how pleased.

He shoved his hands into the sweatpants' pockets. "What?"

"You're bordering on becoming a creature of pathetic misery. Clean yourself up. Deal with this. *Do* something."

"And what exactly am I supposed to do? I found her. I lost her, and no matter what I try, I can't figure out how to find her again."

"Well, I guarantee doing everything you've done all over again is better than ghosting around in here like you've lost your damn mind. You're scaring the hell out of me." She turned to leave, stopped. "You know, when Dad disappeared, you were the one who told me to pull it together. That when the time came, I wouldn't be worth a damn if I let myself fall apart. Seems to me you could stand to take your own advice."

When he didn't answer she snapped, "I'm making you something to eat. Be downstairs in half an hour."

She left, and Jace returned to his pacing out of sheer defiance, but it didn't have the same soothing quality it had held before Valkyrie chastised him. Giving up, he went to take a shower and, he supposed, put on something other than sweats.

He came downstairs exactly half an hour later, freshly cleaned and shaved, wearing actual clothes, and surprised at the difference it made in his mood. Valkyrie was right. He'd been sulking, and sulking wasn't going to help Siren. A tantalizing aroma wafted from the kitchen, and he was relieved to see that "making you something to eat" translated to Valkyrie ordering Chinese. His sister's cooking was not a thing for even the boldest of men to take a chance on.

He helped himself to three eggrolls, some lo mein, and a container of shrimp with vegetables, wondering how long it had been since he'd eaten. He was *starving*.

"Don't make yourself sick," Valkyrie snapped, still obviously pissed at him, "you haven't eaten in a day and a half."

The doorbell rang, and Jace nearly took off the bar countertop jumping out of his seat.

Valkyrie grabbed his arm and pulled him back down. "Sit. Stay. Eat."

Jace sat. He selected a piece of shrimp with his chopsticks and wondered if he should also whine or bark, but decided Valkyrie would punch him before she would find the joke funny.

When she came back, Meredith and Charles were with her, and the look on Meredith's face made him stop eating.

"I will get straight to the point," Charles said. "You know I lent Siren a book?"

"Yes."

"I made a deal with her for it—that within three days of finishing it, she must return the book to me and answer a question, or else I would have the right to retrieve it. The power that binds the oaths I make is stronger than most power that walks the Earth today. It has been precisely three days since she finished the book."

"Are you telling me you can find her?"

"I am telling you that I already have."

CHAPTER

FORTY

Compound, Jace decided, was entirely too apt a word for what he looked down on.

If he'd stumbled across the place without knowing otherwise, he would have assumed it was an abandoned military barracks.

"Thoughts?" Valkyrie prompted.

"I wish Martin DuPont would get his head out of his ass."

The older man stood ten feet away with the other Council members, looking uncomfortable in cargoes and a t-shirt instead of his Council robes.

Valkyrie snorted, twirling a knife in and out between her fingers. "Don't hold your breath. I think this is the first time he's breathed fresh air in a decade. Makes a man all twitchy."

It was the most she'd said in the last twenty-four hours, and her attention was only half on him as she spoke. She was as focused on the compound as he was, and though she hadn't put her thoughts into words, he knew what she was thinking: that if the people who had Siren were the same people who had held their mother, there was a good chance their father was in that compound too.

"I don't understand why he's bothering to get out and breathe the fresh air now."

Once they'd scoped out the location Charles had given him, Jace had been forced to agree with Valkyrie's assertion that they needed to clue the Council in. There were too many people in the compound for him, Val, Meredith, and Random to take on their own. They needed numbers and needed them fast. Albeit fast was a subjective term since it had taken the Council two full days to agree to go after Siren, and DuPont's agreement had discussed Siren in contingent terms that Jace liked not at all. Words like, "unpredictable" and "unstable." They didn't know what had been done to Siren, DuPont explained, so they needed to be certain she wasn't a danger to them.

Focus on Siren. The most important thing right now was getting her out. He would deal with the Council's opinions about her later.

"What is taking them so long?" he growled. "Once we take out the warding, everyone in that compound is going to know we're here, so there's no point in dithering about it."

"But dithering is what the Council does best." Random joined them, standing next to Valkyrie. Nelsen perched on his right shoulder, talons digging into the leather patch worked into Random's shirt. As long as Jace had known Random, he'd never once gotten him to satisfactorily explain how his relationship with the falcon worked. Or, for that matter, where the damn bird had come from.

"Based on Nelsen's scouting, Jace, I think your best bet is the northeastern-most building. It has the highest concentration of warding designed to keep people from breaking in." His gaze flicked to Valkyrie. "*Your* best bet is the central building."

Her gaze zeroed in on the building he mentioned. "Why?"

"It has the most wards designed to keep people from breaking *out*."

Meredith joined them just as the Council broke apart and the rest of the gathered people shifted in response. "They're ready."

Jace lifted an eyebrow. "They don't need to take another vote or possibly consider it over coffee?"

"Don't say that too loud, or they might do just that."

"Good point." He watched the five Breakers in the group approach the warding, nerves rising then settling behind his chest. He looked at Meredith. "Thanks for coming," he said softly.

"Siren helped me once, so I owe it to her." Then she smiled, and there was something almost feral in it, something that hadn't been there when she was younger, and it made Jace wonder just how much of what she had lived through had changed her. "And the Council rarely ever lets us play like this. It's been a long time since I got to shove the truths people don't want to examine back down their own throats."

"You make it sound like we've all got enough inner demons to knock us dead."

"Not everyone," Meredith assented. "But enough do to make this interesting."

It was precisely that sort of attitude, Jace reflected, that made most people avoid Truthfinders.

Ahead, Aspect swelled around the five Breakers, pressure building in the air, filling Jace's ears until it muffled all sound. Then the pressure burst, the perimeter wards crumpled, and Jace moved forward, not giving a damn about DuPont angrily yelling after him. This wasn't an army, and DuPont wasn't his general. The only orders he had any intention of following were his own.

CHAPTER

FORTY-ONE

Time, for the nameless woman, was an impenetrable gray mist. It had become a concept that held little meaning for her, one she knew she ought to be concerned with, but could not remember why.

She remembered so little now, could no longer remember who she was, *why* she was. Her existence revolved around two things: a bright center of pain, and the whirling madness inside that pain that called to her with a siren's pull.

Siren's pull. The phrase amused her, though she didn't know why.

A clang of metal lit the air, and a breeze rushed into the small space she crouched in. She cringed, curling further in on herself, tucking her head into her arm to avoid the bright light filtering in.

"Get her out."

The female voice grated on her ears.

A man with gray eyes grabbed her roughly by her upper arms and pulled her out of the cell. She didn't like the cell, but it was familiar and, faced with the prospect of the unknown, she didn't want to leave. She went limp, feet scraping against concrete, forcing the man to haul her dead weight as she was dragged into the harsh, fluorescent lights of the adjacent room.

She felt exposed, the space around her too large. She wanted to hide again but couldn't, so she opened her eyes and squinted against the light. In the center of the room, someone had drawn a chalk rectangle on the concrete floor, and inside the rectangle was a cage that couldn't be seen with the eyes alone. It flickered and crackled, made of interwoven blue light, six feet tall by three feet wide.

The gray-eyed man kept a firm grip on her arm and dragged her over to the edge of the chalk line. The owner of the female voice walked up, her hair short and brown, her face freckled, something wrong with the right half of her body.

The sight of her sent fury howling through the nameless woman's chest. She lunged at the brown-haired woman, teeth snapping, every instinct in her demanding death.

Pain and a twist of her arm sent her to her knees, trembling and fighting the urge to vomit. Fingers tangled in her hair, yanked her head back.

"Don't," the brown-haired woman snapped. "We don't want her going off prematurely. Just get her inside."

The gray-eyed man smiled, his white teeth gleaming. He pulled her to her feet and threw her at the wall of the cage. She slipped through the wall as if the boundaries of the cage didn't exist, but when she slammed into the inside of the opposite wall, she hit it as if it were concrete.

A rumbling quake shook the ground, throwing her to her knees. She didn't realize this was abnormal until the man and the brown-haired woman shared twin looks of concern, and the door opened a few minutes later to let in a man with wavy brown hair.

"What's going on?" the brown-haired woman asked the newcomer.

"What's going on," he snarled, "is that Jace Winters isn't dead."

Jace. Had she known a Jace? She thought maybe she had, but everything was all jumbled up in her mind, and she couldn't remember.

"Should we move her?"

"Even if you could get her out of that," he snarled, pointing at the cage, "she wouldn't survive the trip. You," he pointed at the gray-eyed man, "get her started. Anne, you and I will finish the job you told me was already done."

"Yes, sir."

The door opened, closed, and she was alone with the gray-eyed man. He touched two fingers to his lips, blew her a kiss, and the molten agony that burned through her made the pain she had previously endured feel like ecstasy in comparison. It brought every nerve ending in her body to screaming wakefulness, battering at her muscles, her mind, her will.

She held the pain inside. Some stubborn part of didn't want to give him the pleasure of hearing her scream. A second wave of pain bit into her and twined with the first. She clenched her teeth, imagined she could feel cracks opening in the molars from how hard they ground together.

A third wave of agony. She closed her eyes, bit down on her tongue.

A fourth.

She tilted her head back and screamed. As the guttural sound escaped, something inside her shattered. A presence, cold and foreign yet achingly familiar, rushed to fill her. She felt as if plunged into both ice and flame, radiating with an intensity that had always been just a step outside of her reach.

Beneath it all, her body shuddered as nerves and muscles ripped apart and then stitched back together, only to be ripped apart again. The power filling her simultaneously destroyed her and rebuilt her, trapping her in an endless cycle of death and rebirth. Her vocal cords shattered beneath the strain of her screams, and even as power rebuilt them, she reacted to the pain with snapping teeth and animal rage. She wanted to hurt that which had hurt her, to sink her teeth into it and watch it bleed.

The cold fire thrumming in her veins caught her intent, swept it up and responded, made the intent its own. Power flowed from her, streaming outward in all directions, seeking the source of her anger. A separate force sucked her power down, fed it to the buzzing strands of blue light that formed a cage around her body, and she was unable to call it back.

Angered by the theft of what belonged to her, she followed her power as it twisted through the strands growing throughout the cage like the roots of some ancient tree, interwoven so tightly no space lay between them. Her power was *there,* soaked into the strands of the cage, held tight against its will.

She snarled and hurled her power at the walls of the cage. It merely slipped into the woven roots of the walls. She couldn't destroy the cage from this side. The gray-eyed man would not destroy it from his. But between them, *inside* the walls, lay power that was still hers. She simply had to reach it.

She pressed her hands to the cage, shoved her power at it once more, trying to forge a connection between herself and her power on the other side. All she succeeded in doing was giving the cage more of her, allowing it to *take* more from her. She needed a true connection, one that would bleed through the strands of the cage.

Bleed. She rolled the thought over in her mind. Now there was something she could do.

She sank her teeth into the soft skin between her thumb and forefinger until sweet copper filled her mouth. She pressed her palm back to the cage, her blood soaking into the strands of the wall, reaching through to touch her power trapped inside it. She felt the exact moment she had that connection, the moment the trapped power felt *her.*

It responded to her, hurling itself at the walls from the inside, until the individual strands that made those walls began to fray and splinter. As the strands unraveled, her power surged throughout the rest of the cage, hammering it in a tidal wave of force and anger, the impact rattling through the cage until the whole of it exploded.

Freed, her power returned to her, and she drank it in greedily, filling the terrible void inside her. She pulled a small chunk of power close, gathered it around her like a cloak, taking comfort in its presence.

The pain that was always with her intensified, and she followed it to its source, turning her attention to the gray-eyed man. He looked at once pathetic, small, and decidedly fragile. Had she really been so afraid of him moments before? She had a memory of running for years, of his face haunting her night-mares, and knew that whatever she could not remember, this man had been a large and unpleasant part of it.

Yet he seemed so insignificant next to the power she commanded. She called that power and thought a single word: *Back.*

Power lifted the man off his feet, flung him back. He hit the concrete wall with the sharp cracking of bones, sliding down to slump at its base. He coughed and wheezed, blood spraying from his lips. He sucked in air, choking, his breathing labored.

The pain that tethered her to him wavered, flickering in and out, in and out, and she saw the moment he decided to let it go, felt the agony slip free of her as if it had never been. Sensation returned to her in glorious detail, exquisite and delicate, no longer the dim, disconnected thing she had previously mistaken for it. She looked down and wiggled her fingers, cringing at the expectation of a pain that never came. Her feet were bare, and so she wiggled her toes too, dug them into the cool concrete beneath her feet, marveling at the feeling of being completely and totally alive.

She laughed, tears of ecstasy running down her cheeks, tilted her head back and issued a howl of joy that traveled up to echo off the ceiling. She looked down at her arms, covered in bruises. The mist of power blanketing her wrapped close against her skin, soothing, and the bruises faded, sinking into her flesh as if they had never been.

A wet cough drew her attention back to the man who slumped, dying, against the wall. She recognized, in a detached way, that she could fix him. With the power swirling to answer her every wish, she could manage it with barely a thought. Life magic was *good* at fixing things. A twitch here, a nudge there, and broken bones would mend, punctured lungs would heal.

And she saw that, just as easily, a different sort of twist would stop his heart.

The woman she had previously been, the one whose memories were distant things, even as they fought for purchase in her mind again, might have turned aside the second realization. That woman had killed when it was necessary, and only then. She would not kill a dying man, unless she told herself it was the kindest thing for him.

Kindness was not a factor for the woman standing in the room now, watching a man cough up his lifeblood.

The part of her that remembered things about her life told her she should let him die on his own. It would not be long now, a minute or two at most. To kill him with power in *this* way was an abomination in the eyes of the society she had joined, and if she did it, she might never be allowed to go back, and that was bad.

But the part of her that was most present didn't remember where *back* was, and it didn't care what others thought. She had been chased and captured and tortured, and the man who had done so did not deserve to exit this world on his own terms, but on hers.

She reached for a strand of power and twisted. The man stopped coughing. Stopped breathing. His life left him in a rush of wind that passed through the woman, enveloping her in euphoria, giving her an inkling of why it could be dangerous for someone with her type of power to kill this way.

It felt like bliss.

Stepping over the man's body, her power reached for the room's exterior door and threw it open. Wind rushed in, carrying with it the sounds of battle. It called to her, called to the power that pushed at the confines of her body demanding release.

A battle. Yes, that would do nicely, indeed.

CHAPTER

FORTY-TWO

The sight of her stole Jace's breath, and he would have taken a hit of concentrated power to the chest if Valkyrie hadn't knocked him out of the way, then taken two running steps and dispatched the assailant with an easy flick of her knife. She shot Jace an irritated, *What the hell?* look that was entirely lost on him, his attention riveted on the far side of the compound.

Siren picked her way through the chaos as if strolling serenely through the gardens of some well-manicured estate, her feet bare, her pace unhurried. She still wore the last things he'd seen her in, jeans and his flannel shirt over a tank top, though the articles of clothing were barely recognizable, torn and bloody and reduced almost to rags.

It didn't matter. She was radiant even in her disheveled state, like some ancient goddess of blood and battle. Her hair had grown far more than was possible in the handful of days she had been missing, hanging in long, tangled waves down her back. Power crackled in the air around her, its presence a mist that surrounded her like a shroud. Spells hurled at her only disappeared into that cloaking mist.

Jace knew with absolute certainty that the barrier inside her was gone, could *feel* it in the sheer unbridled potency of the power surrounding her. He didn't know how everyone around her was alive, how *she* was alive, when she'd been so certain of what would happen when the barrier inside her broke.

He just knew that she was, that she stood a mere hundred feet away from him, and his chest leapt with fierce hope. Two men charged her, one with a sword in hand, the other throwing spells at her in quick succession.

Jace's heart caught in his chest.

Siren smiled. She flicked her hands to her sides and the men crumpled.

Jace read euphoria in her eyes, and fear curdled in his stomach. He remembered stories of Life Aspect users gone mad from death frenzies. He wouldn't lose her, not like this. Not to madness. She had survived the dissolution of her barrier, had survived being kidnapped and likely tortured.

He would see that she survived this, too.

A short sword in one hand, a globe of power spinning to life in the other, Jace fought his way to her, grateful, for the first time in his life, that his father had forced him to become proficient in physical combat.

THE WOMAN WATCHED the two men crumple, felt their lives bleed out, then lowered her hands. Had she thought controlling the power was difficult? Had she feared it would break her body? It only wanted to be used, and she found she wanted very much to use it, that using it was simple.

She paused in the middle of the battle, her power rotating in frenzied circles around her. People fought each other, and though her mind was restless, didn't want to focus, she forced it to sort for her the answer of *why* they fought. She recognized insignias on some of the shirts, identified them as members of the Council. As for the others…an image of a wavy-haired man with a tilted smile rose in her mind, a man who had wanted to be free of both Council and law. These other men must fight for him, then.

She could destroy those who fought for him, could end the battle, rescue the Council members. But was one side any better than the other? Both were terrified of her. She read it in their eyes, and more than one of the spells hurled at her had come from those who bore Council insignias. They would both throw her in a cage again if given the chance. Why not let them destroy each other?

"Siren."

She turned, saw a man with golden hair and brilliant blue eyes, a streak of blood marring the side of his face. He held a short sword in one hand, its blade slicked with blood. His other hand was burned and blackened, the skin cracked and oozing fluids. The sight of it bothered her, but she didn't know why.

It didn't matter. If it bothered her, she would fix it.

Her power twisted about the man's hand, blackened pieces of skin sloughing off to reveal newly grown pink flesh. There. That was better. She turned away from him to wade farther into the battle when someone grabbed her.

She whirled in fury, power crackling about her fist, raised to strike. She stopped a second before her fist connected, staring into the blue eyes of the golden-haired man.

"Siren."

She shook her head. "Why do you keep calling me that?"

Why did his voice sound so hesitant, almost as if he were afraid of her? And if he *was* afraid, why did the idea bother her so much?

"Calling you Siren?" he repeated, questioning.

She nodded.

"It's your name. You don't remember?"

Remember. A man's voice, one she didn't like, *A couple days from now, you won't even remember your own name...*

Siren. Images flashed through her mind. Shopping—no,

working—in a music store, her feet propped up on a countertop as the golden-haired man walked in. Out on the street, running from a monster that hunted her. A large house with iron gates at the road, a raven-haired woman with a warrior's eyes. The golden-haired man again, laughing, making her coffee, holding her, kissing her.

Siren. *She* was Siren, and he was… "Jace?"

"That's right." But he sounded tentative.

"You're afraid of me," she accused.

"No. I'm afraid *for* you."

Siren frowned, eyebrows drawing together. "There is nothing to fear. They can't hurt me anymore."

"That's not what I'm afraid of."

Before he could tell her what exactly he *was* afraid of, an approaching figure caught Siren's eye. Her memory drew up a name for the man: Random. He walked like Random, tossed a cocky smile at her like Random, and yet beneath his appearance her power assured her that he most definitely was *not* Random.

Her power coalesced, and she took a step toward not-Random, fury limning her features.

"Siren, stop." Jace's hand on her arm. "That's Random."

"No," she growled, "it's not." He'd worn the face of Jace's father, the face of a Council scribe, and now, *now*, he was wearing Random's.

Siren shook Jace off and threw a rope of power at not-Random.

Too quickly for her to reel her power back in, too quickly for her to stop, Jace jumped in front of her.

"*No.*"

He screamed as her power latched onto him, intent on the purpose she had given it when she sent it toward a different target. She dropped to her knees beside him, matched her will against her own power's as it pulled Jace's life out of him.

But her power *liked* the taste of death she had given it earlier. It didn't need Jace like she did. It didn't *love* Jace like she did.

"No. No, no, no." But no amount of chanting the word like a prayer could loosen her magic's hold, could stop her from killing the man she loved.

On the other side of Jace, the man who was not Random laughed.

Her fury exploded. She inhaled and filled her breath with power. Then she screamed, releasing a shockwave of Aspect that hit the man in the chest. It slammed him backwards and the sound of his splintering bones filled the air. The residual power of the blast swept out in all directions, an indiscriminate wave of force that lifted every person in the compound off their feet before it slammed them back down, bringing a temporary quiet and stillness to the battlefield.

Siren grabbed the sword from Jace's limp hand and sliced it through the rope of power binding him to her. Pain ripped through her as she severed the connection, but it didn't matter. She was good at pain now.

"Please." She pressed her hand to his chest. It rose and fell with weak, shuddering movements. *"Please* don't die. Please. You can't. You can't leave me here."

She poured Aspect into him and discovered what she already knew. She was too late. The barest spark of life remained inside him, and she didn't know what to do, didn't know how to fix him, because there was nothing physically wrong with his body. No organ failures to reverse, no gashes to mend, no spilled blood to be replaced.

He was in perfect health, and he was dying because she had stolen the essence of his life from him, and she didn't know how to give it back. Desperate, she sank raw power into him, forcing it to breathe for him, to live for him.

Around her, the sounds of movement returned, but they were different this time. Rather than fight each other, the battlefield's combatants turned, as one, to her.

Aspect tore through the air toward her, coming from all sides. Her own power swirled up in a mist to envelope her and Jace, spells disappearing harmlessly into its depths. Her fury bubbled to the surface again. She needed focus, needed to save Jace, and two opposing factions had joined forces to destroy *her*.

She tilted her head back and let out a high, keening wail, releasing her anguish, her fear, her anger.

Those closest to her dropped to their knees, hands clasped to their ears as blood trickled from burst eardrums. She screamed until her breath ran out and the people nearest her lay unconscious. Her power lashed out, seeking heartbeats, tendrils reaching for every single person on the field, not stopping until she felt each heartbeat, each life, thrumming in connection to her.

It would be so easy to kill them.

Her power understood her thoughts, pulsed eagerly in response to them, wanting to slip the leash of her control. She tightened her grip on it and looked down at Jace.

She had to save him. She wanted to go *home* to him, to a life. One did not go home to one's lover after massacring a field of people.

She surveyed that field. People strained against her will, but she hardly noticed, their efforts an itch in the back of her mind. She lifted her hands and let her own will be known.

The people gathered in the field crumpled. Around their immobile bodies, vines sprang from the earth, binding hands and feet to the ground. She left only Valkyrie's, Random's, and Meredith's unbound. When they woke from the sleep she had layered them all in, the people she trusted would be free to sort the right from the wrong.

She turned her attention back to Jace, and her heart sank. The power she poured into him was the only thing keeping him alive, fanning the dying ember of his life. He had no will left.

Siren didn't care. If power would keep him alive, she would give him everything she had. If he needed will, she would give him her own.

She opened the well of her Aspect and let it flow into him,

forced his heart to keep beating, his body to keep functioning. Leaning over him, she whispered, "Live."

Then she kissed him, sinking the entirety of her power, her being, into the command she'd given, and her Aspect carried her will to him.

Siren had the joy of seeing his eyes open, of watching his lips form her name, before her heart stuttered and she dropped dead beside him.

FORTY-THREE

The world came into focus slowly. It was brighter than Siren remembered, even from behind closed eyelids. The inside of her skull had a scoured-sand feeling, her throat and mouth desperately dry.

She lay on her back, surrounded by a pleasant softness, save for something locked around her waist with all the give of an iron bar. She struggled to remove the iron band, panicking as memories of being trapped came roaring to the surface. She flailed, and one hand smacked against something that felt like sandpaper.

"Ow."

At the *ow* something that was pressed against her left side wriggled and let out a whine, and she stopped struggling. Percy. Percy was next to her, and she knew the voice that had spoken.

Jace. His arm was clamped around her waist, and he'd thrown a leg over her too.

"Worried I'm going to run away?" Her voice was scratchy and painful, but it worked, and she needed it to work because she needed him to say something, anything, to convince her that this was real. That *he* was real.

"If you hit me again, *I'm* going to be the one running away. I shouldn't have to stand for domestic abuse."

"You're a poster child for men's rights everywhere." She didn't know how she managed to speak over the cacophony of joy screaming, *Alive, he's alive,* inside her. "Can you get off me?"

"No."

"I have to pee."

"Don't care." He rolled her onto her side so he could glare at her. "You died. I woke up and you were dead. What the hell were you thinking? It should have been me. I was...I was already dead."

"You weren't."

He looked at her.

"Dead," she clarified. "You weren't dead, yet. Just dying. And it was my fault you were dying in the first place."

His arm tightened around her. "Yeah, well, if I'd listened to you when you said that guy wasn't Random, I wouldn't have been dying."

"If I'd been in my right mind, I would have understood that I needed to qualify how I knew that before trying to kill him."

"Are we really arguing over who gets to take credit for me almost dying?"

"Maybe. Look, about the guy who *wasn't* Random..." She trailed off, not quite sure how to say what she wanted to.

"He escaped," Jace said when she didn't continue. "No one's quite sure how since whatever you did put everyone else under."

"About him. He's—I think he's Valkyrie's father. Her biological father." It was something about the way he'd said *my Valkyrie* when he'd asked about her.

"I know. After the battle, when I could sort through the tangle of Aspect traces, I found his. It's the same one I remember from Mom. Valkyrie knows, but Siren? Please don't bring it up to her. She is not in a good place right now.

"The Council's looking for him but they're having about as much success as Dad had for the last twenty years."

Another thought hit her, made her bolt upright. "Lucille? Is she—"

"Fine. She's fine. Safe with Charles."

Thank goodness. She sank back down on the mattress as she sorted through everything that had happened, tried to figure out what was most important.

"The man they're after, the one with Illusion Aspect. He pretended to be your father for a little while. I figured out he wasn't, but he said Elijah is still alive. Did you find him there?"

Jace shook his head. "You and Lucille were the only ones there."

He tucked a strand of hair behind her ear, followed it down to where it now curled to her waist, the quick growth a side effect of the unrestrained use of her Life Aspect.

He looked...wounded.

"Is it okay?" She wasn't asking about her hair. They both knew it, and she was afraid of what answer he might give.

"You *died*."

"I think we established that," she said neutrally.

"If, as you said, *I* wasn't dead, why did fixing me kill you?"

So that's what was bothering him, then. "Physically, you were fine, but your...spirit, I guess you'd call it, had lost the will to live. Life Aspect can do a lot of things, but it can't force a person's will on *that* matter. So I gave you mine."

"You what?"

"I gave you my will," Siren repeated. "I was exhausted from power expenditure, and with my will gone? In retrospect, I guess I'm not surprised I died. Speaking of, how come I'm not still dead?"

"The short version? Ten minutes of CPR and mouth-to-mouth along with about three broken ribs from the previously stated efforts."

Siren breathed deeply. "Nothing feels broken. How long have I been out?"

"Two days." Jace pressed his palm to her ribs. "They started healing after twelve hours. That's when I knew you'd live. That's when I knew you weren't Broken."

Broken. She hadn't even thought of it. She'd read that if a person used too much Aspect, spent it down to the last spark, it was possible to lose it altogether, to never have Aspect again. When it happened, they called a person Broken.

"No," she said softly, "I'm not. Why does that seem to make you sad?"

She let it lie between them for a moment, unanswered, and then said, "At the compound, you said you weren't afraid of me. Is that—I'd understand if that's changed."

He shook his head. "It's not that. The Council has been demanding I turn you over to them since they got back on their feet. I only managed to get you here because Val and Random woke up before everyone else. I have the house warded down so tight the Council can't get through without the Breakers they lost at the compound, and because I suspect they're just waiting me out. They'll fly in new Breakers or we'll come out, eventually, and they know that. *I* know that. I just needed time. For you to get better."

"You should have let them have me. They'll blame you now, too."

"I don't care."

"We can't hide behind these walls forever."

"I'm not letting them take you."

"Jace—"

"No. We can slip out of here. Go overseas, go anywhere. I don't care, as long as I'm with you."

That was...adorably sweet.

"I want you to take me to see them."

His arms tightened around her. "No."

"Jace."

"No."

Siren sighed. They were officially into "Me Tarzan, you Jane" territory.

"I'm not turning myself in, Jace, but I'm tired of running. I want to stay put. I want to stay here, with you. I have a plan, but I have to talk to the Council."

"What's the plan?"

"I need twenty-four hours, Aunt Ella's phone number, and a way out of this house without the Council seeing us leave."

"Which part of that is a plan?"

Since he didn't seem like he was going to let it go, she told him.

"That...could work." She could see the gears spinning in his mind. "Goddess knows if anyone can tell you how to pull it off, it's Aunt Ella."

"So we're agreed, then?"

"What if they don't let you go?"

"They will."

"And if they don't?" he repeated.

"They can't hold me," she said, finally. "If they don't see reason, then we'll leave. I will get on a plane with you to wherever you want, and we'll keep going. Happy?"

"Mollified."

"I'll take mollified. Now can you get off me? I wasn't kidding when I said I had to pee."

Jace helped her up, helped her to the bathroom door because her legs were all wobbly from being in bed for two days.

"Could you get me some water?" Mostly, she asked because he looked like he might hover in the doorway forever if she didn't.

His voice, when he spoke, was a ghost's whisper. "Promise me you'll be here when I get back?"

There was something still...haunted, in his eyes, and she didn't like knowing she was responsible for putting it there.

"I promise."

"Okay." But he stood there a moment longer, staring as if trying to memorize every detail of her face, before he left.

Once she took care of her most pressing business, she had time to register that her teeth felt like they were covered in a layer of fine moss, and she desperately needed a shower. Her now long hair was a tangled mess that would likely require triple-conditioning and breaking several hair picks to fix.

She stripped out of her dirty clothes, rummaged in the vanity drawers until she found a new toothbrush in-package, lined it with paste and hopped into the shower, toothbrush in hand. The water came out blessedly hot, loosening the tense muscles in her back while she scrubbed at her teeth like she could wash away the last week along with the dirt. She covered herself in body wash, resisting the urge to drag her nails across her skin along with the soap, to try and scrape away everything that had happened.

She was on her second round of rinsing conditioner out of her hair when Jace returned. He opened the glass shower door long enough to hand her the bottle of water and then he retreated. He leaned against the sink vanity and stared at the floor, his fingers digging into the marble countertop.

Siren twisted the bottle nervously in her hands but she couldn't bring herself to drink it. She couldn't see Jace's expression through the dark, tinted shower glass, but he didn't look *good*.

"Are we okay?" her voice broke on the last word.

His head jerked up. "We're okay."

He said it, but she didn't *feel* it, and she needed to. Desperately.

"Then why are you out there?"

He stripped out of his clothes, stepped into the shower and took her in his arms. She wrapped herself around him and held him tight. Her body shook with the fear that, no matter what he'd said, they weren't okay.

"I love you," she said. But the words said something else, too, something she wouldn't verbalize. *Please don't leave me.*

He buried his face in her neck and breathed her in. His arms tightened around her. "Don't ever die on me again."

"Promise," she whispered.

"I love you, too."

And there, finally, was the intensity in his voice she needed to believe him.

"Show me."

He took her face in his hands and kissed her.

She felt his Aspect awaken and the hot water beating against her softened and slowed as it reached the hollow of her back. The droplets fanned over her like phantom fingers, caressed her hips before they glided up the sides of her stomach, then higher, higher, to cup the outer swell of her breasts.

She gasped into his mouth and he swallowed it hungrily, pushed her gently against the shower wall as water danced under his control, teasing her nipples to hard peaks. His mouth left hers and skimmed down her neck to her breasts, water-driven Aspect moving down between her legs to rub against the center of her pleasure.

"Jace." Her voice was a breathy moan. "Please."

He lifted his face back to hers.

"Please what?"

His erection pressed against her stomach, throbbing and hard.

"Love me," she said.

His eyes went dark and liquid. "Always."

He gripped her hips, lifted her up, and drove into her. She wrapped her legs around his waist, taking him deeper. He filled her perfectly, and she lost herself in the feel of his skin against her own, of his mouth claiming hers. His Aspect worked her breasts, her clit. Every stroke of his hips as he took her brought her closer to ecstasy.

She held back from the peak, urging him faster, faster, until the ragged catch in his breath told her he was almost there.

"Now," she told him.

He gave a hoarse cry and buried himself in her one final time. Her own orgasm tore through her at the feel of his release, the shockwaves of it cascading through her body.

She unlocked her legs from around his waist and let him lower them to the bathroom floor, her body gloriously wrecked.

"You didn't tell me you could do magic sex."

"Did I forget to mention it?" He nuzzled the side of her neck.

"You did. You really should have led with magic sex."

CHAPTER

FORTY-FOUR

Siren's power radiated out from her, down her arms, through her fingertips, and into the still form beneath her. To her power's initial inspection, there was still nothing wrong with Hank. No physical ailment marked him, and though the Dark Aspect involved in the initial attack on him had long since been removed, he had never woken.

But what had happened with Jace on the battlefield had given her an idea, and so she searched for something that wasn't precisely *wrong*, but wasn't precisely *right*, either. She didn't know how long she sat lost in the trance of her Aspect, but she knew it must have been quite some time, because she felt Jace's nervous tension growing next to her by the second.

Hank was, after all, in a Council-run medical facility, and it had taken Random's peculiar Aspect to get them into Hank's room unseen. Well, his Aspect, and his unparalleled ability to flirt. She could hear Hank's nurse giggling outside the door, more than happy to bend the rules and allow Hank's "granddaughter" some time alone with him. It did, after all, give the nurse time alone with Random.

Thank goodness Valkyrie hadn't come with them. Otherwise, it never would have worked.

Betty Lou's presence, as one of Hank's regular visitors over the last six months, had helped as well. Siren felt guilty for bringing her because she wasn't completely certain that she *could* wake Hank up, and she hadn't wanted to give her false hope.

Contacting her at all had been a risk, but Betty Lou was not high in Aspect Society circles, and what she had or hadn't heard about Siren she was clearly willing to hold judgment on if it meant she got Hank back.

"Siren," Jace whispered. He managed to make the two syllables convey all of his worry and tension and need to get her out of here before something happened.

"Just a little longer," she murmured. She was beginning to doubt her theory was right, that whatever was wrong with Hank was something not even she could fix.

Then she found it, a tiny flaw, an infinitesimal disconnect between the physical and the mental. It wasn't a physical wound, so it didn't call out to her Aspect's instinctual need to heal. What she had found wasn't an injury at all in the traditional sense. More like the tie that bound two halves together had disintegrated.

She saw that the beginnings of a new tie had already formed, frayed tendrils on each side reaching for the other. Given a few more months, Hank would awaken on his own. He didn't have to wait that long, though. He had *her*. Her Aspect latched on to those hesitant beginnings of connection and urged them to grow. They extended rapidly. Each side reached for the other and the filamentous pieces came together, enmeshed, wound around each other like vines tangling into an impenetrable mass.

She poured power into that new connection until it grew strong and dense. She felt his flicker of awareness, and a murmur of power kept him asleep while her Aspect ran through him, correcting the muscle loss and atrophy caused by months of being bedridden. She didn't understand this side of her Aspect that dealt with the mental nearly as much as she did the physical, but she wound through that mental space as best she could.

Instinct guided her to clean up pieces that looked fuzzy and disordered, to bump things back into place here and there. She hoped it would help with the confusion he would undoubtedly feel when he woke up.

She withdrew her Aspect and opened her eyes.

"Is he…?"

"Going to be fine."

The smile that broke across Betty Lou's face could have rivaled the sun.

"He'll wake up in about ten minutes. Once you've been discharged, please give him this." She handed the woman an envelope. "Tell him I missed him, and I'm sorry."

Jace pulled her from the room as fast as he could without physically dragging her. His arm locked around her waist, and he appeared to be strongly fighting the urge to pick her up and run from the building with her. Instead, they came to a stop at the end of a narrow alcove next to the door for the emergency stairs.

"Everything is fine," she murmured.

"I know. Of course everything is fine. Why wouldn't everything be fine?"

"Well, the water fountains we passed spontaneously turned on and the fountain in front of the building is jetting water twenty feet in the air." She could just see it from the window in the narrow alcove where they stood.

His hands tightened around his waist. He rested his forehead against hers and inhaled. Exhaled. The water fountains shut off and the decorative fountain outside returned to normal levels.

"Tell me again that this is going to work."

"This is going to work," she said, with more confidence than she felt. She was powerful, yes, but so was the Council. Aunt Ella had hinted, in her roundabout way, that when the five of them were present in the same room, they were a force even Siren would have difficulty containing. Then she'd made an offhand comment about how Julian wasn't a councilor in truth, though, so their group dynamic was off.

"Of course," she'd continued, "Theo and I will notably abstain from any direct attacks, but we've been outvoted on the legal side, and our lack of participation really won't be that helpful to you, dear."

"Any other advice?"

"Just one thing. A small thing, really. The magic that binds the Council is far older than the European invasion of this country, and little understood. But understand this: to kill even one of us, you would need to kill us all, and *that* would take far more power from you than five ordinary deaths.

"At the height of your power, you could have done so. Now?" She'd shrugged. "I am less certain. But know that I am not ready to die, Siren Savage. And if *I* take the field your success is much, much less certain."

"I have no intention of killing anyone," she'd answered, honestly. She just wanted to be left alone.

"Then let us hope it does not come down to killing," had been Aunt Ella's cheerful, conversation-ending reply.

Jace pulled back just far enough to look into her eyes. "You look like you did when you came out of Aunt Ella's."

"Just…thinking about what she said."

"Are you ever going to *tell* me what she said?"

"No." Aunt Ella had been quite specific that the knowledge she'd provided about the Council's connection—which hardly sounded earth-shattering to Siren—was not to be shared with anyone.

At the look her refusal produced, Siren said, "She *did* threaten to kill me, and I still have no idea how Life and Death Aspect interact." She knew next to nothing about Aunt Ella's power. Like Life Aspect, information on her opposite's affinity was in scarce supply, and Aunt Ella herself wasn't sharing.

"But everything will work out," she reassured him, again. "And if it doesn't, we have a very good exit strategy planned.

And I am now in possession of a lot of money with which to run." Even thinking about the number of zeroes to her name made her uncomfortable. The stock market and compounding interest did stupid things to already stupidly large amounts of money over two decades. When this was all over, she was going to have to figure out how to give at least half of it away.

Jace kissed her. Softly, a little desperately, and she wanted all this to be over so she could stop seeing the haunted look that had been in his eyes since she'd woken up. The look *loving her,* had put there. She kissed him back and tried to tell him, without words, that she was sorry.

"All right, lovebirds, the time to exit the building is now."

Random walked swiftly past them to the emergency stairwell. His Aspect rose and chose its targets, cutting power to both the fire alarm that should have triggered, and the camera at the stairwell's top.

Siren squeezed Jace's hand and pulled him into the stairwell after Random.

Everything would be fine. It *would.*

CHAPTER

FORTY-FIVE

Entering the house she should have grown up in sent chills down Siren's spine. The space didn't feel abandoned, didn't feel as if it had sat empty for twenty-two years, waiting. Waiting for her to come home.

Charles, in care of the estate, had had it annually spelled against the intrusion of dust and pests and other passages of time. He had had nothing removed. The home, and its contents, remained precisely as they had the night her parents had died, as if John and Mara Savage had left the house that very morning, and might return at any moment. Only the traces of their deaths had been removed.

It was creepy. Beyond creepy. It was heartbreaking. She stood in her parents' kitchen, where the last dishes they'd ever washed lay nestled in a countertop rack twenty-years dried. She knew Oracles viewed the world a little differently than everyone else, but she hadn't expected *this*. To walk in and feel like her parents might still be here, that if she closed her eyes she could slip through time and see them.

Jace's strong, warm body pressed against her back and his arms folded around her waist.

"You don't have to deal with it all right now."

"It's *everywhere*," she choked out.

"I know." He squeezed her gently. "I'm sorry."

Maybe doing this here had been a terrible idea. But the Winters' house was too heavily watched to do what she needed, and this house—her house—had been the only place she could think of that might have the space they needed. Valkyrie, who had been a little girl when Siren's parents were still friends with Evelyn Winters, had said she vaguely recalled attending an event or two here.

"Let's just find the ballroom."

The house was not, thankfully, the size of the Winters' home. It did not contain multiple wings, but it was still *large*. She walked through the living area and carefully ignored the book she saw, open and set page-down on the coffee table to hold the place. Whichever of her parents had been reading it, they would never finish, now.

She turned blindly down a hall and started checking rooms. Rationally, she could see she was in a private section unlikely to contain a ballroom, but she couldn't stop. Not until she opened a door and walked straight into a nursery. It was done up in varying shades of soft gray. A little stuffed dog waited in the crib, and a banner strung across the railing spelled out her name.

She broke. She started crying and couldn't stop.

Jace was beside her again. She wrapped her arms around him and pressed her face into his neck. He didn't say anything, didn't demand anything. He just held her.

"If Valkyrie finds that son of a bitch and doesn't call me, I will never forgive her," she mumbled to Jace's neck.

"I'm still having trouble forgiving her for leaving," he answered.

Valkyrie had apparently gone after the Illusion Aspecter, who Siren thought of as Gary the Council scribe for ease of reference, the moment Jace had told her Siren was going to live. Until then, she had begrudgingly guarded the estate's grounds.

"You and I both know even if she was here tonight it

wouldn't change anything," Siren said in Valkyrie's defense. She wasn't angry at the woman for leaving—she understood Valkyrie's all-consuming drive to find the man she hoped would lead her to her father—Siren was just angry she couldn't be searching *with* her, right now.

This house was nothing but hundreds of little reminders of why she wanted—*needed*—to tear Gary apart.

"She could have waited another twenty-four hours. It's not like she has anything to go on. Meredith still has nothing to Track."

Siren didn't argue with him. Jace and Valkyrie had not parted on the best of terms. She thought it had less to do with Valkyrie not being here tonight, and more to do with the fact that the woman was obviously hiding something. Something to do with Jace's father. Confronted with this accusation, she'd staunchly refused to admit anything was out of the ordinary. No, her eyes had simply iced over, and she'd turned on one combat-booted heel and left.

Siren dried her eyes and gave Jace the only smile she could muster. "Come on. We don't have a lot of time left."

No one, Siren decided, could say her parents hadn't had style. The ballroom was done in alternating black and gray tile, which failed to make the space look dark because of the double rows of twelve-foot, arched windows lining either side of the long room. Triple chandeliers descended from a high ceiling.

When she'd seen the mezzanine level that looked down on the space, Siren had all but purred. That, combined with the raised stage at the far end of the room made it perfect for what she had in mind. Jace hadn't liked leaving her, even if he wasn't going far, but in the end, he had.

She found a black wood chair and placed it in the center of the stage, facing the doors at the opposite end. The chair was nowhere near a throne, but it was large and sturdy, and she felt faintly ridiculous as she sat down in it. But appearances—confidence and the assumption of power—were half the battle she fought tonight. So she sat in the chair, and waited.

The Council arrived precisely when Siren expected. Aunt Ella had seen to that. She didn't look at the older woman as the five councilors walked into the empty ballroom, their footfalls echoing off the tile. They had brought no one else with them, none of the Council-employed guards with Battle or other combat-related Aspects.

Siren wondered, briefly, if this was arrogance on their part, or if they'd simply been smart enough to know that throwing people at her wouldn't do any good.

DuPont was the first to break their silent staring contest. "Ms. Savage. The Council is not a servant to be summoned to your side when you deign to speak with us."

Siren lifted an eyebrow. "And yet, here you are."

"You do understand the severity of the infractions of which you stand accused?"

"Perhaps you should explain to me precisely what those charges are."

"You have broken our highest law. The laws you yourself agreed to be bound to. You have used Aspect to take a life."

Siren locked DuPont's eyes and let enough power flash into her own to make him swallow uneasily.

"I killed a man who kidnapped me and performed experiments on me that, according to your laws, are reprehensible. I killed a man who hunted me for years. Who tortured me and put me through pain you couldn't even imagine. All of which he did so that someone else could harvest the Aspect inside me like I was a battery to drain."

"James Gould," DuPont said, using the gray-eyed man's full name, "may have broken our laws, but that does not excuse your breaking them as well."

"And what of Gary? The man who sat in every one of your

meetings, posing as your scribe? The man who engineered all of this, who blatantly told me he harmed Evelyn Winters and is in possession of Elijah Winters? Instead of diverting your attention to that man, one who has broken every single one of your precious laws, you spent your time on me. You surrounded my fiancé's house in an effort to take me into custody by hostile means while I hovered very close to death and you find *that* to be a better use of the Council's time and resources?"

"I am afraid the Council found the information you sent to us on Gary via Mr. Tremayne rather sensational."

"Sensational," Siren repeated.

"We find it implausible the breadth of operation described could exist. Furthermore, for reasons understood to the Council alone, it is highly unlikely that Elijah Winters is the victim of any kidnapping, as we have explained to his daughter on numerous occasions."

Siren, her Aspect wrapped around Jace like a cocoon, needing to know that he was here, that he was safe even though she couldn't see him, *felt* his sharp intake of breath at this announcement. One of the things Valkyrie had been hiding from him, then.

"Given the Illusion affinity of the man you described, it is likely he simply impersonated our employee in order to sow discord in our ranks."

Siren blinked. "And has your scribe reported to work since the incident?"

DuPont's brief silence was all the answer she needed.

"The Council is dealing with the matter. None of which absolves you, Ms. Savage, of your own infractions. It is our majority vote that you are a danger to the Aspect community, and as such will face the maximum penalty for your crimes."

"I would like it noted that I dissent from that ruling," Aunt Ella said.

"As do I," Theo seconded.

"Be that as it may," DuPont said, "the majority vote stands."

"You misunderstand me," Siren said coolly. "I did not invite you here so that you could tell me what you have decided to do with me. I do not consent to decisions made in my absence, which do not factor in the truth of my experiences or allow me to defend myself. I did not invite you into my home so that I could answer to your interpretation of the laws you have created. I did not invite you here to listen to your judgment.

"I invited you here to offer you the choice to listen to *me*. To understand that the things I have done, I have only ever done in self defense because *your* Council, *your* society, *your* laws, have never protected me.

"You hold yourselves above me and you make decisions about me that are based not on the things I have actually done, but on the fact that you are terrified of me. I will not allow myself to be destroyed because of your baseless fear."

"We are not afraid, Ms. Savage."

"No? Then prove it. Do you deny my assertions about James Gould? Do you deny that he kidnapped, tortured, and would have killed me?"

Martin's lips twisted in a grimace. "No."

"Then change your decision, Mr. DuPont. Because the one you have made is sensible only in the context that you fear me too much not to control me."

"We are not afraid," DuPont repeated. "But the decision has been made. You will submit to the laws of this Council or you will be made to submit."

Siren leaned back in her chair and crossed her arms. "If you think you can take me, do go ahead and try."

Siren's shields snapped into place as power struck her. Despite Aunt Ella's and Theo's abstaining from the magical fray, the attack knocked the wind from her, made her tremble inside where she was still raw and bruised.

Outwardly, she didn't blink, didn't flinch. When the first volley was over, she stood and sent her Aspect out in a single, collected wave. It wrapped around the Council. Where ordinarily it would be hardly the work of a thought for her Aspect to wrap around their hearts, to cosset that beating organ and hold it, she had difficulty finding purchase. Finding a way *in*.

She'd never had to work for it before, never encountered this problem. As she searched, her Aspect slipping off them like rain hitting a thick layer of glass, they battered her shields again. She held, again, but it scraped at those raw places inside her, the just-healed places.

Her Aspect roved over the impenetrable layer that surrounded the Council. It was as if there was no individual *person*'s life to take hold of. She remembered, then, what Aunt Ella had told her. That to kill one of them, she would have to kill them all. That they were bound in some way.

They were a *collective*, where magic was concerned.

Her Aspect stilled. She pulled it back, hovered to view the Council from a distance. This time, she barely noticed when their Aspects tore at her shields, the entirety of her attention on the problem they posed, and *there*. To her magic's sight, they *were* one organism. A thread stemmed from each of them, and those threads came together at a central point, a central *heart*, that shifted between them in relation to each individual's movements. That heart took what each of them was and amplified it.

They were strong. Far stronger than simply five Aspect users casting together. But not as strong as they would be if the true fifth member of the Council were present. Julian did not precisely fit. He wasn't a core part of the organism they formed, he was more of a—well, parasite wasn't the right word. It was as if he was something they allowed to live within their structure, but he existed at its fringes. He did not belong, so he neither aided them to the extent their fifth member would have, nor did he receive all the protections that fifth member was entitled to.

Siren's Aspect wrapped around their joined heart, and squeezed.

They stumbled as one and hit their knees as their Aspects flickered out. Siren felt a momentary guilt that she must involve

Theo and Aunt Ella in this threat, because they had *not* attacked her. Yet they *had* chosen to be part of this, this *thing*. They bore some responsibility, she thought, for that.

Unable to resist the pull of her curiosity, Siren descended the stage to the ballroom floor and walked to where the Council's heart hung between them, a glowing, pulsing thing to her magic's sight. She saw the fifth thread, the one that must be Elijah Winters.

It wasn't right. The strand that hovered before her magical sight didn't *feel* like Elijah Winters. True, she'd never actually met the man, only his illusion, but the strand didn't feel...male? She reached out, touched her fingers to that thread, and she understood. Because that thread did *not* belong to Elijah Winters.

It belonged to Valkyrie.

Siren had the sense of a dragon rising behind her, felt it in her bones as the metaphorical wings stretched wide, and Aunt Ella's power reached out to investigate that fifth strand with her. Death's power slid alongside Siren's, immense and ancient, but also gentle. She felt the moment Aunt Ella's power stilled, the moment the woman understood what Siren understood.

Siren turned to face her, the accusation on the tip of her tongue. *Did you know?* But she didn't have to ask it. She could see, by the look on Aunt Ella's face, that the woman hadn't, that the Council *didn't*. Valkyrie, *Valkyrie,* was the Council's true fifth member in terms of the spell that bound them together, and none of them had known.

Siren opened her mouth to ask how that could be possible. Aunt Ella gave a small shake of her head, and Siren snapped her mouth shut. Valkyrie knew, Valkyrie *had* to know, but the woman's insistence on finding her father, the fact she was obviously keeping things from Jace, made Siren certain that however this had happened, it had not been Valkyrie's choice.

Siren turned back to the thread, the line, that was Valkyrie, and wrapped her hand around the base where it connected to the heart.

The entire Council shuddered, and she didn't need Kara's panicked, whimpered, *"Please,"* to make her release it. She'd known the moment she touched that line that if she severed it, Valkyrie would die.

She couldn't *do* anything for Valkyrie now. She could only do what she'd come here to do, say the words she had put together as she prepared for this moment.

"When I first came to you, I was treated with suspicion. Your Truthfinder was allowed to physically harm me without reprimand, and when you found out how much power I carry inside of me—a condition, I might add, forced upon me by illegal experiments carried out by one of *your* Society's members—you wanted to lock me away on the basis that I had the *potential* to be dangerous, despite knowing nothing of my character.

"I could have killed each and every one of you on that battlefield days ago. You know that. You felt it. You feel it now." A squeeze of her Aspect around the Council's heart underscored the truth of her words. "If I were the monster you claim I am, that is exactly what I would do. But I chose then—as I choose now—not to.

"So my answer to your decision is no. No, I am not going to beg you for my life, or let you decide what to do with it.

"This is my counteroffer. Leave me alone, and, with the possible exception of the Illusion Aspecter currently known as Gary, should he be found and the Council fail to bring him to account, I will never kill another person as long as I live. I will never harm another person, unless I am first attacked.

"Should you, or anyone you send, come after me again, I will do whatever I must to ensure my survival and the survival of those I love.

"Is this offer acceptable to you?"

DuPont sputtered. She released her Aspect's clutch on him enough that he could take a full, deep breath. "Ms. Savage, your behavior here is proof that—"

Her Aspect clenched, cutting off his words.

"No matter what you may think of me, or what you intended to do to me, know this: I will not kill you. Should you refuse to rescind your decision, I will leave here. Your Council has counterparts the world over. I am certain at least one of them is bound to be more open-minded than you, given the benefits a person with Life Aspect can bring to a community.

"If necessary, I will travel until I find one that accepts me. But I prefer to stay here. I prefer to confer the benefits of my Aspect on the community that would have raised me, had my parents lived. Discuss it. Make your decision. I'll wait."

She returned to her chair. Holding the Council in her grip tired her, but she couldn't afford to let that show. She channeled her inner-Random and lounged, as if she were sitting because she didn't have a care in the world, and not because she didn't have the strength to stand.

It did not take the Council long to decide. DuPont, when he spoke, looked physically pained by the words.

"The Council has, perhaps, been hasty in its decisions."

"You agree, then, to my terms?"

A stiff nod was her only reply.

"Could you, for the sake of clarity, iterate those terms to me? So there are no misunderstandings."

"Is that necessary?"

"Yes, I do believe it is."

"Very well. The Council will not seek to hold you accountable for the actions you previously took in self defense. We will not seek retaliation. You may remain here without fear of reprisal from us.

"But Ms. Savage? Do not, by any means, think your *display* here today is a lever over us. Should you seek to manipulate this Council to your own ends, should you threaten us in this manner again, we *will* go to war. And we will see who is standing at the end of it."

"I have no interest in manipulating you. That is the Council's area of expertise. Not mine." She raised her voice. "The Council and I have come to terms. Let it be witnessed."

So saying, she broke the spell that hovered high above them, and the empty mezzanine level above revealed itself to be packed with people. She'd gotten the idea from Gary, but the power needed to hide so many people was more than the average Aspecter would be capable of storing up, so there hadn't been a spell that existed that would do what she needed. She'd had to work it from scratch. Well, she'd had the idea and Jace had worked it from scratch, because complex magical theory was what his brain did best. If she could follow his logic well enough, there was no point in her spending days figuring out what he could throw together in an hour.

"So witnessed," the people chorused.

Watching DuPont's face turn pale as Christmas snow brought a genuine smile to Siren's lips. She had expected there was a good chance the Council would accede to her terms, but she'd expected there was an equally good chance they would break their agreement if it was made in a vacuum. So she had ensured their promise wasn't given in solitude.

Her eyes swept up, found Hank's, and mouthed, *Thank you.* Because it had been Hank—and Betty Lou and Random—who had reached out to the people they knew in the Aspect community and filled her home with witnesses.

He gave her his best gruff, typical old man nod.

Siren returned her attention to DuPont and released her hold on the Council. Drawing her Aspect back into her was an instant relief. DuPont, Kara, and Julian turned and walked out of the ballroom without another word. Theo and Aunt Ella stayed.

"Are we having a party?" Aunt Ella asked brightly.

Siren didn't get to say *no* before Random walked through the open ballroom doors, wait-staff following him in with trays bearing champagne and cute little appetizers that were bound to be ridiculously expensive simply because there was so little of them and they were so adorably cute.

"Of *course*, we're having a party, Aunt Ella. We just nearly committed suicide-by-Council. What else would we do?" He looked up at the second floor and waved. "Come downstairs, we're having a party."

Siren couldn't help it. The stress and relief and ridiculousness crashed through her, and she dissolved into fits of laughter.

CHAPTER

FORTY-SIX

It took hours to circulate through the crowd in her home, to meet everyone, dozens upon dozens of names and faces she wouldn't remember, but would try to. They had shown up for her. Oh, they had more shown up for Hank and Betty Lou and Random, but they *had* shown up. These were not the wealthy and elite, the carefully curated Aspect bloodlines the Council so prized. These people were the backbone of Aspect Society, the people the Council often overlooked.

No one wore anything remotely formal, for which Siren was grateful. Circulating among them she felt, if not comfortable—large gatherings really weren't her happy place—at least not out of place. Not judged.

But she was exhausted, mentally and physically, and it was still a relief when the evening wound down, when Hank and Random and Jace ushered the last of the guests out the door. She hadn't really *seen* Hank since he woke up, so when he came up and opened his arms, she flung herself into them and wrapped him in a bear hug.

"Thanks for waking me up, kid," he said, the words spoken in his usual gruff manner. It was such a relief to hear his voice she found herself tearing up again.

"Yeah, well, it's my fault you needed waking up in the first place."

"Aw, now, I know you're too smart to go blaming yourself for what other people do." He patted her shoulder and stepped back. "I, uh, s'pose you won't be coming back to the store now you've got all this."

Siren's eyes widened. "You're firing me?"

"What? No, 'course I ain't firing you. Just figured you wouldn't wanna work any more with this kind of money."

"Hank Trembley, I did not rearrange your entire store and clean out a decade's worth of dust to step back and see it all go to waste. Besides, before all this started, I wanted to talk to you about a promotion."

"Promotion?"

"Yes. I'd like to take a more active role in the buying."

"All right," he drawled. He looked like he didn't quite know what to make of her in that moment, but she needed him to say she could come back to the store, needed the normality, the stability. "Guess I'll see you in the morning then?"

She nodded.

"Store hadn't been open since you left, so, may have a lot to do."

In the chaos of everything, she hadn't really thought about that. "You didn't...you didn't lose the space did you?"

"Nah. Owned it outright for the last decade or so."

Well, that explained how the place was still around with less-than-ideal sales.

"Good," Siren said. "I'll see you in the morning then."

He took a step away, then stopped and looked past her, to where Jace stood by the door, still saying whatever polite things a host said to people leaving their party.

"Things turned out okay with that well-dressed feller then?"

Siren narrowed her eyes. "Things with *Jace* are fine."

Hank grinned. "Told you there wasn't much trouble he couldn't get you out of."

"I got myself out of trouble, thank you very much."

"So I hear. But you gotta admit, you wouldn't have stuck around if I didn't convince you to go to that party with him."

"How do you know that?"

He bobbed his head. "I know the look a person gets when they're thinkin' 'bout running. You already had both feet out the door."

"You're so wise, Hank," she said sweetly. "It must be because you're so very, very old."

He grunted. "If I'm so old, shouldn't you be givin' your elders more respect?"

"I'll take it under advisement."

"Hmph." Hank cast another look at Jace. "He don't treat you right, you let me know."

With that, he gave her another brief hug and left.

She made it all of two feet toward Jace when Random appeared. Now that most of the people were gone, he'd let his façade of cheerfulness fade. He didn't quite have circles under his eyes, but he looked as exhausted as she felt. He didn't even need to say anything, his emotions were so plainly written on his face.

"You don't need to stay," she told him softly. "Go after her."

He pressed his lips together and shook his head. "She doesn't want me to."

Siren chose her words carefully. "I don't know what really happened between you two. And I don't pretend to know what she wants. But if you care about her? I don't think she should be alone right now. Even if she thinks that's what she wants."

Random hesitated.

"*Go.*"

He exhaled, and nodded.

"And Random? When you find her, tell her I need to talk to her. She'll know what it's about."

"I don't suppose you'll tell me what it's about?"

"No."

"Women," he said, in mock exasperation. "You always keep everything so damn close-mouthed. I'll tell her."

Then he was gone. So, she realized, was everyone else. Her gaze traveled across the room, found Jace's.

"It worked," she said. She hadn't really believed it until that moment.

"It worked," he echoed, and she could tell, by the way his shoulders relaxed, and the smile that spread across his face, that he hadn't believed it either.

She ran and jumped into his arms, literally, locking her legs around his waist. He caught her and his arms came under her to steady her.

"I love you," she told him, and kissed him.

"I think," he said, when they broke apart, "I could stand to hear you say that again."

"I love you," she repeated.

"And I love you."

She unwrapped her legs from his waist and slid down to stand, but she didn't let go of him. He had the strangest look on his face.

"What?"

"I was wondering if there was something you wanted to ask me."

Siren frowned. "Ask you?"

"Yes. Your choice of words in your speech was very specific."

Her frown deepened. "We worked them out together. I thought we needed to be specific. To make sure we covered all the bases."

"Oh, we did. I meant the word you used to refer to *me*. Unless," he went on at her blank pause, "you have a fiancé I should know about?"

Her eyes widened. Oh God, surely she hadn't. She ran back through the speech in her mind, and closed her eyes. She *had*. She had called him her fiancé in front of everyone in the room.

"No," she managed. "I don't have another fiancé you should know about."

She still couldn't read the expression on his face. They'd never talked about marriage. She had no idea if it wasn't something he was interested in at all, much less with her.

"So are you going to?'

"What?"

"Ask me?"

"Are you really going to make me? Now?"

"I've never been proposed to before. It's an experience I'd hate to miss."

"What are you going to say?"

"I can't tell you the answer before you ask. That's not how this works."

"Well, I don't think you can just demand that I propose to you. That's not how it works either. That wasn't the plan."

He smiled at her, his eyes dancing with laughter. "What was the plan?"

"I was going to buy champagne. We were going to drink it and have mind-blowing sex and I'd ask you in the height of passion when you'd be too drunk on sex hormones to say no."

"I like that plan." He caught her lower lip between his teeth and nipped it, lightly. "Let's go enact it."

She placed her palms against his chest, halting him when he would have picked her up.

"Maybe I want to know what your sober answer is." She took a deep breath and met his gaze. "Jace Winters, will you marry me?"

She would remember the smile that lit up his face for the rest of her life.

"Fuck yes, I will marry you." His hands roamed down her back, settled on the curves of her hips. "But I don't want to rob you of your original plan. We should probably still act that out."

He kissed her. His tongue parted her lips, glided against her own, and a ribbon of heat curled low in her stomach.

"I think we're all out of champagne," she said, breathless.

"I guess we'll have to make do with just the mind-blowing sex. Try not to be too disappointed."

"With you? Never," she said, and kissed him again.

WONDER WHAT'S IN STORE FOR RANDOM AND VALKYRIE IN BOOK 2?

The Bonus Epilogue for Siren's Song (in which Valkyrie tramples all over poor Random's heart, yet again) is available exclusively for my newsletter subscribers. You can sign up here:

https://michellemanus.com/newsletter/

If you enjoyed the book, do consider leaving a review at your retailer of choice. Reviews really are the best way you can help support your favorite authors.

You can find me on my website michellemanus.com, or get in touch with me via email at michelle@michellemanus.com

Thanks so much for reading!

ALSO BY MICHELLE MANUS

The Aspect Society Trilogy

Siren's Song

Valkyrie's Call

Truthfinder's Promise

The Nyx Fortuna Series

Guardian of Chaos

Guardian of Shadows

Guardian of Madness